# Rescuing Josiah (Special Forces: Operation Alpha)

## PREY SECURITY: CYBER TEAM
### BOOK FOUR

## JANE BLYTHE

**Cover designed by Q Designs**

Dear Readers,

*Welcome to the Special Forces: Operation Alpha Fan-Fiction world!*

If you are new to this amazing world, in a nutshell the author wrote a story using one or more of my characters in it. Sometimes that character has a major role in the story, and other times they are only mentioned briefly. This is perfectly legal and allowable because they are going through Aces Press to publish the story.

This book is entirely the work of the author who wrote it. While I might have assisted with brainstorming and other ideas about which of my characters to use, I didn't have any part in the process or writing or editing the story.

I'm proud and excited that so many authors loved my characters enough that they wanted to write them into their own story. Thank you for supporting them, and me!

READ ON!
    Xoxo
    Susan Stoker

*Acknowledgments*

I'd like to thank everyone who played a part in bringing this story to life. Particularly my mom who is always there to share her thoughts and opinions with me. My wonderful cover designer Amy who did an amazing job with this stunning cover. My fabulous editor Lisa for all the hard work she puts into polishing my work, and Detra who does an amazing proofread. My awesome team, Sophie, Robyn, and Clayr, without your help I'd never be able to run my street team. And my fantastic street team members who help share my books with every share, comment, and like!

And of course a big thank you to all of you, my readers! Without you I wouldn't be living my dreams of sharing the stories in my head with the world!

# CHAPTER

*One*

May 11th
6:29 P.M.

The sound seemed to echo through his body.

For some reason, it hurt the most.

Which was ridiculous given that actual bullets pierced his body.

Tearing through flesh like it was nothing.

But worse even than the thunderous sound of gunfire were the screams.

Barely human howls coming from men he considered family. Men he served with, men he fought alongside, men with whom he'd forged a bond that was supposed to last a lifetime.

Men who now fell around him.

Dying.

Dead.

Gone.

Beneath him, the ground was hard. The sand clung to his damp skin, a rock dug into his back, but he didn't bother to move, though.

He wanted to, damn, did he want to shove to his feet and start firing back at those who had killed his team, but he didn't seem to have the energy to move.

Everything hurt, and he could feel the life spilling out of him.

Dying like the others, only more slowly.

One tiny detail altered their fates.

He was still wearing his body armor. The others had removed theirs because they were supposed to be safe here. Safe on a base even though they were in hostile territory.

Now he didn't even remember the reason he'd left his on when the others didn't.

Shouts sounded around him.

More bullets flew through the air.

Then people were all around him. Well-meaning people, performing first aid, putting pressure on his wounds, and offering words they thought might comfort.

They didn't.

Nothing could comfort him right now.

As his body was jostled, he saw them. Bullet-ridden bodies that had once been living, breathing men. Gone now. Taken out in an ambush that had to have been led by a traitor. That was the only way to explain how they'd been attacked on what was supposed to be a secure military base.

It didn't matter now. They were gone. All of them. Except him.

He alone had survived.

And he wished he hadn't.

When he began to fight against the hands of the people

attempting to save his life, they tried to stop him. They didn't understand that he didn't want to live without his team.

A horrible wail filled the air. A desperate sound made of pure grief-filled agony. It took him far longer than it should have to realize it was coming from him.

"Josiah."

The soft, sweet voice was out of place. It didn't belong here. Hadn't been there the day he'd lost his entire team.

"Wake up," that same angel voice insisted.

Panic lashed at him, inflicting the same burning pain a whip would.

No.

She couldn't be here. It wasn't safe. They'd get her, too. Shoot her, kill her, leave her beautiful body riddled with bullet holes on the hot sand.

He had to get his weapon, he wasn't going to let them have her, too.

Not her.

A hand touched his shoulder, trying to prevent him from getting his weapon, and he snapped out one of his hands to stop them, surprised by the sudden burst of strength he had when just moments ago his body had felt heavy and useless.

She whimpered. A muted, pained sound, and Josiah turned toward her, needing to put a stop to it. That sound hurt worse than everything else combined.

One blink changed everything.

The sand disappeared, replaced by a hard plastic chair, the heat morphed into the dry, cool of AC air, and the bodies littered around him became a couple of people giving him odd looks. Fearful looks.

Beside him stood the woman whose voice had spurred fear unlike any other to flood his system. Her hand rested lightly on his shoulder, and his much bigger hand circled her wrist in a grip he knew was causing her pain, because the face that looked down at him held a tightness that wasn't usually there.

"It's okay," she murmured softly, "it was just a dream. You're safe. I didn't mean to touch you, I know you don't like that, but ..." She trailed off and indicated the few people about them, all looking at him expectantly.

Right.

The wedding.

They were at the courthouse so he and one of his co-workers could get married. Not because they were in love, but because they were going undercover to try to bring down an organ trafficking ring that had been operating for several years now.

Things had taken a personal turn earlier in the year when one of their coworkers had been snatched by the ring. Ava Hendricks had managed to escape with the help of a Navy SEAL, Nathaniel Trevino. The two were now happy and in love, and wanted to start their future, but they couldn't because of the ring.

Fellow teammate and former Delta Force operator, Tobias Ashford, had also fallen in love when he'd gone back into the field for the first time in years to help raid one of the trafficking ring's clinics. There, he'd met imprisoned nurse Isabella Baker. Despite a rocky start, the two had also fallen in love and were expecting a baby.

Then last month, another of his teammates, Teresa Dash, was targeted. The timing had been good, or bad depending on how you looked at it, because her teenage crush had popped back into her life around the same time.

The two had worked through their issues, and Teresa had decided to give Micah Hart a second chance.

Three teammates, three new relationships.

Three chances of happiness and a life that he would never allow himself to have.

They were why he was here now. Why he'd decided going undercover was their best bet at getting to the elusive head of the trafficking ring. Desiree Tilly had lost her husband and three of her four children to a rare genetic disorder that caused a protein buildup to affect organs. Organ failure had occurred, and they had all passed away.

All but a daughter.

One Desiree Tilly refused to let go of.

While they could all understand the desperation that had led her to start up a black-market organ ring, none of them could condone it. Hundreds of people across the globe had been abducted, killed, their organs stolen, and sold to the highest bidder. The woman had to be stopped, and he knew he could be the one to do it.

But Chelsea Pierce was not supposed to be part of it.

His plan had been for him to infiltrate the ring alone. Posing as a dying man willing to do whatever it took to live, he was going to get himself an appointment with someone inside the ring, and then work his way up the ladder until he got an appointment with Desiree Tilly herself.

Only he'd been outvoted.

Chelsea had insisted that nobody would believe that a retired SEAL, who had served his country and lost his entire team in combat, would seek out a black-market trafficking ring. Not for himself anyway. But she'd believed that if the ring thought he was doing it to save someone he loved, it might be more believable.

So here they were. A day later, at the courthouse,

getting married. To make this work, they needed everything to be as legitimate as possible, since quite obviously, Chelsea was not in fact dying and in need of a black-market organ to survive.

The justice of the peace who would sign off on the marriage certificate was watching him with suspicious eyes, like he wasn't sure if he should pick up the phone and call the cops.

While Josiah hated the idea of Chelsea being in danger, he didn't hate her specifically. Despite his reputation for hating everyone and everything, the only people he truly hated were the men who had stolen the lives of his team-mates and the man who had set them up.

What he did hate was letting anyone get even vaguely close to him.

Including touching him.

It took more effort than he would have expected to slowly uncurl his fingers, one by one, from around Chelsea's slender wrist. The look of understanding in her gray eyes almost made rage explode out of him.

How dare she understand him.

Why couldn't she keep her distance like everybody else?

The rest of his team were polite, but they respected his boundaries and didn't try to force friendship that he didn't want onto him.

Not Chelsea, though.

Never her.

She was always trying to engage him in conversation, trying to be nice to him, and get closer to him. She baked him sweet treats, she gave him a Christmas gift every year, she brought cake and candles, and insisted everybody sing him "Happy Birthday". She was everything good and sweet in the world, and everything he wanted to avoid at all costs.

Only now as he stood and faced what was without a doubt the scariest mission of his career, and that had nothing to do with bringing down an organ trafficker, she was everything he couldn't avoid. Everything he had to pretend he wanted, because to the outside world, this marriage had to appear real, even if it was going to be annulled the second Desiree Tilly was in custody.

Doing this with anybody else would have been easy to pretend, to fake it, do what had to be done for the greater good.

But Chelsea Pierce was his Achilles heel.

Something he couldn't allow anyone—especially her—to realize if he wanted to go back to his solitary life once this was over. That life, devoid of as much human contact as he could, was the only thing that kept him sane, kept him breathing.

Keeping people out wasn't just self-preservation, it was the only thing keeping him alive.

$\sim$

May 11<sup>th</sup>
    6:50 P.M.

This was never going to work.

Chelsea Pierce glanced sideways at Josiah as they walked back outside after what had to be the absolute shortest wedding in the entire history of humanity.

Why had she thought this was a good idea again?

At the time, it had seemed so simple. No one would believe that Josiah Fleet, an honorable man who had just about every military medal it was possible to receive, was suddenly going to go seeking out traffickers to save his own life. That she was absolutely certain of. It wouldn't convince anyone, and if they were going to make contact with the traffickers, they would have to seem legitimate.

After all, Desiree Tilly and her ring knew that Prey was onto them, knew that Prey was hunting them, and knew that Prey would do whatever they had to in order to destroy them. Including sending someone in undercover.

So this had to seem real.

Enter her.

She was confident that if they could convince the trafficking ring that she and Josiah were in love, then they could convince them that they weren't there to betray them but to save her life.

But getting Josiah to look as though he tolerated her, let alone liked her, let alone loved her, seemed to be getting more impossible by the second.

Waking him up from a nightmare had been a bad idea, but it had also been necessary. She'd spent enough time around special forces guys to know that you didn't touch them when they were dreaming, that if you did, it could end extremely badly.

Only this time she hadn't had a choice.

The justice of the peace was ready to sign their paperwork with them, and Josiah had dozed off in a chair in the hall while they were waiting. It wasn't like she could just leave him there and do this herself.

Not that she would admit it to him, but her wrist throbbed from where he'd gripped it almost tight enough to crush bones. There would be bruises later, and she should probably ice it to help with the swelling, but she also didn't want to do anything that would draw attention to it because she didn't know how Josiah would react.

He'd never hurt her on purpose, that wasn't who he was. Angry at the world, yes. Closed off from everybody else, yes. But he wasn't a bad guy, he was just scared, and she tried to do everything within her power to show him that he didn't need to be scared around her. If he could just lower his guard the tiniest of bits, she could scale up it and scurry down the other side. That way, he'd never have to face anything alone again.

Too bad he didn't seem inclined to lower those barriers. Not even a millimeter.

"Uh, well, that didn't go too badly, I guess," she said, trying to lighten the mood a little bit.

It didn't work if the expression on Josiah's face when he whirled around to glare down at her was anything to go by. "Don't *ever* touch me again when I'm asleep," he growled, his voice low enough that no one around them would hear it.

"I'm s-sorry," she stammered. Again, she knew that Josiah would never deliberately hurt her, but that didn't mean that when he scowled like that, he wasn't a scary-looking guy. "I didn't know what else to do. I tried calling your name and it didn't wake you up. We had to go in there and sign the papers. I did what I thought was the right thing."

"You thought wrong," he snapped.

"Okay," she agreed, mainly so they didn't have an argument right out here on the street. They had no idea if they were being followed, but if they were, they had to look somewhat believable as a couple.

The whole plan depended on the trafficking ring believing that she and Josiah had been secretly in love and dating for months, but were unable to be vocal about it because of Prey's no fraternization policy. In reality, there was no such thing, after all, founder and CEO Eagle Oswald himself had fallen in love with an employee. Okay, so Olivia had taken the job under false pretenses, but she had been an employee, and everything had worked out in the end.

Still, that was a believable reason why they hadn't announced a relationship, and there were now fake medical records showing her kidneys were failing and she needed an urgent transplant. Their lie was that they'd married so that Josiah was legally allowed to make medical decisions for her as her next of kin.

If they could make the charade look believable, they would attend some fake medical appointments over the next few days and hopefully hook the trafficking ring. Then they just had to reel them in, and this would all be over.

As badly as she wanted this to be over so all her friends would be safe and free to move on with their lives and their new relationships, Chelsea couldn't help but feel a little like she was going to be left behind. Everyone else in Cyber Team, except her and Josiah, was now in love, and it was only this case and the threat hanging over their heads because of it that everything hadn't already completely changed.

It was coming, though.

Changes. Big ones.

And she wasn't quite sure how she felt about it. Happy for her best friends, of course, Ava and Teresa deserved to be happy, and so did Tobias. But where did it all leave her?

"Let's go," Josiah snapped, turning on his heel and walking off without her.

She hurried to catch up with him, something that was hard to do without actually breaking into a run, because his legs were much longer than hers, his six-foot-four frame towering over her five-foot-two.

"You don't look like someone who just married the woman they love," she whispered when she managed to catch up to him.

"Because I'm not and I didn't," he grumbled.

Although those words were true, Chelsea couldn't help but feel a pang in her heart. Everybody other than Josiah himself knew she was hopelessly in love with him. What she'd first thought was just a crush that would pass quickly had only grown over the years they'd known one another.

Some people might wonder what she could possibly see in the rude, grumpy man who had made it his life's mission to keep everyone at a distance. But once you knew about his past, all he'd lost, the betrayal, it all made sense, and you couldn't not feel sorry for him. That's what kept her unreciprocated feelings alive. Josiah Fleet was hurting, and she wanted to take that pain for him, shoulder some of it so he didn't have to carry the heavy burden alone.

If she was being honest with herself, maybe she thought that this, playing at being a couple, spending one on one time together, might make her dreams a reality. Or at the very least, bring them a little closer to being real.

Now, though, it was painfully obvious that wasn't going to happen.

Not now, and likely not ever.

Only when she tried to convince herself to give up on the idea of Josiah never being more than a coworker, she couldn't seem to do it. It felt wrong to give up on him. He didn't let himself have anyone, and while he might not want her presence in his life, she was here, and she wanted to help if he'd just let her in.

Giving up on Josiah would be dooming him to life of loneliness and pain.

She couldn't do that. No matter how much he wanted her to.

Slipping her hand into his, he didn't curl his fingers around hers and hold onto her, but she didn't let that stop her. Naïve or not, she was going to be here for this man whether he liked it or not. She wasn't going to leave him alone to drown in a sea of pain.

"I know you hate this. I know you hate ... me." She had to swallow down her emotions as she said that out loud. It was true, but she hated it. "I know you wish I wasn't here, that you were doing this alone, and I'm sorry for changing everything up. But I won't be sorry for caring about you, Josiah, so don't try to make me. Just like I won't be sorry for caring about Ava and Nathaniel, and Tobias and Isabella, and Teresa and Micah. I care about them, and I want to make this work, which means that we have to find a way to make it look like we're together. That means you accepting that I get to decide who I care about and you can be mad about it all you want, but you are one of the people I care about."

Nothing was going to change that.

Maybe she was naïve, and maybe she was a romantic who always tried to see the good in everything and everyone, but she was also stubborn. Stubborn enough to not let Josiah push her away yet. She could take whatever anger he dished out over these next days or weeks, however long it took to get to Desiree Tilly. She was stronger than she looked, and she'd made a promise to herself the first day she'd met Josiah and been hit by the force of his internal pain.

No matter what he said, no matter what he did, no

matter how hard he pushed her away, she was going to be there for him. A steady presence in the sea of his agony, grief, and betrayal. Something he knew would always be there.

He could be rude and angry if he wanted, but she was going to keep meeting his energy with her own patient and caring one.

# CHAPTER

*Two*

May 11<sup>th</sup>
    8:03 P.M.

Giggling.

Every time she did it, it felt like a hammer hitting his chest.

A weird way to describe someone else's laughter, Josiah got that, but no one else laughed in a way that affected him.

Pretty much everything everyone did annoyed him. A fact of life since his team had been gunned down around him, and he learned that someone he should have been able to trust had betrayed them in the worst possible way.

How else was he supposed to feel about the fact that his entire team was dead because someone had switched sides? No one else got it. Not his family, not his new team, definitely not Chelsea. Maybe Eagle Oswald did. The man had also been a SEAL until a betrayal had cost him his team and his leg. It was why, as soon as Josiah woke up in that hospital room on the other side of the world, his first call hadn't been to his parents or one of his brothers. That first call had gone to Eagle, and he'd asked for a job.

He hadn't needed anyone to tell him his career as a SEAL was over, he knew it. Had known it when he was bleeding out in the Middle East sand. He couldn't go back home, take a job at a bank, or a store, or even become a cop. He had to do something that would carry on the work he and his team had signed up for, and working for the world-renowned Prey Security seemed like the best way to do that.

But he never could have anticipated that one of his new teammates would be a pretty brunette, with huge gray eyes, and the warmest smile he'd ever seen. A woman who was always happy, supported everyone, and treated him with kindness when he deserved the opposite.

How was he supposed to fight against her sunshiny smile?

And yet how could he not?

The alternative was letting her charm work, her sunshine wear down his walls, and then she'd be on the other side of them, and he'd be left vulnerable again. Losing someone else was not an option. There was no way he could survive that. So he was ruthless in his endeavors to shove everyone out of his life, including his own family.

"It's like they took my dream house right out of my imagination and made it a reality," Chelsea said again, awe in her voice as she walked around their new home. This was where they'd be for the remainder of their assignment. The townhouse was pretty, sure, if you cared about that kind of thing. His apartment was nothing more than a small table with a single chair, and a bed. He spent little to no time in it, and more often than not, slept at Prey so he could focus on work.

Work was what kept him going.

Work was how he honored his fallen teammates.

Work was the only thing that kept him sane.

And yet ...

A tiny little voice at the back of his mind whispered a truth he wasn't ready to acknowledge yet. Would never be ready to acknowledge. Something else at work got him through each day, and it was currently giggling as it walked through the living room they were going to share.

The house was fancier than he would have chosen, but Prey had put this together for them. The house was four stories, with a gym in the basement, a living room, dining room, kitchen, and library on the ground floor, three ensuite bedrooms on the second floor, and an entire master suite on the third.

Unfortunately, they would have to share that room.

Chelsea had been right about one thing earlier, he did hate this, but he also had to make it look believable. They could be being watched, and if they were, it had to be clear that he and Chelsea were a couple now. Legally anyway. Nothing more. Never anything more.

"Would you stop giggling?" he snapped, unable to take a second longer of the sweet, musical sound. It was too pure, too innocent, too everything he wasn't, and it continued to chip away at his hardened heart. Which was absolutely unacceptable.

"Sorry."

The smile slid off her face, and Josiah immediately regretted his harsh words. It wasn't that he wanted to hurt Chelsea. The opposite in fact. He liked her more than he wanted to, he just knew he could never allow anything to happen between them.

No one was ever going to get close to him again.

The pain of losing someone ...

Damn, it had almost killed him to lose his entire team in one fell swoop, and if he ever had to go through anything like that again, there was no doubt about what it would do to him. It would kill him. Simple as that.

Still, hurting Chelsea ... it left a bitter taste in his mouth. She was the absolute personification of good, sweet, pure, and innocent. She was an angel, and touching her would destroy her. He'd destroy her. Because while she was an angel, he was the devil. His darkness would smother her light, and he couldn't let that happen to her. One day, she'd get over her crush on him and find someone who could love her like she deserved, and there was no way he intended to corrupt her and steal her chance at happiness.

"We should get our bags unpacked, and then I'll cook us some dinner," Chelsea said. Although the light in her eyes had dimmed, he saw her determination to not let his bad attitude ruin hers.

If she were anyone else, she would have gotten sick and tired of that bad attitude of his long before now. She would have wiped him out of her mind, been polite with him at work, but nothing more.

Only this woman didn't know how to not care about others.

Angel. There was no other way to describe her.

"We're not sharing a bed," he said abruptly. The thought of lying beside her, all her soft skin on display, so close, so tempting, and knowing he could have another dream and hurt her worse than he'd done earlier was too much for him.

"O-okay," she stammered. "I guess you could take one of the other bedrooms then. I know you'll want to be a floor below me in case they try anything, then they'll have to go through you to get to me."

"No," he growled. That was a much better idea, certainly a smarter one, but for some crazy reason, he couldn't stand the idea of that much distance between them. "I'll sleep on the floor."

"Oh, no, that won't be comfortable. There's probably a couch or something up there. Or we could order you an air mattress if you don't want to share the bed."

"We're supposed to be in love and newly married, I don't think an air mattress popping up on our credit cards sends that message."

"They don't have access to that kind of stuff, they're not us," Chelsea said, so brimming with confidence. "They get their medical information through moles at hospitals, but they don't have the same resources as Prey does. They'd never know, and I don't want you sleeping on the floor."

Josiah merely grunted, and when his phone rang, he yanked it out of his back pocket.

The name on the screen was one of his brothers, he had three, one older, two younger, and he hadn't spoken to any of them since his team was killed. Didn't stop them from calling, though, damn stubborn family. Didn't they get by now that he didn't want to talk to or see them?

"You can answer that if you want," Chelsea said, heading for the stairs. "I'll start putting away my clothes, then I'll cook dinner."

"Ice your wrist first," he snapped. If she thought she was doing a good job of hiding from him that he'd hurt her earlier, she was sorely mistaken.

"Oh, uh, yeah, sure, good idea. It's not too sore, though, you didn't hurt it too much, and you were right, I knew better than to touch you when you were having a bad dream." Her expression was apologetic, like she was the one who had hurt him rather than it being the other way around. She was right, she shouldn't have touched him. But she was also right when she'd said earlier that she didn't know what else to do.

In the end, it was his fault for falling asleep waiting for their appointment. Over the years, he'd gotten used to not having a regular sleep schedule. Usually, he took short naps a few times throughout the day rather than sleeping through the night. It kept him in a near constant state of one step away from exhaustion, but it was the only way he knew how to live these days.

Watching as Chelsea hurried up the stairs, he found he couldn't take his eyes off her. What the hell had Eagle been thinking, okaying this plan? Didn't he get that Chelsea was too innocent, too naïve to do an undercover operation like this? She didn't have the ruthlessness needed to be able to play a character under pressure, knowing that one single slip-up could end your life. She should be tucked away at Prey, protected and safe, not here with him, walking willingly into the lion's den.

The phone in his hand had stopped ringing, but it buzzed with a voice message, and he sighed.

He already knew what the message would say.

Usually, he would ignore them, delete them straight away, but today he found his finger bringing up the voicemail. Tonight he needed to suffer a little, he'd hurt Chelsea, been rude and angry with her when all she'd ever been with him was kind and caring. Hurting her to keep her away was necessary, but it never felt good.

Today, it felt particularly bad.

Holding the phone to his ear, when his brother's voice —his brother's *angry* voice—came from the phone, his knees wobbled a little. Hearing from anyone in his family was a double-edged sword. He still loved them, of course, but he couldn't let them back into his life. Cutting them out kept him in control. It meant that losing them wouldn't hurt so badly. His parents were getting older, sooner or later, they'd pass away, and he needed to know he could handle it without falling apart.

No one realized what a tightrope he walked each day, how close to a catastrophic breakdown he really was.

"What the hell is wrong with you, Josiah? How could you be so selfish? Six years. Six years you've refused to see us, to speak to us. I know you went through hell, man, but punishing your family because of it is crazy. Josh was married this weekend, and you weren't there for it. Another family milestone missed, and Mom is heartbroken. She wants her baby boy back. You're killing her, I hope you know that. That's it. We're all married now except you. No more weddings for you to attend, no way to make it up to Mom for her broken family. If I didn't love you, I would hate you. Call Mom. Please. You want us to beg, I'm begging. Call Mom."

Jackson's plan to make him feel like the most horrible son in the world had worked. But his brother didn't get it, his whole family didn't understand. How could they? They hadn't felt a bullet pierce their body while watching the men they served with fall around them like dominoes, their empty eyes staring sightlessly at the sky.

His brother was wrong, though, he was married too. To a woman he could never deserve in a thousand lifetimes.

A woman he was going to destroy the same way he'd destroyed his mom and his family.

Death and destruction seemed to follow him wherever he went.

❧

May 12<sup>th</sup>
    7:44 A.M.


Okay, she could do this.

She could step out of this room and act like she had it all together. Like she wasn't a bundle of nervous energy, uncertain what the right thing to do or say was.

Yesterday, after she'd gone upstairs to unpack, she hadn't seen Josiah again for the rest of the night. She'd cooked dinner for the two of them, set the table, and thought they could talk a little, about neutral topics of course, before they sorted out the sleeping arrangements.

Turned out she shouldn't have worried about them.

When she'd finally tracked Josiah to the gym in the garage, she'd found the door locked. He'd ignored her calls that dinner was ready, and eventually she'd given up, gone back up to the kitchen, and eaten alone.

Stupidly, she'd still clung to some hope that the evening could be salvaged.

After cleaning up and putting his food away in the fridge in case he wanted to eat it later, she'd settled into the living room to watch some TV. Her hope had been that he'd come up, heat his food, and they could talk in there while he ate.

But he never came.

Eventually, she'd gone up to bed alone, not the way she'd thought she would ever spend a wedding night. This wasn't a real wedding, and it wasn't like she'd expected them to have wild, passionate sex, but was wanting a little bit of company really so bad? Couldn't Josiah have given her that at least?

Instead, he'd never even come up to the room.

It had taken her at least an hour to fall asleep, and he still wasn't there, plus every time she woke during the night, the room was empty. When she got out of bed thirty minutes ago, it was clear he hadn't even brought his suitcase up to the room.

She tried not to let it hurt. This wasn't a real marriage, and they weren't really even friends, although not for lack of trying on her part. She wasn't expecting a magical change in Josiah just because he was pretending to care about her, but she needed something. Needed him to at least make somewhat of an effort.

Since she was supposed to be sick enough to be in dire need of a transplant, after her shower, Chelsea hadn't bothered to do much more than pull her hair back into a simple ponytail, because she knew that made her look younger, and leave her face free of makeup. She'd even chosen a simple outfit, just denim capris, and a button-up short-sleeved blouse. They had a doctor's appointment this morning, so she had to look presentable, but if she were gravely ill, she wouldn't be worrying too much about her appearance.

Determined not to let Josiah's bad attitude destroy her own, she pasted on a smile and walked out of the ensuite. The bedroom was still empty, but Josiah couldn't hide in the gym all day. He had to accompany her to the appointment, and she was determined that they set a few ground rules.

Fake or not, for the moment they were married and living together. They had no idea how long it would be before the trafficking ring contacted them, and there was a chance that it would never happen, but she had no intention of being ignored that entire time.

Josiah didn't like this arrangement, he didn't have to,

but he still had to accept it. And that started with eating meals together. It was only a small thing. He could hide in the gym the remainder of the time when they didn't have appointments to go to, but meal time was going to be together time, whether he liked it or not.

To that end, she headed down to the kitchen. Because she liked to torture herself, apparently, she stopped to check each of the three bedrooms on the next floor down on her way, just to see if Josiah had decided to use any of them. They were all empty, the beds neatly made, and when she reached the ground floor, she spotted Josiah's suitcase right where it had been when she went up to bed.

He hadn't really spent the entire night in the gym, had he?

The door to the basement was in the kitchen, and she was heading there anyway, so she eased it open and slipped down the stairs. Josiah's truck was parked down there, and one of the doors was partly open. Had he slept in his car last night? Was that really the lengths he was prepared to go to just to avoid her?

That stung.

If he had really been that against sharing a bed with her, he could have used the floor like he'd planned or the couch in their bedroom like she'd suggested. He could have used any one of the other three bedrooms. He could have slept on the couch in the living room.

Instead, he'd slept in his car.

She'd known he didn't want her here, but that was taking things to the extreme.

Since she could hear him working over a punching bag in the gym and assumed he would have locked the door again to keep her out, Chelsea didn't bother saying anything, just hurried back up to the kitchen to make breakfast. Chances were, he wasn't going to eat with her, but she was going to make him breakfast anyway. There had been real pain on his face last night when he looked at his phone and saw who was calling.

As difficult as he made it to feel sorry for him sometimes, she reminded herself that Josiah was hurting. He didn't lash out for fun, or because he was a cruel person, and he didn't push people away because he didn't care about them. It was all self-preservation.

When he was at his least likable, it was when he needed compassion the most.

So she chopped up enough ingredients to make two omelets, and refused to let her hurt feelings push her to retaliate with anger at Josiah ignoring her. He'd accepted her presence in this op only because Eagle and Raven had agreed that her plan was more likely to yield results than his.

Just as she was dishing up their plates, she heard footsteps on the stairs.

Dragging in a deep breath, Chelsea painted on a smile and turned to face the door.

Josiah paused slightly when he spotted her standing in the kitchen, and from the scowl on his otherwise handsome face, she knew he'd been hoping she wouldn't be in there and he could sneak away and get ready, then only have to deal with her when it was time to leave.

"Perfect timing, breakfast is ready," she said as she carried both plates over to the table.

"I was—"

"You were what? Going to skip breakfast like you skipped dinner?" she asked, daring him to go ahead and leave this room without having consumed the food she'd cooked for him.

"Didn't skip dinner," he grumbled, but he opened the

fridge, grabbed a carton of orange juice, and brought it to the table.

"Oh? Because I don't remember you answering me the dozen times I yelled through the door to tell you dinner was ready. I don't remember you sitting at the table with me to eat, and I don't remember hearing you come up while I was watching TV." It wasn't that she wanted him to feel bad, and she wasn't trying to be childish, but he had to understand that while this was hard for him, that didn't make it easy for her. She'd never done anything like this before, and it was scary knowing she was willingly walking into danger. The least she needed right now was a little bit of support from the man who was, for better or worse, her partner for the foreseeable future.

"Had some extra energy I had to work out," he mumbled as he poured them both juice, returned the carton to the fridge, and then took the seat across from her.

Had some extra *emotions* to work out, he meant, but she didn't correct him. At least he was here now, and she intended to take this moment to get a few things straight. This was turning out to be harder than she'd thought it would be, but she wasn't backing down, wasn't giving up.

Maybe she wasn't up to the enormous task before her, but she was going to give it her best shot. She wasn't giving up, and Josiah had to accept that.

"Yeah, we need to talk about your skipping meals to work out. I know you don't like this, but we're here together, and I don't want to be completely ignored. I'd like us to agree on sharing meals. I won't ask anything else from you. If you want to spend the rest of your time in the gym, or on your laptop, or sleeping in your car, that's up to you. But can we please sit down together to eat our meals?"

Josiah's brown eyes were wide with surprise. He obviously hadn't expected her to be so upfront about her needs or confront him on ignoring her. Thing was, she might be naïve at times, and she was for sure a romantic at heart. She went out of her way to look for the good in people, but that didn't make her a pushover. She could stand up for herself and she was doing it now.

"I didn't sleep in the car," he said.

"Well, you didn't sleep upstairs in our room, or in any of the other rooms, or on the couch, and your car door was open when I went down to look for you this morning."

"Just sat in there to work out some cramps," he muttered, refusing to look at her as he stabbed his fork into his omelet with more force than was necessary. "Overdid it in the gym."

"Then don't do that again," she said simply, pleased that he'd been honest with her. A teeny tiny little baby step, but at least he'd let her in with that one little thing. Maybe this wasn't as completely hopeless as she'd thought. Josiah was never going to reciprocate her feelings. He wasn't going to magically fall in love with her, but maybe he'd let her be his friend. That wasn't all she wanted from him, but it was better than nothing.

Better than seeing him slowly die inside even as he kept breathing.

# CHAPTER

## Three

May 12<sup>th</sup>
   10:22 A.M.

His foot bounced as they waited.

He should stop it, betraying any of his nervousness could be misconstrued by Chelsea as meaning more than it did.

Of course, he was nervous. He was taking a woman into a situation that wasn't only unsafe, but that she was untrained and unprepared for. Chelsea was tough, he wasn't denying that. She handled the things they saw in their line of work without losing her cool, but seeing it on a computer screen and living it were two completely different things.

This wasn't her world, and yet she was about to be thrust into it.

At full speed.

Without a parachute on.

"It's going to be okay, Josiah," Chelsea said gently.

They were sitting side by side in the waiting room at the hospital. This was the same hospital they already knew had a connection to the trafficking ring. It was the hospital Ava had attended mere weeks before she was targeted and abducted. The same hospital that several other young, healthy adults had a connection to before they also turned up missing.

Since they needed the trafficking ring to find out that Chelsea was supposedly sick, Prey had vetted one of the doctors here and briefed him on their plan. The man would take them on as patients, make sure to talk about the case as much as he could without drawing undue suspicion, and keep them updated if he felt like anyone was accessing his files.

Because this mission was so critical, they had to take it a step further than that.

If they could get themselves a meeting with the trafficking ring, that would include having some of the ring's own medical personnel take a look at Chelsea. While of course they were not going to actually do anything to damage her kidneys badly enough that she was legitimately in need of a kidney transplant, they had to do something so that she at least passed for sick when they got their meeting.

That's what had his foot bouncing anxiously this morning.

Chelsea didn't seem worried about literally playing with her health. Or at least if she was, she was doing a better job at hiding it than he was. He was terrified that whatever the doctor suggested they do to make Chelsea appear ill would have long-lasting implications for her health. They had to walk a fine line, make her ill enough not to rouse suspicion, but not make her sick enough that she walked away from this with irreparable damage caused.

It should have been him.

He didn't care if he walked away with lasting damage to his body. His sole purpose in living was only to honor the memories of the men who had died at his side that day six years ago. That, and to protect himself from more pain.

But he didn't care when he died.

He didn't care if that day was tomorrow, next week, next year, or fifty years from now.

Actually, that wasn't quite true. He'd much prefer to die next year than in fifty years' time.

"We're here to make you sick, not better," he growled under his breath so the other patients in the waiting room didn't overhear.

"Not *sick* sick, just enough to fool them," she soothed like that was any better.

Before he could say anything, the door to the doctor's room opened, and Chelsea's name was called. They both stood, and he was startled enough by the easy way she slid her hand into his that his fingers automatically curled around hers.

If he held on a little too tight, that was only because he wanted to be supportive. Not because he needed her. She was the one taking most of the risks, he was little more than glorified muscle.

"Good morning, Mrs. Fleet, Mr. Fleet," the doctor greeted them as they entered his office, and he closed the door behind them.

Hearing someone call Chelsea his last name sent an unexpected shaft of ... something ... through his chest. It wasn't anger, but it wasn't really pleasure either. In fact, he couldn't decide if he hated it or liked it. But it was a reminder that he had a role to play, and while the doctor was in on it, he'd better start getting used to playing the role of doting husband.

Pulling out a chair for Chelsea, he helped her into it, then took the seat beside her. "Whatever you're going to do to her, I don't want it to be something she can't come back from," he blurted out.

A hand landed on his knee, and since he knew it was Chelsea's, and she was also just playing her role, he didn't look down at it.

Wanted to though.

Because it didn't feel like she was just playing a role.

She'd had a crush on him pretty much from the beginning, but he'd always thought that it would eventually fade when she realized her feelings weren't reciprocated. Only it hadn't. He often caught her sneaking what she thought were little, unobtrusive glances at him, and saw the love shining brightly from her eyes. Despite his terrible attitude, she'd found something in him compelling enough to develop feelings for him.

She saw something in him he couldn't even see in himself.

He was too consumed with grief, guilt, and rage to feel anything even remotely human anymore. But whatever lingering light that was left in his world, it was there solely because of the woman sitting beside him.

"I've been thinking about what we should do," the doctor said. "A quick rundown of the signs of kidney failure are swelling of the legs, ankles, and feet, urinating less, itchy skin, tiredness, trouble sleeping, loss of appetite, nausea and vomiting, muscle cramps, and headaches. Most of those things can be faked without the need to do anything. If you can get a meeting with these people, Mrs. Fleet can easily pretend to be nauseous and tired, there's no way to prove or disprove she's having muscle cramps or headaches. Same with the loss of appetite and urinating less. So, I thought we would focus on one specific symptom, while also setting you up to have fake dialysis at home. Although we will have to insert a catheter into your abdomen," the doctor said apologetically to Cheslea.

Josiah felt his insides clench at the thought.

Of course, he'd known they'd need to do something, but inserting a catheter....

It made him feel sick.

"What else?" he snarled at the doctor, noting how the man paled at the venom in his tone.

"Josiah," Chelsea rebuked. "He's just worried, sorry about that. What was the other symptom you thought we should focus on?"

Eying him warily, the doctor focused his attention on Chelsea instead. "The swelling. We'll need to send you along with some blood and urine samples if you get a meeting. You'll have to figure out how to swap out the samples they take from you with the ones we'll give you. But if they do a physical exam, the swelling in your legs will give credibility to your claims."

"And how do we do that?" he growled.

"I was thinking we could give Mrs. Fleet prednisone," the doctor replied.

"Steroids?" he demanded, not liking the idea one little bit.

"Prednisone is used to treat many different issues, including ones that would be easily explainable if they found out she was taking it. It can cause swelling in the legs and feet, exactly like we need it to."

"But it might not," Josiah countered.

The doctor nodded. "We'll have her on a fairly high

dose, because she won't be taking it for a prolonged period, I'm fairly certain that we can simulate the swelling from kidney failure with the prednisone."

"What other side effects does the drug have?" Josiah asked.

"High blood sugar, increased blood pressure, infection, low adrenal gland function, which would actually help with some of the other symptoms Mrs. Fleet would have to fake, like nausea, vomiting, loss of appetite. Mood and behavior changes, and stomach bleeding. Which again, blood in urine would help with your claims of kidney failure."

"Absolutely not." Josiah shoved away from the table. This was too much. Too dangerous. It was one thing to take an untrained civilian into a dangerous undercover operation, it was quite another to willingly inflict this kind of potential damage on her body.

"This was always going to come with dangers," the doctor said. "You knew that. You want me to help you simulate organ failure. The only way to do that is to use medications that might cause damage to her body, and a whole lot of lying. I don't enjoy being part of this, but since it's for such a good cause, I'm doing everything I can to ensure that Mrs. Fleet is safe, both with the medications I'll give her, and in trying to ensure she passes whatever examinations they give her to keep your cover. In the end, the only person who can decide if this is worth the risk is Mrs. Fleet herself."

Josiah wanted to order Cheslea to tell the doctor this was too much, that she'd go back to Prey and let him take on all these risks, but he already knew from the stubborn glint in her eyes that she wasn't going to let him do that.

"Whatever we need to do, I'm up for it," Chelsea said, her voice calm and sure. "These people have already hurt so many, and they made it personal when they went after the people I care about. It's worth the risk."

May 12th
    4:17 P.M.

There was no way she would regret her decision, but Chelsea definitely felt yucky as she stretched out on the couch in the living room of her and Josiah's rented townhouse.

They'd been at the hospital for hours this morning, talking things through with the doctor in more detail, having the catheter inserted, and setting up fake dialysis appointments. Prey had virtually unlimited resources, and they would hire someone to come by daily with a fake machine so that no real time or resources were wasted on their charade.

Despite her fear about what this might do to her body and the danger she'd be walking into, she knew she'd made the right choice. Life was about taking risks, and while she'd never been much of a risk taker, she was glad she was doing this. For years, she'd sat nice and safe in front of her computer, tucked away in Prey's secure building. It had never really occurred to her that danger lurked so closely until Ava had been abducted.

Of course, she knew the world was a dangerous place. She couldn't not get that when she spent her days scouring intel that would be used to help keep Prey teams alive as they went on dangerous ops and gathered the information they needed to rescue innocents, or capture and sometimes kill dangerous people. But doing that from the safety of her computer and seeing it happen in real life were so very different.

Ava's abduction changed everything.

Then Tobias going back into the field after a back injury, which ended his career, because the trafficking ring had gone after one of their own had inspired her. He'd been willing to put his health on the line, and in the end, he'd come out of it finding the woman he wanted to spend the rest of his life with.

And Teresa had been willing to allow herself to be abducted by the ring a second time to try to get them intel. If her tracker she'd been working on had failed, she could have lost her life, but that hadn't stopped her.

Her friends, her teammates, they were brave enough to make tough choices for the greater good, and she wanted to be the same. Maybe she was a bit more naïve than the rest of them, maybe she was a bit softer, but she could be brave, she could be strong, she could even be tough.

She had to be, because she wanted this trafficking ring destroyed.

This was her part to play in making it happen, and there were going to be no regrets. If she felt a little sick for a while, it was a small price to pay. Certainly a much smaller price than Ava had paid. She'd had a kidney stolen by the ring. A smaller price than Isabella had paid, she'd been tortured and sexually assaulted by the guards while forced to play nurse to the ring's victims. And they'd taken part of Teresa's liver, but still she'd been prepared to take them on again.

They'd all lost so much, and all she had to do was take some medication that made her feel a little queasy.

Easy peasy.

"Here."

Startled, she looked over the back of the couch to see Josiah walking out of the kitchen carrying a steaming mug in his hands. When they finally got home from the hospital, she'd gone up to take a shower and change, then settled on the couch in the living room, while he'd disappeared, she assumed to go back to the gym and work out his excess energy.

Honestly, she hadn't expected to see him again until dinner time, and given how she was feeling, she probably would have ordered something rather than cooked. But it wasn't even four thirty yet, still at least an hour away from when she'd drag herself to the kitchen or give in and order takeout.

"Coffee?" she asked as she took the mug.

"Tea. Lavender. Supposed to relax you or something." He shrugged and looked away, like he was embarrassed.

Not that he needed to be.

Being thoughtful was nothing to be embarrassed about, it was just normal, common courtesy behavior. Still, for six years, Josiah had been working at pushing people away, keeping distance between them, so it was no wonder he was feeling uncomfortable now, he wasn't used to doing this kind of thing anymore.

"Thank you. I love lavender tea, it's actually my favorite." Holding the mug up to her nose, she breathed in deeply, letting the soft scent soothe her. Trying out different flavors of tea was always fun, and the first sip she'd taken of lavender many years ago had her hooked.

He grunted but then held out his hand. "Painkillers."

For a moment, Chelsea thought about assuring Josiah that she wasn't in too much pain, it was more just like general discomfort taking over all of her body, but he was making an effort, trying to take care of her, and she found she couldn't say no.

"Thank you," she said again as she took the pills, popped them into her mouth, and swallowed them down with a sip of her tea. "Mmm," she moaned in delight as the sweet lavender flavor touched her tongue. "This is perfect. I didn't even realize I needed it until you made it for me."

Another grunt, but she would have sworn that Josiah's cheeks pinked slightly. "Let me take a look at your stomach," he said, already dropping to his knees. He didn't wait for her to lift the hem of her oversized T-shirt to give him access to the small wound and device that was now attached to her, although not as it would be if she were really having dialysis.

"Doesn't hurt, just a little annoying," she assured him, because his brow had furrowed and she wasn't even sure he was aware that one of his large hands rested against her stomach, his thumb brushing small circles around the tube.

This right here was why she'd fallen so hard for this man. He was angry at the whole world, she got that, but it was because of what had happened to him, because of all he'd lost. Josiah was a good man who didn't know how to deal with his trauma and was so terrified of suffering any more loss that he had erected a thousand-foot razor wire-topped fence around his heart.

But he was suffering alone, and he didn't have to.

She was here, and she'd help if he could just let her.

"I am feeling a little ... blah, though. So I thought I might just order us some dinner rather than cook. I guess that means you're off the hook for eating with me tonight." She could use the company, but the deal was that if she cooked, he ate with her. If she wasn't, she couldn't expect him to hang around, that wouldn't be fair.

His gaze snapped up to meet hers. "You hate ordering food."

Surprised he knew that about her, she gave a small nod. "Guess I've been too spoiled over the years. My mom loved cooking, so we hardly ever ate out, and Teresa loves cooking, too, so since we live together, she usually cooks for all of us."

Josiah cleared his throat, and she didn't need to know him well to know he was uncomfortable again. "I already got a pot roast cooking."

There was nothing he could have said that would have surprised her more.

Nothing.

Not even if he told her he was a Martian who'd come to take over the Earth.

"A pot roast?"

"We had all the ingredients," he said, dropping his gaze again to stare at her stomach. "I put in carrots, potatoes, onion, and parsnip. I thought you might not feel like cooking, and I didn't want you to have to order takeout if we could avoid it."

"That's so sweet, thank you," Chelsea gushed.

Josiah just grunted and shrugged, moving her T-shirt back down to cover the tube. Before he could stand and move away, she grabbed hold of his hand, keeping him close. Not ready for there to be much distance between them. Even though he would have preferred to do this alone, she was part of it, and he was all she had for a support system. She was all he had, too.

"I mean it. I know you don't like any of this. I know you don't ... like me—"

"Stop saying that," he growled.

"Saying what?"

"That I don't like you. I never said I didn't like you."

"I just assumed. You don't like anyone." She got that it was to protect himself and not personal, but still, Chelsea believed that Josiah no longer had the ability to like people.

"The only people I hate are those responsible for killing my team. Are you responsible for that?"

"Uh-uh." She shook her head for emphasis.

"Then I don't dislike you," he grumbled as he gently tugged his hand free from her hold. "I'd better go check on dinner."

"It takes at least four hours or so to make a pot roast," she called after his retreating back. She heard his grumble, but it was a half-hearted one at best, and she giggled in delight at the revelation he'd just given her.

He liked her.

Josiah actually liked her.

Not in the way she wanted him to, but he'd told her he didn't dislike her and mentioned his team in front of her when he usually never spoke about them at all.

Maybe things weren't completely hopeless, maybe together they really could work together to bring down the organ trafficking ring, and come out the other side as friends.

# CHAPTER

May 13th
9:53 A.M.

"If you don't feel up to this, we can—"

"What?" Chelsea cut him off. "We can what?"

Josiah dragged his fingers through his hair. He'd been right to want to keep Chelsea as far away from this mess as he could. This plan would have been so much easier if he was working it alone. So he didn't have to worry about anyone else. The last time he'd worked in the field with a team ...

They all wound up dead.

Slaughtered.

Their bodies riddled with bullet holes. Empty eyes staring at nothing. Still. Too still.

Dragging in a somewhat shuddering breath, he forced himself to remember that Chelsea would not wind up like that. As much as he hated her being part of this in any way other than her sitting safe and sound at Prey in front of her computer, there was no way she would wind up shot to death.

It wasn't what these people did.

Both of them were wearing the same trackers Teresa had used to lead them to her when the trafficking ring had been targeting her.

Knowing Chelsea would be rescued promptly if the worst happened and they were abducted, didn't seem to still the churning anxiety in his gut.

Taking care of Chelsea last night when she felt sick had forced him to accept the fact that while maybe he was ready to be back in the field if he was alone, there was no way he was ready to deal with a team. He should never have allowed Prey to agree to let Chelsea be part of this with him.

There were ways he could have disregarded his boss' wishes. Like disappearing, going off-grid, or taking what he knew and making his own attempts to get a meeting with Desiree Tilly. The worst that could have happened was that he lost his job, and while he didn't think that would happen because he knew he had Eagle Oswald at his back, even if he had been fired, it wasn't the worst thing in the world.

He'd already lived through that.

"Look, Josiah, I know you don't like that I'm here, and I'm not going to lie and say I'm not scared, because I am."

Chelsea's soft admission had his heart rate jumping up.

Her fear ...

It affected him in ways he didn't like. Didn't want.

From the moment he first met her, he knew she was going to be trouble. There was something engaging about her, appealing, she drew him in even as he wanted to stand alone.

Alone was safe.

You couldn't lose anyone if you were alone. There was no one to lose.

"You know how I can do this even though I'm scared?"

Shaking his head at her question was automatic.

A hand slipped into his, slim fingers curling around his own. "Because you're here. You won't let them hurt me."

How could she have such honest faith in him?

There was no way she didn't know at least the basics about how his team had been slaughtered. If she knew, then she had to know he hadn't saved them. If he hadn't saved his team, there was every chance he wouldn't save her either.

"Mrs. Fleet."

The nurse's call had them both standing. Despite how uncomfortable Josiah was with Chelsea's unfounded confidence in him, he reached for her elbow to steady her, genuinely concerned about her ability to stay upright, even though she had assured him this morning that she was feeling better than she'd been yesterday afternoon when she started taking the drugs.

The problem was, she looked sick. He had no idea if she'd used makeup or something to create the effect or if it was genuine. That bothered him. How was he supposed to take care of her if he didn't know what signs were real and what weren't?

What happened if he failed her, too?

"We're here," Chelsea called out, placing her hand over the one he had gripping her elbow, likely way too tightly. She squeezed once, then leaned in and murmured, "We can do this, Josiah. *I* can do this. Scared or not, I am capable of playing this role. Have a little faith in me."

The thing was, it had nothing to do with having faith in her abilities or lacking it. When he was still a SEAL, he'd put his life in the hands of his team, he'd never once doubted their ability to watch his six the same way he watched theirs. Despite that trust, that faith, he'd still lost them.

Wishing there was any way he could do this doctor's visit without Chelsea by his side, they both followed the nurse down a short corridor and into the doctor's office. It was a different room from the one they'd met in yesterday, but it was supposed to be a visit with the same doctor. The falsified medical records that Prey had put together showed that Chelsea had been declining for months, and that the Prey doctor she'd been seeing—who didn't really exist— had referred her to the hospital because she had progressed to the point of needing a transplant.

There was every chance that the trafficking ring wouldn't buy that any of this was real, and he still believed he would have had a better shot at doing this alone, but they were here now, and they would have to sell this story with everything they had.

Both he and Chelsea faltered slightly when they entered the room the nurse guided them to, and found a different man sitting behind the desk. The man was older, close to retirement age, he was thin, almost too thin, completely bald, and wearing a pair of wire-rimmed glasses that accentuated his almost birdlike beak of a nose.

He was one of them.

The calculating gleam in the doctor's blue eyes as he gave them both a scrutinizing once over told Josiah everything he needed to know. This doctor was here to feel them out and see if they might be open to the idea of getting an organ through the trafficking ring.

That, or he was here to try to set them up.

Whatever play the ring was making, he and Chelsea were in too deep to just back out.

Not that it seemed like Chelsea wanted to anyway.

"Oh, you're not Dr. Marcus," she said, her tone perfectly confused, whether on purpose or because she was genuinely confused, he had no idea. Maybe he should have gotten to know Chelsea a little better before they jumped into this, because he was finding it almost impossible to read the woman, and that could spell disaster.

"Dr. Marcus had to pass this case on to me," the man said, rising and walking around his desk. "I'm Dr. Wood. Pleasure to meet you, Mrs. Fleet, Mr. Fleet."

"Nice to meet you too," Chelsea said with a gracious smile, holding out her hand to shake the doctor's.

Josiah merely grunted. They weren't undercover as different people, so he didn't have to pretend to be someone he wasn't. All he had to do was be himself and pretend that he was in love with Chelsea.

"Is Dr. Marcus okay? He's not ill or anything? He seemed okay yesterday, and again when he called early this morning to set up another appointment, so I do hope he hasn't been in an accident or anything," Chelsea said. There was nothing in her tone that indicated she was feeling the fear she'd mentioned to him not even two minutes ago. Seemed she was braver than she gave herself credit for.

"He's fine. I actually asked to take over this case after viewing your file. Dr. Marcus specializes more in the treatment of kidney diseases, but I'm a transplant specialist, Mrs. Fleet," the man said with what Josiah could only consider to be fake sympathy. The gleam in his eyes remained calculating and predatory.

If he had to guess, Josiah would say that Dr. Wood went through files at the hospital looking for prospective buyers. People who might have the means to pay for a black-market organ. Unfortunately, he still wasn't sure if it was because he genuinely believed they might buy one despite them working for Prey, or the ring was trying to play their own game.

"O-oh," Chelsea stammered, sounding totally shocked, and this time he knew she was faking.

Damn, she was one hell of an actress.

Wide gray eyes turned to look up at him, before returning to the doctor. "Does that m-mean you think I-I need a t-transplant?"

"Please, come and sit, Mrs. Fleet, and we can discuss everything in more detail," Dr. Wood said, oozing fake charm as he once again reached for Chelsea's hand.

This time, Josiah had to force himself not to rip the man's arm right off.

Nobody touched Chelsea without her permission.

If she hadn't darted out her free hand to grasp his, he might very well have done something stupid, but her touch grounded him, soothed the roughest edges of the rage that boiled constantly inside him.

"I know you're scared, Josiah, I am too, but we should listen to the doctor before we panic," Chelsea said, her voice like a cool wave crashing over him, subduing a little more of his red-hot fury

Not trusting himself to speak without growling at the doctor to get his hands off Chelsea, he merely nodded and placed his hand in the small of her back to guide her toward the desk.

They were halfway there when she wobbled.

Josiah was already reaching for her when it happened.

Her eyes rolled back in her head, and she collapsed.

∾

May 13<sup>th</sup>
    10:03 A.M.


They had him.

Chelsea was positive of that.

This Dr. Wood guy was here to feel them out, see if they might be willing to purchase an organ from the trafficking ring. If he was involved in the ring, they needed to get this office bugged. The more intel they could give to Prey, the better their chances at getting to Desiree Tilly and dismantling the entire operation.

What better way to get a few moments alone than to fake faint?

As she knew he would, Josiah's arms caught her before she hit the floor, and he scooped her up, cradling her with a gentleness that might have surprised anyone else, but not her. She'd always known, under the layers of anger he'd covered himself with was a big heart hidden away.

"Put her down here," Dr. Wood said, and Josiah carried her a few steps before setting her down in what was likely one of the chairs at the desk they'd been heading for anyway.

Someone picked up her wrist, and she knew it was the doctor checking her pulse.

A growl rumbled from Josiah, who still had an arm wrapped around her shoulders. Leaning into him was the easiest thing in the world, and she had to fight against a smile at the protective vibes he was giving off.

He could pretend all he wanted not to care about her, or the rest of their team, but she knew without a shadow of a doubt that he cared about them more than he was comfortable with.

Caring about people meant opening yourself up to the potential pain of losing them, and that wasn't something Josiah could handle.

"What's wrong with her?" Josiah demanded.

"Looks like she just fainted," the doctor replied.

Because she didn't want to be admitted to the hospital, it was vital she spend as little time being examined by anyone as possible, Chelsea gave a small moan and opened her eyes slowly, as though they were heavy.

"Josiah?" she mumbled, making her voice sound faint, thankful for the years of acting classes she'd taken as a kid. Her parents had been older by the time they had her. After trying all their married lives, they wound up getting pregnant with a late-in-life baby, right before her mom hit menopause. Because they were older, they weren't able to be as active with her, but they made sure she had every opportunity to try out anything she wanted. One of those things had been acting classes, and she'd taken them through middle and high school.

Now she was eternally grateful that her parents hadn't denied her anything.

"Yeah, Chels, I'm here." Fingers swept across her forehead, then smoothed a lock of hair, tucking it behind her ear.

"What happened?" she asked, keeping her voice small.

"You fainted, Mrs. Fleet," Dr. Wood told her.

"Oh. I just ... my head ... I guess I got lightheaded," she said softly.

"Have you been eating? Drinking enough water?" the doctor asked.

Scrunching up her nose, she shook her head. "I skipped breakfast this morning because I wasn't sure I could keep anything down." Actually, that was true, and she was sure it was a mixture of nerves and feeling a little nauseous from the medication she was taking.

Dr. Wood tutted. "That won't do. I understand it's difficult to eat when you're feeling ill, but your body still needs fuel. I'm going to grab some fluids, set up an IV, and it should be done by the time we're finished talking. If you're not feeling better after that, we can talk about admitting you to the hospital."

While she nodded her assent, Chelsea knew there was zero percent chance she was going to agree to stay any longer than she had to.

But they now had the perfect opportunity to plant the cameras and microphones she had hidden in her purse. All she needed was a couple of minutes without the doctor in the room to get them set up, then she'd let the IV run, and see if they could get the doctor to admit he worked for the trafficking ring.

"I'll be right back," the doctor said, patting her hand and making another growl rumble through the big man standing beside her.

Knowing they didn't have time to waste, the second the door closed behind the doctor, she jumped to her feet, already unzipping her purse so she could scramble through it and find the cameras.

"What the hell?" Josiah snarled.

"Shh, hurry," she muttered. She didn't have time to explain, they had a couple of minutes at the absolute most. "Here, I brought two cameras and a microphone." Locating them, she shoved them toward her angry husband. "You'll know better than me where to put them so that he won't find them."

Taking a step toward her, getting right up in her

personal space, Josiah's voice was low and cold, deep with rage, when he spoke. "Did you just fake passing out?"

"Of course. Like I said, I brought a microphone and some cameras to plant in here. I thought if I pretended to faint, I could get us a couple of minutes alone, and it worked." Chelsea offered him a bright smile, but it died on her lips when she saw the rage dancing in his dark brown eyes.

He was angry.

Really angry.

It wasn't like it was a big deal.

Certainly nothing he should be furious about.

She took an instinctive step back. Not because she thought Josiah would actually hurt her, but because there was too much rage rolling off him and she was about as unconfrontational as it was possible for a person to get.

"We have to hide these now," she said quickly, pushing the small devices into his hands. "He's going to be back any second. What's done is done, there's no point in stressing over it. It worked, and we can bug his office. Please, Josiah."

With a snarl, he snatched the microphone and cameras from her hand and made quick work of planting the monitoring devices, then he stalked toward her, a dangerous look on his face.

Only this time she didn't move away from him.

If anything, her body drifted closer.

There was no denying he was utterly furious with her, although she wasn't quite sure why exactly that was. Josiah was a dangerous man, he was highly trained, and had years of experience. If he wanted to, he could snap her in half as though she was nothing more than a twig.

And yet she didn't fear the man. This whole protective rage thing he had going on made warmth spread through her. Whatever his reason for being angry with her, all it did was prove to her that he cared.

"Don't you *ever* put yourself in danger like this again," he growled as his large hands closed around her shoulders, and he gave her one fierce shake.

While she could see he was completely serious about that, it kind of defeated the entire purpose of what they were here to do. This whole thing was dangerous. He was risking his life every bit as much as she was. She might be the one who had to pretend to be sick, but he was the only thing keeping them both alive. Chelsea was putting her life in Josiah's hands, and it was something she was more than happy to do. She trusted him, even if he didn't trust himself.

Both their heads snapped toward the door as they heard the sounds on the other side, and she quickly dropped back down into the seat she'd been in. Before Josiah could move back to stand beside her, the door swung open, and instead of trying to dart back to where he'd been when the doctor left, Josiah kept moving forward, making it seem as though he'd been pacing this entire time.

Apparently, Dr. Wood liked that, because he nodded approvingly at Josiah. "Don't worry, son, we're going to do everything we can to get your wife healthy again."

Josiah just grunted.

"Sorry about him, he's just worried," she said, making sure her voice sounded a little thready.

"No need for apologies, Mrs. Fleet. I can see how concerned he is for you. He must love you a great deal," the doctor said as he walked over to her and picked up her arm, readying it to set up the IV.

If only that were true.

What she wouldn't give to make Josiah fall in love with her.

But Chelsea had long ago accepted the fact that it was never going to happen. Her love would remain unrequited, and she seemed helpless to shut down her feelings, move on, and find someone who could love her back.

"Thank you for understanding." She shot the doctor as warm a smile as she could muster.

"Love leads people to do things they wouldn't normally consider. It changes people in ways they don't even understand." Dr. Wood met her gaze squarely. "I understand that better than most, Mrs. Fleet. That's why I'm here."

# CHAPTER
## *Five*

May 13th
    2:37 P.M.


His fists slammed into the bag over and over again.

Pain radiated up his arms.

It wasn't enough.

Didn't matter how many times he hit the damn bag, the fear inside him didn't abate.

Josiah hadn't felt as scared in a long time as he had in the moment when Chelsea collapsed in his arms.

Faking.

It had all been a trick.

Anger.

He'd been furious with her. Didn't she get that it was bad enough she was undercover with him, risking her life, without the skills necessary to give her a good chance of survival? Obviously, she didn't if she could take things a step further and tempt fate.

What if the doctor had admitted her? What if he'd run more tests that they were unprepared for? Chelsea wasn't sick, her kidneys were fine, if the ring found out that she was faking, she would find herself on a table ready to be carved up. He would, too, not that he cared about his own life, but Chelsea's ...

After watching his team get gunned down around him, surviving only because he hadn't yet taken off his body armor when the others had, he'd shut down. Ruthlessly rid himself of all emotions except for anger. It was the only way to survive.

But today he'd felt fear.

Terror.

Actually believed that something was wrong with her, that the medication she was taking to simulate some of the symptoms she should be having with kidney failure had made her sick. Or worse.

She'd been so cavalier about the whole thing, too. Jumping up as soon as they were alone and pulling out her gadgets. It wasn't a bad idea, and if she'd told him ahead of time what she intended to do, he might even have gone along with it.

Probably wouldn't have, but there was the slimmest of possibilities.

More than likely he would have taken the microphone and cameras in his pocket, pretended to leave something behind, then when the doctor was with Chelsea in the hall, go back to get it and plant their surveillance devices. That would have been the safest option, but Chelsea didn't seem to care about safety.

It was like she had some sort of death wish.

Logically, he knew that she did not. They'd known one

another for years now, and there was no one sweeter, more caring and kind, with a bigger heart, than Chelsea Pierce. She was every bit as sunshiny as the sun itself, and she saw the best in everyone. Despite all of that, she had a good head on her shoulders, she was smart and funny, observant and attentive to detail, and great at her job.

She was doing this because the trafficking ring had targeted their team, and she wanted to do her part to help stop them. He got all of that, and yet he couldn't seem to find his usual distance.

Josiah was aware that most people looking in from the outside would say that he kept himself separate from his team, that he didn't care about them or even like them. While it was true he did maintain an emotional distance, he liked every one of them just fine. He'd stepped up when Teresa needed their team to remind her she wasn't alone, and he watched over his team even when they weren't aware of it.

Keeping himself separate from them was the only way he could survive. Already he'd lost one team, he couldn't handle losing another.

Yet here Chelsea was, deep in the middle of an undercover operation, messing with his head because he cared about her a whole hell of a lot more than he should.

Caring about her left him open to more pain.

Pain he couldn't handle when the wounds left behind by his teammates' deaths still felt raw and open, not even partially healed.

Even now, hours later, after they'd finished up a meeting that had gone as well as they could have hoped for, the fear of losing Chelsea hadn't abated. Didn't matter that the morning had been a success, that Dr. Wood had come as close to admitting he had a way to get them a black-market organ without outright saying those words. If Chelsea had actually had a bad reaction to the drugs she was taking, in his mind it would have been a failure.

When had her life become more important than their op?

If he was being honest with himself, it always had. From the moment Raven agreed with her plan to come undercover with him, he was prioritizing her safety over everything else. He wanted this ring shut down, but not at the expense of Chelsea's life.

Picking up the pace, he slammed his fists into the bag repeatedly, refusing to give himself a break until his body began to weave with exhaustion.

What he needed was to get some proper rest, but he couldn't seem to get his brain to shut off. Sleep was bad enough for him on his best day, and being with Chelsea under these circumstances, he was absolutely not having any best days.

Of all the people in the world, she was the only one who could make the barriers he'd built around himself shake. She couldn't make them crumble, he couldn't allow her to do that, but she did make them shake a little, weaken. Not even his own family could do that. While he didn't enjoy cutting them out of his life, he had to do what was necessary to survive, and that meant no emotional attachments.

Not even with the woman he knew was sitting upstairs alone.

She might not have said the words, but Chelsea had clearly been hoping he would celebrate the morning's success with her when they got back to their rented townhouse. Unable to handle spending any time around her without exploding on her again like he had in Dr. Wood's office, he'd stalked straight down to the basement gym. He'd been going at the bag long enough that his hands ached, his shoulders ached, every muscle in his body felt tight, and sweat soaked his clothes and stung his eyes.

Knowing he couldn't keep going indefinitely, and if hitting the bag was going to rid him of the fear still floating through his system, it would have done it already, Josiah admitted defeat. Much as he'd like to push his body to its absolute limits, he also had to remember that he was responsible for Chelsea's safety. She didn't have the training needed for this kind of operation, and if he wound up passing out from exhaustion she would be a sitting duck.

Ripping the tape off his hands, Josiah tossed it into the trash and headed for the stairs. The higher he got, the tenser his body became. Chelsea was up there somewhere, and he had no idea what he was going to say to her when he saw her. It would be safer to say nothing than to go into another rage about her putting her life in danger this morning, but Chelsea wasn't big on silence.

By some miracle, both the kitchen and the living room were empty, and he took advantage of that and ran up the next flight of stairs, picking the closest bedroom to disappear into. Chelsea must be up in their bedroom, and he didn't want to run into her. Part of him was ashamed he'd snapped and yelled at her in Dr. Wood's office, the other part insisted he hadn't pushed hard enough to make her see her plan had been reckless and dangerous.

The longer he could avoid her the better.

Stripping out of the jeans and sweater he'd worn this morning, he removed his boxers and then leaned into the shower to turn the water on. While he waited for it to warm up, he checked the straps on his body armor.

It never came off.

Ever.

Nobody knew that he wore it literally everywhere he went. Hadn't taken it off since the day he'd been released from the hospital after the attack that killed his team. If anyone found out about it, they would insist on him seeing a therapist to talk through his issues, but the way he saw it, a therapist wasn't going to stop a bullet, but his body armor would. His team had lost their lives because they'd taken theirs off, he'd survived because he hadn't. No amount of talking about his feelings was going to change that.

So he wore the body armor. Hid it beneath sweaters that he wore no matter the weather. He'd rather be too hot than risk getting hit by a bullet.

Steam filled the air, and he stepped under the spray. With his body armor on, the water couldn't properly reach his muscles, work out the tension in them, but he didn't care. The feel of it on his skin was enough to help him relax, and he knew he was going to have to find a better way of handling his emotions.

Chelsea had taken a step away from him in that doctor's office this morning, she'd been afraid of him. That wasn't what he wanted. But the thing was, she *should* be afraid of him. He was so consumed by anger that he was every bit as much a danger to her as the trafficking ring they were trying to dismantle.

~

May 13th
    3:13 P.M.

.  .  .

The shower was running.

Of course, Josiah managed to time it for when she went upstairs to grab a sweater because she'd gotten chilly.

Chelsea thought he would have been over his anger at her for fake fainting this morning. Everything had worked out okay, there was no need for him to be so stressed about it. If the doctor had tried to admit her, she just would have claimed she was tired and needed to go home to rest. Nothing bad was going to happen to her, well not in the hospital this morning. The only thing that could make this all fall apart was if the ring caught on to the fact they were lying, and honestly, it was Josiah's anger in the doctor's office that had put them at risk more than her well thought-out gamble.

If she could just get him to stay still long enough to talk things through with her, she was sure she could assuage whatever fears it was that he had.

But he'd been hiding out in the gym ever since they got home.

She had tried to hint that it might be nice if they cele-brated their successful appointment with Dr. Wood by getting some takeout, or making lunch together, maybe enjoying the hot tub in their courtyard garden. Really, she would have settled for anything, even just chilling and watching a movie. Only he hadn't taken any of her hints, leaving for the basement the second they were through the door.

A couple of times she'd gone down to check on him, just to make sure he was okay, and she'd heard him pounding away on the punching bag that was in the gym. As much as she'd wanted to interrupt him, remind him she was okay, and ask him to come and spend a little time with her, she'd chickened out every single time.

Something about the fury burning in his dark eyes in Dr. Wood's office held her back.

Not because she thought Josiah would ever lay his hands on her no matter how angry he was, he wasn't that kind of man. It was just ... she had no idea how she was supposed to help him let go of that anger.

She wanted to, though.

Badly.

Some days it was all she could think about. And right now, here with Josiah, the two of them sharing a home, pretending to be married, it was hard to think about anything else. As much as she wanted to play her part in helping bring down the organ trafficking ring, she equally wanted to help Josiah however she could.

Problem was, she didn't have the first clue how to start.

With a sigh, she shook her head, passed the room with the shower running, and headed back downstairs.

It was boring being stuck here with nothing to do. She wanted to spend time with Josiah, maybe that would help her figure out how she could best help him, but he didn't seem inclined to spend any time with her.

Seemed that one evening of taking care of her when she was sick was all she was getting out of him.

Better than nothing she supposed as she flopped down onto the couch and picked up her book. And at least she was feeling better today. The medication still had her feeling slightly nauseous, and definitely lacking an appetite, but it wasn't anything she couldn't handle.

That's what Josiah didn't seem to get.

He thought she wasn't cut out for this kind of work. Granted, she had no official training, beyond Prey's self-defense training, which she got was nothing but a drip in the ocean compared to what Josiah had, but she could handle a weapon, and she did know a lot of self-defense, so she felt she could hold her own if it came down to it.

But it wasn't going to come down to it.

This was about playing a role and that was something she was good at. As she'd proved today. The whole fainting thing had worked exactly like she'd wanted it to. Josiah worried because of what had happened to his team, she understood that, but this wasn't the same thing at all.

Even if the worst happened and they were caught, all they had to do was activate Teresa's trackers and Prey would come for them.

Easy peasy.

Now how could she convince Josiah of that?

Especially if he wouldn't even talk to her.

Fixing her attention back on her book, she was just going to have to wait for Josiah to come to her. Badly as she wanted to, you couldn't help someone who didn't want to be helped, and right now, Josiah didn't want to be helped.

No more than a couple of minutes later, a phone began to ring.

It wasn't hers, because she had different ringtones for every person in her contact list, and none of them were playing right now.

Must be Josiah's phone. She hadn't even realized it was there, she assumed he'd had it with him in the basement, and that it was now upstairs in the bedroom or bathroom. Wanting to make sure it wasn't Prey, she set her book down and crossed to where the sound was coming from, finding Josiah's cell phone on a small end table.

There was a name on the screen, and it said it was Josiah's mom. Not Prey, but still a call he would want to take.

Worried that the call wouldn't last long enough for her to get the phone all the way upstairs, she scooped it up and answered. Josiah wouldn't mind, he'd want to speak with his mother, it could be something important.

"Hello," she said, bringing the phone to her ear.

"Hello?" the voice on the other end said. "Who is this? Is everything okay? Where's Josiah?"

"Mrs. Fleet?"

"Yes."

"I'm Chelsea, I work with Josiah." She couldn't mention the undercover operation they were on. Not only was it sensitive intel not to be shared with anyone outside those involved, she didn't know how close Josiah was with his mom and whether he'd told her he was undercover. She certainly didn't want to worry his mother, who had already almost lost her baby boy once before.

"Why are you answering my son's phone?" Mrs. Fleet asked. It wasn't that she sounded angry about it, if anything she sounded worried, and definitely confused.

"Josiah is in the shower." When the woman gasped, she realized how that sounded and rushed to explain. "Oh, that came out weird. I didn't mean it like it sounded. We're not together or anything. Like a couple. Definitely not a couple. We're just working, it's complicated. I'll go get him," she finished lamely as she started up the stairs, realizing she'd just babbled like a fool to the mother of the man she was hopelessly in love with.

A soft chuckle came down the line. "It's okay, dear. You sound very sweet. If you could get my boy for me that would be wonderful." The woman's voice hitched on that last word and Chelsea wondered what that was about.

"Of course. I'm heading upstairs now. I'll knock on the

door and let him know you're on the phone. He can either hop right out or call you back."

"No!" Mrs. Fleet yelled. "I'm sorry, dear. I didn't mean to shout. Would you please make sure you give him the phone without the option to hang up and call me back?"

"Umm … sure. Yes, of course." She had no idea why it was important, but maybe his mom really had called because there was some sort of family emergency. "I'm just at the bedroom door now and I can hear the shower still running. Hold on for a moment and I'll pass you over."

Lowering the phone, Chelsea eased open the door. The bedroom was empty as she had expected, and she crossed it to knock on the door to the attached bathroom.

"Josiah?" she called out. "Your mom is on the phone."

After waiting a few seconds and not getting an answer, she put her hand on the doorknob. She wouldn't look at him, that would be totally unprofessional and definitely violating, but she knew the layout of the bathrooms because she'd already explored the entire house. If she only opened the door a crack and kept her head turned to the side, she wouldn't be able to see anything she shouldn't.

"Josiah," she called out again as she edged the door open a couple of inches. "Your mom is on the phone. She wants to talk to you. I think it might be important."

The water shut off, and the next thing she knew, the door was ripped out of her hand, startling her. She snapped her head around to look at him, only for her mouth to drop open in shock.

He wasn't naked.

Well, not completely.

Everything down below was hanging out for all to see, but he was wearing a Kevlar vest that was dripping with water.

Had he worn it in the shower?

Why would he do that?

"What the hell are you doing in here? And why did you answer my phone?" he snarled at her as he snatched it out of her hand.

From the rage simmering in his voice, maybe she should rethink her whole Josiah would never hurt her idea.

# CHAPTER

## Six

May 13th
3:22 P.M.

His mom was on the phone.

Chelsea was standing before him, eyes wide, face pale.

Water streamed down his body.

Other than the body armor, he was naked.

Not that Josiah cared, that was the least of his problems right now.

What the hell had Chelsea been thinking, answering his phone?

So far, she hadn't answered his roared questions, just stared at him with her terror-filled eyes as the seconds ticked by.

From the phone he'd torn from her hand, he could hear his mother's voice calling his name. There was everything in her tone from desperation, to worry, to fear, and he realized he was simultaneously scaring the two women in the world who meant the most to him.

Disconnecting the call solved one of his problems, but not the other. Chelsea still stood there as though she was frozen in shock, and he hated that she was afraid of him. Again. For the second time today.

"I'm sorry," she said softly.

"You should be," he growled. "What gave you the impression it would be okay to touch my phone?"

"Thought it might be someone from Prey."

"My mother's number is saved in there. Her name would have been on the screen. You knew it wasn't someone from Prey," he snarled.

A fine tremor shuddered through her body, and he was struck by how much smaller she was than him. He had over a foot in height and probably a hundred pounds on her. Plus, he was acting unhinged, no wonder she was afraid of him.

"I didn't think you would be upset about a call from your mother." Despite her obvious fear, she met his gaze when she spoke.

Quickly, Josiah spun around.

The last thing he wanted was to see the terror in her big gray eyes.

Or pity.

Because now she knew.

For six years, he had kept from everybody around him that he was paranoid about taking a bullet. That he couldn't even stomach the idea of taking off this vest, much less actually go about doing it. Since he didn't let anyone get close to him, it hadn't been hard to keep it secret, and that Chelsea might have found out while they were living together had never occurred to him.

Why would it?

They weren't here to have sex or strip for each other.

They were here to do a job, and there was no reason for her to have stepped into his bathroom today.

*She didn't.*

*Not really.*

*The door was mostly closed.*

*The only reason she saw you was because you got angry and showed your hand.*

The voice whispered insidiously in the back of his mind, and Josiah dragged his fingers through his hair, tugging hard enough to make his scalp sting.

Good.

He needed the pain.

Something he could control, unlike the mess unraveling around him.

"Get out," he ordered as the phone, still clutched much too tightly in his hand, began to ring. His mom. He knew that without even having to look. Now that she'd heard his voice, she wasn't going to give up on trying to get through to him.

His heart ached.

Physically ached.

There was nothing more in the world that he would love than to be four years old again, crawling into his mother's arms and knowing he was safe, that the big, bad world couldn't touch him there, and letting her hugs and kisses soothe whatever pain or fear he was suffering.

But he wasn't a four-year-old child any longer. He was a fully grown adult and one who knew that nothing in the world could fix what had happened to his team. No amount of mother's kisses could bring back men from the dead, or rewrite history. And that was the only thing he needed.

"Josiah—" Chelsea's small hand rested on his shoulder, right beside where the vest covered his skin.

That touch was everything he craved and everything he couldn't have.

She knew now. There was no going back. Chelsea knew that he had lost part of his sanity out there in the sand, surrounded by his teammates' bodies. There was no way she would ever be able to look at him the same way again.

No longer able to see him as anything other than a ball of rage contained by flesh and bones.

"Get out," he roared.

The hand withdrew, and a moment later, he heard the door close behind him. Josiah would have sworn he also heard a whispered apology from Chelsea before she disappeared, and that she would apologize to him when he was the one in the wrong filled him with remorse.

Without thinking, he slammed his hand into the mirror, glass shards raining down around him as dozens of small cuts began to leak blood.

Good.

He deserved to hurt for hurting Chelsea.

The phone he still clutched in his other hand buzzed to indicate a voicemail, and because he wanted to punish himself, he unlocked his cell and tapped on the voice message.

*"You better not have hurt that poor girl, Josiah Darren Fleet. She didn't do anything wrong, and you know better than to raise your voice like that. I raised you better than that. So help me, if you do not reply to me right now, I am calling your boss, demanding your location, and driving straight over there to put you over my knee. I don't care that you're bigger than me now. It's bad enough you ignore your own*

*family, but yelling at that poor, sweet girl is just unacceptable."*

His mom was right, of course. Once again, he'd allowed his fear to explode on Chelsea, who absolutely did not deserve it. Of all the people in his life, she was the one who made a constant effort to try to get closer to him. Yeah, his parents and brothers called often, but it was Chelsea he saw day in and day out, who got to him more than he would ever admit with each kind word and soft smile.

Because he had no doubt his mom would follow through on her threat, he typed out a quick text. Talking to her wasn't something he could handle, and if he called with the intention of leaving a voicemail, she would pick up the call, so text it was.

**Of course I didn't hurt her
Chelsea is fine
But**

Although the idea left him trembling, he knew he owed her an apology.

More than that.

An explanation.

It might not be easy, but she had twice this morning been the recipient of his anger, and he didn't like knowing he'd scared her. Just because he hadn't put his hands on her didn't mean that he hadn't inflicted damage.

Damage he was responsible for fixing.

**I owe her an apology**
**Which I will give her**

Actually, he owed more than just Chelsea an apology. His entire family deserved one, but he wasn't in a place yet where he could face them. He loved them, and he couldn't put them in danger by placing himself back in their lives.

**I'll be waiting for my apology as well**
   **I still like roses**
   **And chocolate**
   **I love you, son**
   **And I'm still here when you're ready**
   **We all are**

His mother's words made his eyes sting with tears he wouldn't allow to fall. He didn't deserve her kindness, her love, not after everything he'd already put her through.

For six years, he had done everything in his power to avoid his family. Barring them from his hospital room. Blocking them on all social media. Changing the locks on his door. Refusing to see them when they tried to surprise him by showing up unannounced.

They had never given up on him, though.

Not a single one of them.

To say he didn't deserve them would be a massive understatement.

Ignoring the blood on his hand and the pain pulsing through it, he straightened his back and braced himself for what he had to do. Facing the prospect of offering apologies to his family might not be something he was ready to tackle, but he couldn't put off apologizing to Chelsea.

If for no other reason than because they were undercover together and he was supposed to be her husband, who was willing to buy black-market organs because he loved her so much. Nobody would believe that if she was afraid of him.

Only as he stalked out of the bathroom, Josiah knew it wasn't the case that had him going to apologize to the woman downstairs.

Truth was, he couldn't stand the idea of Chelsea being scared of him. Knowing that she was, felt like a thousand fire ants crawling all over his skin. He had to make things right, had to tell her he was sorry, and try to explain in a way that she would understand without exposing all the wounds he kept hidden from the world.

And if he couldn't, he would lose the best thing he had in his life.

May 13th
    3:30 P.M.

What was she going to do with him?

Chelsea paced the living room, knowing she needed to do something but not sure what that something was.

Maybe she should go back up there?

No.

He'd told her to leave, and she wanted to respect his

wishes. Besides, he'd likely be talking to his mom, maybe she could calm him down.

Only ...

Had he been upset about her seeing him in the vest, or because she'd answered his phone? Both?

It hadn't seemed like he was pleased about her answering, although she honestly hadn't thought she was doing anything wrong. Why wouldn't he want to talk to his mom? What if there had been some sort of emergency? But maybe he didn't want to talk to his mom. Since Josiah kept everybody at arm's length, she had no idea what his relationships with his family were like.

If he would just *tell* her what he needed, then this would be so much easier.

Did he know that she'd do her best to give him whatever he asked for?

She was hopelessly in love with the man, even knowing there was every chance he was never going to love her back. If he needed someone to talk to, she was right there, she'd be the friend he needed and not ask for anything in return.

At the sound of footsteps on the stairs, Chelsea spun around and saw Josiah strolling down them.

Naked.

Well, aside from the vest. Which he still wore. Even though it must be sodden from his shower and feel so uncomfortable against his skin. If he wore it in the shower, then he wore it all the time. She'd never known that. Then again, he'd made sure of that. He always wore a sweater, even in the summer, and he wasn't close to anyone on their team so no one would even suspect.

Her gaze zeroed in on his hand.

Was that ...?

"You're bleeding," she accused, storming toward him. "What happened? What did you do?"

"It's fine," he said dismissively, only it didn't look fine from where she was standing.

"Men. Special forces men," she added. They thought they were infallible, downplayed everything, and acted like bleeding out was the same thing as a paper cut. "Come and sit down, let me go grab a towel and some bandages."

Not giving him a chance to disagree, Chelsea took Josiah's elbow on his good side, guided him to the couch, and then hurried off into the kitchen. Beside it was the laundry room, and under the laundry sink was the first aid kit. She grabbed it and a couple of towels, then paused in the kitchen to fill up a bowl with some water.

When she returned to the living room, she found Josiah right where she'd left him. His back was ramrod straight, and that wasn't the only thing hard and straight. His erection stood at attention, and there was no way she could tend to his wounds or have any sort of conversation with him like that.

"Okay, I can't talk to you like this," she informed him.

"Like this?" Josiah's brow furrowed like he had forgotten the fact that he was naked, although she had no idea how that was possible.

While his thighs were thick and muscular, his erection impressive, and she had no doubt that beneath the Kevlar he was absolutely ripped, she felt a little uncomfortable seeing him naked. Not because she wasn't wildly attracted to him, but because she was.

And he wasn't attracted to her.

Although the erection did hint otherwise.

"Can we do something about Mr. Woody?" she asked with a giggle, indicating his thick length. If she stared at it for much longer, she was going to start dreaming about how good it would feel thrusting inside her, and once she went down that path, she wouldn't be coming back.

"Oh." Josiah looked down, shrugged, grabbed a throw blanket from the armchair beside the sofa, and tossed it over his lap. "Better?"

"Uh, yes." Chelsea nodded, but she was still picturing that huge length of his. Already she'd had a vivid imagination, spent hours daydreaming about her and Josiah in bed together, now her dreams were going to be a whole lot more accurate. "I can't believe you came down here naked."

Another shrug. "Wasn't even thinking about it."

"Well, your little buddy was obviously thinking about something," she muttered as she sat beside him and reached for his injured hand.

"You."

"Huh?"

"You. It was thinking of you."

Her cheeks heated in what she knew had to be one pretty major blush. "You think I'm pretty?"

"I think you're gorgeous."

Her gaze snapped to his, needing to see if he was just messing with her.

From the way he didn't shy away from meeting her gaze, she didn't think he was.

That Josiah might be attracted to her was more than she could ever hope for. It took pretty much every bit of self-restraint she possessed not to strip off her clothes and crawl onto his lap, take him inside her, and make him fall in love with her.

Since she absolutely could not do that, Chelsea began to clean away the streaks of blood on his hand so she could assess the damage.

"Sorry I answered your phone. I didn't mean to upset you, I just didn't realize it was a big deal. I'm sorry, though, I won't do it again," she assured him. If she'd known that it was going to make him so angry, she would have ignored the call.

The hand she wasn't working on clenched into a fist. "I'm sorry I scared you. I don't want you to be afraid of me."

"I'm not afraid of you."

"I yelled at you twice today. Once at Dr. Wood's office, and once in the bathroom, I saw the way you looked at me after."

There was so much recrimination in his voice that she abandoned her work of cleaning away blood, and did climb onto his lap, although she ignored the erection prodding her side. Framing his face with her hands, she feathered her fingertips across his temples.

"Look at me, Josiah."

Somewhat reluctantly, he brought his gaze up to meet hers.

"I am not now, nor have I ever been afraid of you. I was confused in the doctor's office because I was expecting you to think bringing along surveillance equipment was a good idea, and yet you freaked out. Is that why you were hiding from me in the gym? You were worried I was scared of you?"

He gave a slow nod.

"Could never be scared of you," she assured him. "Upstairs just now, in the bathroom, I wasn't scared of you, I was worried about you."

"Worried?"

Letting her hands drop lower, she ran her palms over the thick Kevlar vest. "Of course I'm worried about you. I care about you, Josiah. You know that. Everybody knows that. This isn't normal. I mean, I can guess why you're wearing it, but I don't think it's helping you. Does your mom know? Anyone else?"

Since she was sitting on his lap, Chelsea could feel the way his entire body went tense. "I don't talk to her."

"You mean like very often?"

"I mean like at all."

"You don't talk to your mom at all? Is that why you got so angry with me?"

"They call all the time. My mom, my dad, my brothers, but I can't ... I don't ... since what happened, I haven't seen them or spoken to them."

"Josiah, that's six years," she said, her heart breaking for him. How could he deny himself what he so badly needed? His family was willing to rally around him, and he was shutting them out the same way he shut out her, their team, and everyone at Prey.

All he did was shrug, and Chelsea threw caution to the wind and wrapped her arms around Josiah, hugging him tight. He didn't return the hug, his arms hanging stiffly at his sides.

But he didn't push her away.

And to her poor little heart that loved this man with everything it had to give, that was everything.

"I'm extra sorry about answering your phone. I didn't realize you didn't speak with your mom. Josiah, she seemed worried about you."

"She was worried about you."

"About me?"

"Told me she'd find out where I was and come and spank me if I had hurt you."

"You'd never hurt me," she said with confidence she felt down to her bones.

"You don't know that, Chelsea."

Was he really worried he might? He had to know himself better than that. "Yes, Josiah, I do know that. You wouldn't hurt me. But would your mom really spank you?"

Her question surprised a bark of laughter out of him, and he shook his head. "Never. Not in a million years. When I was a kid, she usually lectured and then gave us a time-out or grounded us. She was always fair, though."

"Because she loved you." As much as she'd be happy to stay right where she was, Chelsea knew Josiah would hear her better if she slid off his lap and returned to cleaning up his hand. "She still loves you. You have so many people who care about you. You're not alone. Even if it feels like you are because we don't understand, you're not. We might not have lived through what you did, but we all care about you. Please try to believe that."

The only way she was ever going to get her shot with Josiah Fleet was if he could accept the fact that he deserved to be alive, that he deserved to live a long, full, and happy life, and got out of his own way.

She just didn't know how to convince him of that.

# CHAPTER

## Seven

May 14th
1:43 P.M.

"No tricks today," Josiah warned as they took their seats in the waiting room.

Things had been surprisingly good between them since their talk yesterday. Not that he'd said much, well, not really, but admitting he hadn't spoken to his family in years, hadn't communicated in any way save for the text to his mom, was a lot for him.

More than he was comfortable with.

Only with Chelsea, it didn't feel as uncomfortable as he expected.

She wasn't afraid of him. If it weren't for the fact that she'd climbed onto his lap to soothe him, he might not have believed it. But she wouldn't have done that if she feared him. Wouldn't have touched him with gentleness, uttered soft, reassuring words, and told him she understood.

Chelsea was right, no one could truly understand what

it was like to survive an onslaught of bullets that took out the entire rest of your team. Men you respected, considered brothers, trusted in a way most people would never trust another human being. To lose them was devastating, but to be the only survivor ... that hurt more than anything else.

He should be dead right now.

For the last six years, he had wished daily that he'd died alongside his team.

But today ... today instead of wishing he was dead, he worried about who would be here with Chelsea right now if he'd died that day. Someone else would have done this undercover mission, he was sure of it, and Chelsea may or may not have volunteered to tag along. If she had, whoever was with her couldn't have cared more about her safety than he did.

Not possible.

"No tricks? You're no fun." Chelsea pouted, but amusement danced in her big, gray eyes.

Those eyes reminded him of storm clouds, but not the dangerous kind that brought damaging winds and flooding rains, the kind that came after a long, hot summer's day, clearing away the heat and refreshing the landscape.

That's how she made him feel.

Refreshed. Almost clean. Almost.

"You're incorrigible," he muttered, but one side of his mouth couldn't help but kick up into something that almost resembled a smile. Her answering smile was nothing short of a burst of sunlight, and because he was supposed to be in character now anyway, Josiah didn't resist the urge to reach out and brush his knuckles along her cheek like he normally would.

Somehow her smile got brighter, as did his urge to kiss her.

One taste.

That couldn't hurt anything.

Could it?

Of course it could. More than that, it could destroy the delicate balance he maintained only by ruthlessly keeping his emotions in check.

Thankfully, before he could do something stupid like throw caution to the wind and finally kiss the woman who had the power to decimate his control, Chelsea's name was called, and they both stood.

While he could claim the only reason he reached for her hand was because of their charade, that would have been a lie. The reason he took her hand was simple. Because he wanted to. Nothing more and nothing less. The more time he spent with her, the harder it was to maintain control.

"How are you this morning, Mrs. Fleet?" Dr. Wood asked as he ushered them both into his office. The man had had his secretary organize this appointment at the last minute, they weren't supposed to meet with him again for another week. Since the meeting was at the hospital and not some undisclosed location where the trafficking ring might try to ambush them, they were both assuming this was going to be good news.

"Well, I'm feeling okay, as good as I can hope for right now, but ..." Chelsea trailed off, chewing on her bottom lip and darting glances to him and then back to the doctor. If he didn't know better, he would believe that she was scared of something, definitely nervous. Who knew the woman was such a good actress? If she'd told him of her skills, maybe he wouldn't have worried quite so much about taking on this mission with her.

Maybe.

But probably not.

Most likely, he would have worried just as much.

"Yes?" Dr. Wood prompted. While they couldn't say the man was cold and calculating, he also wasn't warm and fuzzy. Not the kind of doctor you felt truly cared about you as a person, but not one who made you feel like a bother either. The kind you usually trusted because they were friendly enough and also professional enough that you believed they could save you.

"Is it bad news?" Chelsea blurted out as he guided her into a seat.

"Bad news?" Dr. Wood asked.

"We weren't supposed to see you again until next week, but your assistant called and said we needed to come in today," Chelsea explained. "I was hoping that didn't mean you had bad news for us."

"Oh no, not at all," the doctor rushed to assure her as he rounded his desk and dropped into his plush leather chair. "The opposite in fact."

"Opposite?" Josiah demanded as he took the room's only other chair, the one beside Chelsea, and threw the doctor a glare. Thankfully, he did not have to play much of a role because his acting skills were not up there with Chelsea's. They were passable, but this wasn't the usual work he'd done as a SEAL, or working as part of Prey's Cyber Team.

"I work here at the hospital, but I also work for a private clinic," Dr. Wood began.

"Okay," Chelsea said slowly.

They needed to hear the doctor spell something out if they were going to get the man arrested and thrown in prison. So far, the cameras and microphone they'd planted in his office had yielded nothing concrete that would help with that goal.

"We have some connections that the hospital doesn't have," Dr. Wood continued. "And sometimes we are able to procure organs that traditional methods are unable to."

"What does that mean exactly?" Chelsea asked.

"Sometimes we have families who wish to bypass a little red tape."

"Red tape?" Josiah growled.

"Some people who have lost loved ones want to make sure that those organs actually make it to a person in need," Dr. Wood told them with what could only be described as fake compassion. There wasn't a drop of sincerity in his words. "Unfortunately, sometimes red tape gets in the way of that."

None of that was true, of course. The organ registry did everything in its power to get the limited number of donated organs to those who needed them the most. Unfortunately, there was a massive shortage of people willing to donate their organs, which left an opening for trafficking rings just like the one Dr. Wood worked for to step in and take advantage of dying people and their loved ones.

"You mean bypassing the law?" Chelsea asked in a soft voice.

Before the doctor could answer, Josiah growled out a question of his own. "Is it a better chance at finding her a match?"

Dr. Wood met his gaze squarely. "Yes. Much better." The doctor offered no answer to Chelsea's question, so they couldn't get an outright admission that he was breaking the law, but his non-answer was, in fact, answer enough.

"How do we get an appointment at this clinic?" Josiah asked.

"I've already put your name on the list," the doctor assured him. "You understand that since this is a private clinic, the costs might be a little higher than if you were to wait for an organ through more traditional means."

Not a little higher. Way higher. Given the cost of receiving a transplant was already astronomical, he had no doubt the costs of buying a black-market organ would be in the millions. Not that it mattered to them, Prey would foot the bill, and once the trafficking ring was disassembled and Desiree Tilly and all who worked for her imprisoned, they would get the money back. No doubt get all the money the ring had and use it in some way to help the families of those who had perished at the ring's hands and those who had survived their horrors.

"Money is not an issue," he said, a little surprised by how strong and confident the words came out. They were what the doctor needed to hear him say to ensure they got themselves a meeting with this "clinic," but he also meant it with absolute honesty. When it came to Chelsea's safety, there was nothing he wouldn't pay or do to ensure it.

"I'm happy to hear that, Mr. Fleet, very happy to hear that. If you're happy to proceed, I will ensure all of Mrs. Fleet's records are sent to the clinic so we can begin the search for a match of our own. Of course, she will be kept on the more traditional lists as well. Best of both worlds."

"Do it," he agreed. "I won't lose my wife." Chelsea might not really be his wife, but he couldn't lose her. She was the only sunshine left in his life, and these last few days had forced him to confront feelings he usually kept buried with ease. He just had no idea what place she had in his life or what place he wanted her to have.

~

May 14th

4:58 P.M.


"So ..." Josiah said slowly as they both climbed out of the car.

"Yeah?" Chelsea prompted when he didn't continue. She was worn out after this afternoon's appointment. It had gone so much better than they could have hoped for, pretty much as perfect as possible, but it had been exhausting. Making sure that every word out of her mouth was appropriate and what one would really say if they were truly in the situation she was pretending to be in. Balancing knowing about the ring, but Dr. Wood now coming right out and admitting he was part of it, monitoring every facial expression, and the pressure not to fail, it had worn her down.

Now they were back at their rented townhouse, she expected Josiah to go and hide out in the gym like he usually did, and she intended to take a nap. Since she had no idea if he'd eat dinner with her or not, she would probably make something quick and easy, but right now she was too nauseous to worry about food.

"Did you want to ... if you weren't planning on doing anything else ... I was wondering if you wanted to ..." Josiah rubbed a hand along the back of his neck, his gaze darting about like he was nervous.

And he was.

Her big, tough, standoffish, always in a bad mood, retired Navy SEAL was nervous.

Amused, Chelsea held back a giggle, she didn't want to put him off whatever it was he was trying to ask, because she was dying to know what it was.

"I don't have plans," she supplied, not real ones anyway.

A nap could definitely wait until later, and while she wasn't feeling amazing, she wasn't feeling so bad that she couldn't do whatever it was Josiah was trying to ask her to do.

"I was thinking maybe we could celebrate. Our success. Like you wanted to the other day." Josiah said the words cautiously, almost like they tasted foreign in his mouth. It was also pretty clear that he was expecting her to say no, like he'd already blown his chance by taking himself off to the gym after yesterday's appointment with Dr. Wood.

Only there was no way he could ever blow his chances with her.

Chelsea wanted him more than she wanted to breathe. She'd been smitten from the first moment she laid eyes on the broody SEAL, but she'd fallen in love with him a little bit at a time over the last several years. Each time she saw the pain in his eyes, pain he tried so hard to hide. Each time he did something that gave away how much he cared about their team. Seeing how hard he worked, how dedicated he was, how he gave his all to each case that crossed their desks, it all had her falling a little more until she got to the point she was at now.

Hopelessly and eternally in love with Josiah Fleet.

"I would love to celebrate our successful visit with Dr. Wood with you," she told him enthusiastically. "What did you have in mind?"

Seemingly caught off-guard by her response, Josiah froze.

She giggled when she realized he hadn't thought any further ahead than actually asking her.

"Pizza and a movie?" he asked hesitantly.

"Pizza and the hot tub?" she suggested instead. The medication she was taking to simulate some of her kidney failure symptoms had her muscles feeling tense and heavy.

A long soak in the warm water sounded like heaven. "Or pizza, hot tub, and movie."

Never in her life would she have guessed she'd see this big, muscled, mountain of a man squirm. But that's exactly what he was doing, and she could guess why.

"You can leave the body armor on, I don't mind. I want you to feel safe, and I want you to feel relaxed. You're both with me, Josiah." Stepping closer, Chelsea hesitated for barely a moment before she reached out and placed her hand on Josiah's forearm. Beneath her palm, his muscles were coiled with tension, but he didn't push her away so she called it a win. "I'm going to go change, we can soak for a bit in the hot tub, then order pizza and watch a movie."

If he really didn't want to, she wouldn't push him, but she hoped he would agree.

After a long moment, Josiah gave a sharp nod.

Victory.

"I didn't bring anything to wear for swimming, so I'll just have to wear my boxers," he informed her, and she had to bite back a moan as images of his long, thick length, standing erect, flooded her mind.

"Uh, that's okay," she said quickly, praying her cheeks weren't flaming, giving away where her mind had gone.

Although the small spark in Josiah's dark eyes told her they were, and he knew exactly what she had been thinking about. "Go and change, I'll get everything ready," he gave her a little nudge toward the stairs, and they both started for them.

She was a little slower than usual, and she half expected Josiah to brush past her, but he didn't. Instead, he stayed behind her, going at her pace. In the kitchen they parted ways, and she took the next two flights up to the master suite.

By the time she got there, she was a little breathless, a lot excited, and even more nervous. This was as close to a date as she was ever going to get with Josiah, and she wanted it to be ... perfect.

This might be her only chance to convince him that he wasn't just safe with her, he could be everything with her if he just let himself believe it. While she knew she couldn't force Josiah to reciprocate her feelings, she wanted so desperately for him to see her as more than a colleague.

Wishful thinking, but she couldn't help herself.

Throwing off her clothes, she ferreted around in the drawers until she found two swimsuits. One was a sexy bikini, tiny scraps of hot pink material that she was sure was enough to drive any man wild.

But that was the thing.

She didn't want Josiah drunk on lust, she wanted him to see her as more than just a woman he could make out with. She wanted him to see her as a woman he could fall in love with if he could just let go of his survivor's guilt. That was what he was suffering from. She'd done some reading up on it and was as sure as she could be without having a degree in psychology or psychiatry.

Decision made, Chelsea went with the other swimsuit. It was still a bikini because that was all she owned, but it was more modest, cute rather than sexy, in a pretty shade of baby pink. Slipping into it, she twisted her hair up into a messy bun on the top of her head, covered the catheter site with a waterproof bandage, then headed back down the stairs.

By the time she stepped out onto the deck, Josiah was already there. He had the hot tub bubbling away, and he'd set up an array of snacks and drinks. Fruits and cheeses, all neatly sliced, sat on a large platter, and bottles of water, juice, and soda were lined up along the outdoor table.

Then there was her sexy SEAL. He was wearing boxers that did little to hide his tree trunk-like legs, and his huge length, and he still had on his Kevlar. He stood facing the door, arms crossed, waiting for her. When he saw her, his nostrils flared, and heat blazed in his eyes. She watched her usually together guy drag in a breath before he took a step toward her.

"I'll help you in," he said, his tone brisk, but the hand that grasped her elbow trembled slightly, and she knew how far outside his comfort zone he'd stepped for her.

"Thanks," she said, trying to keep her tone light, free from any sort of pressure. The last thing she wanted to do was spook him and send him running.

Rather than helping her in, he pretty much lifted her in, then somewhat reluctantly climbed in to join her. As the warm water bubbled around them, Josiah sat there so stiffly that it took everything she possessed not to lean over and massage the tension right out of him.

It was only knowing that would make things worse that had her restraining herself.

There were a million questions she wanted to ask him, about his past, what had happened with his team that had him needing to wear the vest continuously, she only knew about the loss of his team in generalities, not specifics. There were other questions she wanted to ask, too, about his family and his childhood, about the things he liked and was interested in.

Basically, she wanted to gather every shred of information she could about this man.

But she didn't ask any of those questions, because

Josiah was already pushing himself to his limits, and he was doing it all for her.

So instead, she settled into the water, tipped her head back, and let her eyes fall closed. "It's okay, Josiah. We don't have to talk. We can just be."

At her words, she felt him settle even though she kept her eyes closed. For now, it was more than enough just to enjoy his company. She had no intention of pushing him, just proving to him that she was someone who could be trusted.

Only then would he contemplate handing over his trust.

# CHAPTER

*Eight*

May 14th
  11:51 P.M.

*Laughter.*

*The sound filled his mind, and Josiah snapped his head around to try to find the source.*

*There.*

*Under a canopy that did little to protect them all from the searing heat of the desert sun.*

*It was his team. Laughing at something Pun had to say. The man was always telling a joke, making the most ridiculous puns, hence the nickname. They needed that out there, though. Needed someone to brighten up their days with a little bit of humor.*

*Walking toward his team, Josiah startled when he saw that he was already there.*

What the hell?

*Picking up the pace, he hurried toward the small group of*

*men, himself included, ignoring everything else happening around him.*

*For some reason, it seemed important to get to them quickly.*

*He had to stop it from happening.*

*Had no idea what it was, but somehow it felt vitally important that he put a stop to it.*

*When he reached the men, still laughing at some joke Pun had made, he saw that the men were all removing their body armor. They believed they were safe. They were on the military base, so why wouldn't they be safe?*

"No!" *Josiah yelled.*

*They couldn't take those vests off. Couldn't.*

*Doing so would have deadly consequences.*

*As he watched, none of the men reacted to his screamed warning. They were acting like they couldn't see or hear him at all. But that didn't make any sense because he could both see and hear them.*

*They were close enough to touch.*

*Reaching out his hand toward Ham, standing the closest, he was shocked when his hand passed right through the man.*

"Ham," *he pleaded.* "I'm right here, man, you have to listen to me. Keep your vest on. Don't take it off. That Kevlar will be the only thing that's going to save your life."

*As he spoke, the horrifying details came rushing back. The assault that was about to come. The bullets that would fly through the air, piercing the men standing around him. All except himself. Because for a reason he could no longer remember, he hadn't taken off his body armor when the others did.*

*A cruel twist of fate.*

*This should have been where he died. His blood seeping*

*into the sand along with the blood of his team. His brothers in every way that mattered.*

*But he wouldn't die out here. He'd survive, and have to live with the horrors of watching his team being slaughtered.*

*"Please," he begged, already knowing no one could hear him because this wasn't really happening. He was trapped in a dream. A nightmare. Forced to watch his team die all over again.*

*How many times would he have to watch this play out?*

*Hadn't he already suffered enough?*

*His own screams joined the pain-filled ones of his team as the roar of gunfire filled the air. He watched in horror as the men dropped around him one by one. He watched himself go down, too, only those bullets wouldn't pierce his lungs, his heart, he was protected by a fluke. One that doomed him to live out the rest of his life when he wanted to be dead.*

*Once he'd watched himself fall to the ground, Josiah tore his gaze away from the pools of red staining the sand. Turning his head in the direction that the bullets had come from, he saw them.*

*Men.*

*Half a dozen of them.*

*If they hadn't had a traitor to allow them access to the base, they never would have been able to kill so many. Most of those men had escaped that day. When the other men and women on the base responded, the shooters had fled. Two had died in the return fire, but four of them had escaped in a vehicle, one that the traitor had set up for them.*

*He heard its engine roar to life, and when it took off across the sand, he took off after it.*

*Time lost all meaning, the world disappeared around him, it was just him, the Hummer, and the sand.*

*Nothing else.*

*It wasn't getting away. Not this time.*

*Those men had to pay.*

*They had to suffer for stealing his brothers from him, for not killing him, too. They had to die horrible, slow, agonizing deaths. Maybe that would soothe some of the roughest edges of his rage.*

*Somehow, despite knowing that a person could not run faster than a vehicle, couldn't even keep pace with it, he began to gain on the Hummer. And as it pulled up outside a rocky cave entrance deep in the desert, he got close enough to grab one of the men.*

*Startled, the man swung his weapon at Josiah, but he merely huffed a mirthless chuckle, grabbed the weapon, and slammed it into his raised knee, snapping it in half.*

"That's not going to help you, not this time," *he told the man who was staring at him with wide, defiant eyes.*

*Slamming his fist into the man's head, dropping him to the ground, he turned on the others. They fired off shot after shot at him, but he merely laughed as the body armor he wore repelled every one of those bullets.*

*Then he was on them, slamming his hand into four more heads, and one by one the four men dropped.*

*The weapons they'd used to kill his team, innocent men who put their lives on the line every single day to rid the world of filth like them, were next. He snapped them all like they were nothing, and then he took the offending pieces of metal and used them to bind the wrists of the men.*

*He wanted them to watch as he killed them. Wanted the anticipation of knowing what was going to happen to them to sink in as they watched helplessly, with no way to escape their fate. It had been sealed the moment they made a deal with a traitor to attack the base and kill his brothers.*

*Sliding out his K-BAR, he admired the sharp blade, and*

*with a wicked grin, he pounced on the first of the men. They'd slipped away before, disappeared back into the shadows, lived when they should have died.*

*Today, they were going to die the deaths that should have been theirs.*

*The man he approached yelled something, but Josiah couldn't make out the words through the bloodlust pumping through his veins. The first swipe of the knife through flesh did little to satiate it, so he sliced again and again. Blood was everywhere, splattering him, staining the ground around him, covering the body of one of his team's killers, but it wasn't enough.*

*More.*

*He needed more.*

*More blood to be shed to get justice for his team.*

*Turning on the next of the cowering men, he tossed his knife aside. This time he wanted to use his bare hands. Curling his fingers into fists, he pounded them into the man before him. Each strike was rewarded with a grunt of pain, and they fueled him, urging him on, and by the time the body before him was no longer recognizable as a human being, he was breathless, but riding the high of vengeance.*

*Time to move on to man number three. Josiah's weapon appeared in his hand as he stared down at the next on his kill list. The man cowered, begged, tried to get away, but there was nowhere for him to go.*

*Opening fire felt so good.*

*Bullets pinged into their target until it was riddled with holes, and blood soaked the earth.*

*Wasn't enough.*

*Never enough.*

*It all had to go.*

*All had to die.*

*It was the only way.*

*The only way.*

*One more of his team's killers still breathed, and that wasn't acceptable. Tossing his weapon onto the ground to join his knife, he advanced on the man. This one he intended to rip to pieces with his own two hands. With rage lending him strength he'd never normally have, he knew he could do it.*

*Placing his hands on the man's leg, he yanked and was rewarded with the sound of tearing flesh and the most delightful howl of pain as the leg ripped from the man's body. His other leg came next, and then both of his arms.*

*Pleas fell from the man's lips, but nothing was going to deter him. Didn't they know he was more monster than man now? It was part of the reason he pushed everyone out of his life, he was too full of a fury that could never be quenched. He was a danger to the people he loved, and it was all these men's fault.*

*Placing his hands on either side of the man's head, Josiah looked him dead in the eye as he yanked it from the man's neck.*

*This was what he had to do.*

*He had to slaughter everyone and everything that had taken so much from him. That was the only way he was ever going to find any measure of peace, no matter how small it might be.*

*So when a voice called his name, a voice that was too sweet, too innocent to have anything to do with the death and destruction that had stolen the lives of his teammates, he turned on it.*

*Lost in a red haze of fury, he didn't think.*

*Just reached out and grabbed whoever had made the soft sound and wrapped his hands around its neck.*

$\approx$

May 15<sup>th</sup>
   12:28 A.M.


The whimpers were so riddled with pain that they woke her from a deep sleep.

Blinking open sleepy eyes, Chelsea's gaze zeroed immediately in on the figure on the floor.

Despite there being a couch in the master suite, as well as a king-size bed, she was sure they could have avoided each other in, Josiah had decided he would sleep on the floor. The only way she had agreed without an argument was if he let her gather every spare blanket and pillow in the house and make him a little nest of sorts. His own cozy little place to sleep that was as comfortable as she could make it without him being in a bed.

When she'd fallen asleep, he'd still been awake. He wasn't making a noise, and he wasn't on his phone or anything, but she could tell he was still alert. Maybe watching over her until she succumbed to sleep.

Which she'd done all of an hour ago, she realized as she glanced at the glowing clock on the nightstand. How long Josiah had been asleep she had no idea, less than an hour, but long enough for him to start dreaming.

Throwing back the covers, she swung her legs over the side of the bed and stood. Josiah wasn't just dreaming he was having nightmares. The closer she got, she could see he wasn't just moaning and groaning in his sleep, he was thrashing about as well.

Dreaming about losing his team?

That was her best guess, and she hated that he had to

relive that traumatic experience repeatedly every time he closed his eyes. Did he have nightmares often? While she hoped he didn't, she suspected that he did.

There was no doubt he was having bad dreams, and the faint pain lingering in her wrist reminded her what waking Josiah while he was in the middle of a nightmare would mean. It would be a recipe for disaster, he wouldn't know where he was, and he'd lash out only to feel bad about it when he was fully awake. But what else was she supposed to do? Leaving him to suffer was not an option as far as she was concerned. What was the worst he could do anyway? Hurt her wrist again? She could take that if it meant ending his nightmares.

Cautiously, she reached out and brushed her fingertips across his temple. "Josiah?"

For a moment, he stilled, and she thought she was going to be able to wake him without issue.

"Josiah, it's Chelsea. Wake up, you're having bad dreams," she said, feathering her fingertips over his forehead. He felt a little warm, and his skin was dotted with sweat. Whatever he was dreaming about was bad, and she hated that for him.

He still hadn't lashed out in any way, and when his head suddenly snapped in her direction, she thought she had avoided disaster. His eyes opened, and she smiled at him, but it took her barely a second to realize something was wrong.

No sooner had the smile curled her lips up than anxiety had them dropping down to form a worried frown.

There was something wrong with his eyes. They were empty, he was looking through her not at her. Not really seeing her at all. His eyes might be open, but he wasn't awake, he was still caught up in whatever nightmare had grabbed hold of him.

Before she could back away and think of a different way to wake him up, he moved, faster than she'd ever seen a person move before. His hand snapped around her throat, and he launched up onto his feet, backing her up until she was slammed against the nearest wall. The hand gripping her neck was there to kill her, she knew that because there had been no hesitation, it just grabbed around her throat and squeezed hard enough to cut off her air supply.

Trying to get out of his hold would be impossible, and she didn't want to hurt him because he didn't even know what he was doing. He wasn't seeing her, he was seeing whatever haunted him.

Talking wasn't an option, not with the way he shut off her ability to breathe, so instead, she just reached out and framed his face, her fingers tracing soft circles against his now icy cold skin. When her thumb brushed along his bottom lip, the hold on her neck faltered, loosening a little, enough that she could drag in a much-needed breath.

"It's okay, Josiah, you're safe," she said, voice rough, sucking in more mouthfuls of air in case he didn't snap out of his dream and tightened his grip again.

The dark eyes staring sightlessly through her blinked once, slowly, and then cleared, and she knew the exact second that reality crept in because his expression turned horrified.

"I tried to kill you," he said, voice tight with regret. "Are you okay?"

Without giving her a chance to answer, he leaned down and scooped her up, carrying her to the bed, and piling up the pillows against the headboard before setting her down against them.

"I'm sorry, I knew sleeping in here was a bad idea, if I—"

"Shh," she murmured, voice still rough as she leaned over and touched a finger to his lips. "You didn't try to kill me."

Gaze lingering on her throat, which she was sure was already red and bruising, he shook his head. A large hand circled her wrist, and he moved her hand away. His touch was gentle, and there was so much guilt and regret in his eyes that she couldn't stand it.

Throwing herself at him, Chelsea wrapped her arms around his shoulders, her legs around his waist. She didn't care that her throat ached a little, all she cared about was soothing Josiah's pain and not letting him blame himself for something he hadn't even known he was doing.

"You were dreaming. I knew the risks of waking you, you told me last time not to do it again, and I did it anyway. It's my fault, not yours. It. Is. Not. Your. Fault," she said firmly, over-enunciating each word.

"But I hurt you." His voice was as rough as her own, only his was clogged with emotion.

"Not on purpose. What were you dreaming about?"

The tension in his body somehow increased at her question, and he tried to grab hold of her, pry her off. "We need to call an ambulance. You need to go to the hospital. There could be damage to your neck and swelling. This charade is over. We'll have to find a different way to bring down the trafficking ring."

"Well, that escalated quickly," she said with a giggle as she clung to him tighter so he couldn't dislodge her.

"Are you ... laughing?"

"Mmhmm. I don't need a hospital, and we are definitely not backing out when we've made amazing progress.

I am okay. Look at me, Josiah." Pulling back enough that she could see his face, she waited until he met her gaze before continuing. "You have to talk about it. If you can't talk to me, then you have to find someone else. You can't keep going on like this. You're hurting."

"What I deserve," he whispered so softly she barely heard the words.

"It sure as hell is not," she growled. No one got to talk about the man she loved like that. Not even himself. "You deserve all the good things in the world."

"I should have died with them." Those words were said with such belief that she buried her face against his neck and breathed in his soothing, woodsy scent, to assure herself he was actually standing here alive.

"I'm glad you're not dead," she murmured.

"They took off their vests, and I didn't. I was supposed to die out there along with my team."

"That doesn't mean you don't deserve to be here. Doesn't mean you still can't live a long and happy life. You can hate what happened and still be glad you're alive, both at the same time." Chelsea silently begged him to believe her. She'd never give up on him, but you could only help someone who wanted to be helped, and right now Josiah wasn't sitting in that camp.

"So much anger inside me. I'm not safe to be around."

"Of course you're angry. You have *every* right to be angry. But I want you to feel other things too. I want you to feel happiness, peace, enjoyment, and excitement. I want to help however I can. Please, Josiah, I'm right here, talk to me. Let me in. Just a little bit."

Hands skimmed the length of her spine, then dropped once again to hang limply by his sides. "Can't. You're too sweet, too innocent. You've never experienced anything like what my team and I lived through, you won't understand."

"Oh, Josiah," she said sadly, lifting her head again so she could read his expressions. "Don't you get it? I don't have to understand what you lived through, I don't have to get what it was like to be a SEAL, I don't have to have lost people I cared about in such a horrific way. Because I understand *you*. There's no way you can't know that I'm in love with you and have been for a long time. Everybody knows it."

Throwing caution to the wind, Chelsea leaned in and pressed her lips to his, needing him to know without a shadow of a doubt that the love she felt for him was not conditional. It was freely given with no expectations of anything in return.

# CHAPTER
## *Nine*

May 15<sup>th</sup>
12:39 A.M.

She was kissing him.

The crazy woman was kissing him.

Like he hadn't wrapped his hands around her delicate throat and almost squeezed the life out of her not even five minutes ago.

More than that, she'd told him she was in love with him.

With *him*.

How was that even possible? How could a woman who was as good, and sweet, and kind, and loving, and open as Chelsea Pierce possibly love a man like him? What could she possibly even see in him?

"Make love to me, Josiah," she whispered as she pulled back. Desire danced brightly in her gray eyes, along with arousal, and he didn't understand how she could be totally fine with him almost killing her.

And locked in his dream as he'd been, he *had* been trying to kill her.

It wasn't that he wouldn't love to lose himself for a while, bury himself so deep inside Chelsea that he couldn't help but absorb some of her goodness, her light. But there was no way he was going to cause her more pain.

The truth was, he had zero to offer her. Not now and not ever.

Because he knew Chelsea wasn't really wanting just sex. She wanted a commitment, a future, she wanted him to love her back, and allowing himself to love her was like asking the universe to take her from him.

Not a risk he was willing to take.

Not with someone as special as Chelsea.

"Chels," he said slowly, lifting his hands to grip her hips and still them when she began to rock them against the erection straining against the flimsy boxers he wore. "You're something special, you know that, right? You're beautiful and smart, you're caring and kind, you go out of your way to see the best in people. You're the brightest of light shining on the darkest of days."

"Why do I sense a but coming?" she asked, but she didn't sound angry. If anything, her voice was full of tender affection.

"Because you have to know I have nothing to offer you. If things were different, if I was different, then I'd ask you out in a heartbeat. But as the man I am right now, I don't have anything to give you."

"But I'm not asking you for anything."

"Look, I know you think you can do just sex, but I know you, and I know you're looking for more than that. You want the whole fairytale, white picket fence, happy ever after, and that isn't something I can give you."

"Pretty arrogant of you to assume you know more about what I want than I do." She arched a brow at him to emphasize her point, and he had to shake his head at this sassy woman. She might be all sunshine and sweetness, but she knew how to stand up for herself, and he respected the hell out of that.

"Not saying I know more about what you want than you do, but we've known each other for years, and I know you're a hopeless romantic. You think you can fix me, and that's ... that's not possible." If he knew a way to fix himself, he would have done it by now. Truth was, he was too broken to ever find enough pieces to put together to make a whole, and Chelsea deserved only the best.

"Oh, Josiah, once again you've got it all wrong. I don't want to fix you, you don't need fixing, you're not broken. You're hurting, you're suffering, and all I want is to be there for you, to love you." Leaning in, she brushed her lips across his again in a searing kiss that seemed to brand his soul. "Now make love to me, please."

"Trying to do the right thing here, Chels," he told her, restraining his urges to tear her clothes from her body and sink inside her regardless of whether it was a good idea or not.

"Stop trying to be all noble. I don't want noble."

"But you want making love, you want soft and sweet, tender and loving. If I have sex with you right now, it's not going to be any of those things."

Instead of putting her off, his words only seemed to turn her on, and she ground her center against his rock-hard erection, then leaned in to nip his bottom lip. "I don't care how we do it. I love all the different sides of you. Take me however you want me, because I'm already yours, and nothing you say or do, no matter how much it panics you, can ever change that."

Her acceptance snapped whatever control he'd been clinging to, and with a growl, he managed to pry her off him and toss her onto the bed. She bounced as she hit the mattress, but he was already ripping off his boxers and then reaching for her clothes.

They had to go. If she was determined to do this, he wanted to see every inch of her delectable body. Her gaze was locked on his length as he yanked her sleep shorts and panties down her legs, then shoved up the tank top she was wearing to bare her breasts and cover the nasty red marks he'd left behind on her neck.

"Like what you see, Chels?" he asked as he pushed apart her thighs and settled between them.

"Even more than I liked it the other day," she said, then gasped as he didn't hesitate to dive right in, licking and nipping at her sensitive flesh like he was going to die if he didn't drown himself in her taste.

She was so responsive, each time his tongue circled her bud, or teased its way inside her, she gasped and moaned. Her fingers tangled in the sheets, and her head tossed restlessly against the pillows.

"Josiah, I need—"

"Know what you need, Chels," he told her as he plunged two fingers inside her, making her cry out. Hooking them so they brushed across the rippled flesh that would make her see stars, he pumped them in and out as he closed his lips around her bundle of nerves and sucked hard.

Chelsea came apart for him, screaming his name.

Not giving her time to float down from the orgasm he moved up her body. "You on birth control?"

"Mmhmm," she said with a nod, her eyes still glassy with pleasure.

"I'm clean. Haven't been with anyone in almost two years." Not since he realized Chelsea was in love with him, and the appeal of finding a random woman who liked rough sex lost its appeal.

"I'm clean, too, we don't need a condom," she told him, and that was all the permission he needed.

Sinking into her was like heaven, a surreal feeling he'd never experienced before, didn't even know existed. She was so hot, so tight, so utterly perfect, and he was so close to coming, but he wasn't letting go until his girl came again. He wanted to feel her clamp around him, locking them together for a few far too brief seconds.

Setting a brutal pace, Josiah balanced his weight on one hand and grabbed one of her breasts, kneading it roughly, then tweaking her nipple before his hand moved to touch her where their bodies joined together.

Chelsea gasped as he rolled her bud between his fingers. "Josiah, it's too much," she whined, but she lifted her legs and hooked them around his hips, drawing him deeper.

"Don't think anything is too much for you," he told her as he began to circle the sensitive bundle of nerves and picked up the pace. Chelsea said he could take her however he needed to, and he was filled with desperation to claim her in the only way he could.

Her fingers clawed his shoulders, no doubt leaving behind scratches he would wear with pride. Too bad they couldn't be permanent. Something to remind him that someone loved him despite his self-loathing.

A high-pitched scream fell from Chelsea's lips as her internal muscles fluttered and then clamped around him as her orgasm hit. It set off his own, and it exploded inside him with fiery pleasure that licked along his every nerve ending until it consumed him.

It was almost too easy to want this, too easy to let himself believe that he could keep Chelsea in his life.

"Mmm." A content sigh rumbled through Chelsea's chest. "That was ... no words. You broke my brain and my vocabulary."

Pulling out of her was harder than it should be. If he could just stay here, connected to someone in such an intimate way, the anger held at bay by Chelsea's unwavering love and devotion, then maybe he could find the peace that eluded him. Peace he didn't feel he deserved.

But it had to be done.

"Stay, please, sleep beside me, just for tonight. Let me hold you and remind you that you're not alone," Chelsea whispered, her eyes begging him, and he found he couldn't say no to her.

With a single nod, he stood and disappeared into the bathroom to get a towel to clean her up. Once that was done, he stretched out beside her, pulling the covers up to tuck them both in.

Immediately, Chelsea snuggled against his side, one of her legs thrown over his, her hand resting on the Kevlar above his abdomen, her cheek above his heart. She didn't seem concerned about how hard and unyielding the body armor was, just settled down to sleep.

On the other hand, he lay there, unsure where he should put his hands, wanting to wrap his arms around this woman and hold her close, pretend she could be his, but scared to tempt himself with what he could never have.

If only things were different.

Only once her breathing evened out and she drifted off to sleep did he allow himself one moment of weakness.

Touching his lips to the top of her head, he swept a hand down her back, tracing the length of her spine. "Thank you for not giving up on me when I've already given up on myself," he whispered.

～

May 15th
   8:10 A.M.

"Thanks for trusting me last night," Chelsea said, turning from the stove where she was cooking up bacon and eggs for breakfast once she heard Josiah enter the kitchen.

Since she was looking at him, she saw how he froze, got that deer caught in the headlights sort of look that told her he was both uncomfortable, but trusting her more without even realizing it because he hadn't filtered out his expressions. Instead, he'd let them play out across his face, something he wouldn't have allowed even as recently as yesterday.

His subconscious was beginning to trust her even if his conscious mind hadn't.

Progress.

Small but there nonetheless and she loved it.

Even if Josiah never fell in love with her, and honestly, despite the fact they were growing closer, she still didn't see it happening, at least he could walk away from this undercover operation with a reminder that he had friends. Feeling all alone and actually being all alone were two totally different things, and Josiah had an entire team at his back, all he had to do was turn around and see them.

"Trusting you with what?" he asked, starting to move

again. He came to the stove, nudged her out of the way, and nodded toward the table, which she took as an indication that he wanted to take over cooking breakfast.

"You slept beside me," she explained. Sex with Josiah had been everything she'd known it would be, but the fact that he'd agreed to sleep in the bed with her for the remainder of the night was even better. Another indication he was starting to trust her.

Plus, there was what he'd whispered to her when he thought she'd fallen asleep.

*Thank you for not giving up on me when I've already given up on myself.*

She'd been right on the cusp of sleep when those words had filtered through her mind and settled in her heart. She would never give up on him, and that wasn't contingent on him ever falling in love with her. After everything he had been through, he deserved to have someone who was unconditionally on his side, no matter what.

"You asked," he said with a shrug, trying to brush it off, act like it wasn't a big deal, but she knew that it was a big deal. For both of them.

"I'm glad you remembered to put on clothes after your shower," she teased, not wanting to dwell on the heavy stuff. The more she drew it to Josiah's attention, the more time he was going to spend trying to talk himself out of believing in her.

A laugh came from the stove, and she froze.

Laughter.

Real laughter.

She'd known Josiah for years now, and she had never once heard him laugh. Not like this, not all free and genuine.

Tears blurred her eyes as she stared at him. How badly

she wanted him to be able to move on from the past. It would always be there, he would always miss his team, always feel anger at what had happened to them, likely always feel some survivor's guilt for living when the rest of them had died. But he didn't have to revolve his entire life around his loss. He could be happy, find joy, maybe even find love one day, with her or with someone else.

"I don't think I like the idea of the rest of our team getting a look at how ... impressive ... you are," she added with a giggle of her own, wanting to soak in this carefree moment because she didn't know when or even if the next one was coming.

There was actual amusement sparking in his dark eyes when he turned to carry two plates piled high with eggs and bacon to the table. "Definitely don't want that. Wouldn't want to make Ava and Teresa feel bad about what they got stuck with. Isabella either."

Chelsea's mouth fell open.

Not only had he laughed, but he was making jokes.

This version of Josiah made her fall in love with him all over again. If she'd thought he was handsome when he was all serious or scowling, seeing him like this, smiling and relaxed, he was drop-dead gorgeous.

"I think I definitely was the winner," she agreed.

A little of the joy seeped out of him, worry clouding in. "Chelsea, remember I—"

"Shh," she hushed, picking up her fork and digging into her meal. "I know. I don't have any expectations, Josiah, so don't go putting pressure on yourself that isn't coming from me. You know how I feel, but you also know I would never want you to do anything you don't want to do. If you don't ever love me back, I've made peace with it. I still enjoy your company, still want to be your friend, and still will always be here for you."

After a pause, he gave a single nod, then took his seat at the table, and they ate in companionable silence. They didn't need to talk, she was busy soaking up Josiah's company, and she was sure he was busy having an internal debate with himself about whether or not he should be sitting at the table with her.

But he stayed, and that was a win as far as she was concerned.

Together they cleaned up after breakfast, rinsing off dishes and loading the dishwasher, wiping down the table and counters. Then they headed into the living room, and Josiah set up his laptop. They had a video conference with their team this morning, and while she wanted this case wrapped up as quickly as possible, she was going to miss being alone with Josiah.

Right at eight thirty on the dot, the call connected, and a moment later she was looking at the smiling faces of her team. Ava and Teresa were the two very best friends anyone could ever ask for, and Isabella was quickly becoming a friend as well. There were no better bosses out there than Raven, and since meeting Isabella, Tobias was trying to integrate more into the team, making an effort to form friendships rather than just being a colleague.

The organ trafficking ring didn't stand a chance against them.

"How are you both doing?" Raven asked.

"We're doing great," Chelsea assured their boss.

"And you're feeling okay?" Raven asked her.

"A little tired, sometimes a little nauseous, and there is definitely some swelling appearing in my legs and ankles," she replied. Beside her, Josiah had tensed, and she knew he was thinking about his hands around her neck this morning. He'd already been up when she woke, so he hadn't seen them this morning. The red marks weren't visible because she'd chosen a dress with a high neckline just for that very purpose.

"Good, happy to hear you're not suffering too badly. We all appreciate the sacrifices you're making. The sacrifices you're both making," Raven added, her gaze shifting to Josiah.

"Do you have anything?" Josiah asked in his usual brisk tone, the lighter one from breakfast was gone, and her heart sank a little.

"We've been going through the footage from the surveillance cameras and microphone you planted in Dr. Wood's office, and we're compiling a list of all hospital employees that he might be working with," Raven replied.

"We hacked into his hospital account and were able to get our hands on some of his communications," Ava added.

"Isabella was the one who cracked his code," Teresa told them, and Isabella blushed but nodded.

"Helped to know some medical-specific terminology," Isabella said.

"That's great," Cheslea gushed. If they wanted to shut this ring down permanently, they needed to get as many of the people involved as possible. Of course, another ring would rise up to take its place, but that would take time, and lives would still be saved by dismantling this ring.

One thing she'd had to learn when she took this job was to celebrate the wins however small they might seem. There was more evil in the world than most people realized, and no matter how many terrorists or traffickers you took out, there would always be another to take their place, but that didn't mean you still hadn't achieved something.

It was that same attitude she needed to use now with Josiah.

Walking beside him wouldn't be an easy road, especially since he was going to be fighting to shove her off it every step of the way. But each win was a win no matter how small it might be. And over the last couple of days, they'd had several wins.

The future held whatever it held. It wasn't their place to try to figure it all out, just to take the intel you had at the moment and work with it, make the best of it.

Even if the best that came from her time alone with Josiah was one special night where he felt safe enough to fall asleep beside her, then that was a win.

But she'd never stop hoping for more.

Hope for the best, but be content with what you had.

# CHAPTER

## Ten

May 15th
    8:43 A.M.

He was finding it difficult to stay focused this morning.

Not a problem Josiah usually had when it came to work.

When work was all you had in your life because you had ruthlessly cut out your family, the family of your lost teammates, and refused to allow any new connections to form, it made sense that you threw everything you had into it.

For six years, it had been his only reason for getting out of bed in the morning. The only way he could honor the memories of his fallen teammates was to make the fact that he had been spared mean something.

Then something inside him shifted.

A petite brunette with stormy gray eyes and a heart of gold. Her dedication to standing beside him and offers of friendship meant he could no longer just shut himself away. Physically or emotionally.

Every time he turned around Chelsea was there, physically, or he could smell the sweet lavender scent of her perfume or hear her puttering about the house. But it ran deeper than that. Somehow, she had him starting to believe that there could be more to life than his self-imposed exile.

It was a terrifying thought.

His survival and his sanity relied on his not letting anyone get close. He didn't enjoy cutting his family out of his life or giving in to his growing feelings for Chelsea, but he had to do what he had to do.

Didn't he?

"Josiah." Chelsea poked him in the leg, and he blinked as he looked over at her.

Like it had all morning, his gaze zeroed in on her neck. He couldn't see her skin beneath the high neck of her dress, but he knew beneath the soft pink material, there had to be bruises. Bruises he'd put on her delicate skin.

The reminder was exactly what he needed right now. A reminder of the damage he could cause if he weakened and let Chelsea in. Already he was slipping. It was getting easier to spend time with her, he'd joked with her at breakfast, laughed, and enjoyed the comfortable silence. How much further could he slip over the next few days or weeks?

"Yeah?"

"Raven asked about uploading a virus onto Dr. Wood's computer the next time we go there," Chelsea explained patiently. "They want to try to see how he's communicating with the rest of the trafficking ring. The code works for other hospital employees, but he has to have another way of contacting the ring. I said I think next time we're there, we can figure out a way to get you alone in the room so you can upload the virus. And don't go acting all outraged like you don't want me to be in danger."

Snickers and chuckles came from the computer, and he knew the rest of their team was watching the exchange, waiting to see how he was going to respond.

Of course, he wanted to explode and absolutely forbid Chelsea to follow through on whatever idea was currently running through her head. The last thing he wanted was for her to be in danger.

But ...

That's why they were here.

This whole thing was dangerous, and he'd agreed to be part of it even if the idea of Chelsea in danger had always made him feel sick. He trusted her. At least in this. She'd proven herself to be a talented actress, and to be brave and strong. She was handling all of this like a champ, and implying otherwise felt like insulting her.

"We can do that," he agreed.

"We can?" Chelsea's eyes widened in shock enough that he couldn't help but smile.

"You're right, it's dangerous, but not any more than what we're already doing. We'll work out a plan that minimizes risks," he said, refocusing on the screen.

"Perfect," Raven said. "We'll leave you two to work on that. Update us once you have your plan worked out so we can assist in any way necessary. This is the list of employees we were able to identify through the coded messages. We'll brief you both on all of them, and if you get any chance to make a connection with them run with it."

As members of his team began detailing the information they had so far compiled, Chelsea leaned slightly closer. Not enough that anyone on the call would notice, but enough that he felt the heat of her body seep into him.

"Thank you," she murmured.

"For what?"

"For not freaking out, for believing in me, for wanting to work with me instead of against me."

Her words were simple, but he felt the weight of them. The weight of her gratitude for something as simple as him working with her as the partners they were supposed to be.

There was no way in hell he couldn't imagine what it would be like to truly be Chelsea's partner. She was headstrong, sure, and he was quickly learning that she was a risk-taker, but he was also learning that he liked seeing that side of her.

For all the years he'd known her, he'd always believed she was too soft, too sweet, too innocent for the work they did. While he believed she could handle it, he'd never thought she could take what they did and make it work out in the real world, where there was real danger, real threats.

But she could.

From the looks of things, she could handle anything. She certainly took his anger in stride.

Why couldn't things be different?

Why couldn't he be a normal man, one who wasn't a threat to be around, one not consumed by rage and guilt? One who didn't spend more time wishing he were dead than actually living his life?

If he was then he could reach out and take hold of everything Chelsea was offering.

Then again, if he were that kind of man, it would have meant his team had never been slaughtered. He'd still be a SEAL, and he never would have met Chelsea.

The shaft of unexpected pain that pierced his soul at the idea of never having met Chelsea, of her never being part of his life, told him he was already in a lot deeper than he wanted to be.

Try as he might, Josiah couldn't keep his mind on the

information his team was giving him, and he prayed Chelsea was taking more of it in. Working with Chelsea was so different than serving with his SEAL team had been. Those guys had been like brothers, and he'd cared about every single one of them, although he was closer with some than others, but their presence had never distracted him. It hadn't taken all of a whiff of lavender to make his blood heat and his heart beat faster.

She didn't even realize how deeply she affected him.

Although as he shifted in his seat, trying not to let anyone know he wasn't paying attention, his gaze caught Chelsea's, and she smirked. A cute little one-sided smile that told him she knew exactly what she did to him, and she liked it.

A lot.

Eventually, the call ended, his team said goodbye, he and Chelsea promised to keep them apprised of any changes on their end and assured everyone that they would be safe. Once he closed the computer, his attention swung to Chelsea. It was still early, and they didn't have any plans for the rest of the day.

Only his mind seemed to conjure up dozens.

Used to his own company, and focusing all his energy on work, it was weird to find that he hadn't minded sitting in the hot tub with Chelsea the day before, or watching movies with her, and he certainly hadn't minded sinking into her tight heat last night. Although that one had to be a one-off. No way could he hold onto any semblance of sanity if he let himself touch her and taste her again.

"Want to relax in the hot tub again?" Chelsea asked as though reading his mind.

"If you want to," he replied, trying not to sound too

eager. The last thing he wanted was for her to find out just how much power she had over him.

"Up to you." She arched a brow at him, and he knew she was already well aware of the power she wielded.

Since she wasn't going to let him out of making a decision, he nodded. "The hot tub is fine."

"I'll go up and change." She pushed to her feet and was already halfway to the stairs when her cell phone began to play some old lullaby. "Oh, my mom is calling." She squealed in excitement, as she hurried over to snatch up her phone. "I'll go change as soon as I'm done," she told him before answering the call.

Watching how excited she was just to talk to her mom made his heart ache. Before he lost his team, he'd had a great relationship with his mom. She'd always been fair, always been someone he could talk to, and he'd never gone through the teenage embarrassed by his parents phase, because his mother was just such a decent person, there was nothing to be embarrassed about.

He missed his mom.

His parents.

His siblings.

It was time to stop pretending that he didn't.

Time to stop pretending he could go on like this forever as well. The more time he spent with Chelsea, the less terrifying the idea of living seemed. But was he really ready to take the plunge and try to start living again?

~

May 15<sup>th</sup>
9:34 A.M.

. . .

"Mama," Chelsea greeted her mother as she answered her phone. There was just something about talking to her mom that made her feel like a little girl again. Her parents were almost in their eighties, and they needed her more and more to help out with things, but she would always be their little girl.

"Hello, my darling," Mom said. "Your daddy and I miss you. How are you doing?"

Since talking about her undercover operation with anyone outside of Prey, even her parents, wasn't an option, she sank down onto the couch and considered her words. She hated lying to her mom, always had. Even as a teenager, she'd struggled to tell those typical teen lies. Deciding to be as truthful as possible without mentioning the trafficking ring, she tucked her feet up underneath her.

"I'm doing okay, Mom. A little under the weather, and we're really busy with a case, but I'm okay." The last thing Chelsea wanted to do was stress her parents out. Her dad had had a heart attack almost a year ago, and while he was doing well, his health still felt a little shaky. She worried about both of them a lot, since they'd had her in their early fifties, and she was approaching thirty, she knew their time left together was limited. It was important to her to enjoy every moment she could get with them.

"Happy to hear that, my darling. I worry about you."

"There's no need to worry about me."

"You've always been a romantic, Chelsea, always waiting for the perfect love story. I don't want love to pass you by because you think you're waiting for something better."

Both her parents knew about her crush on Josiah. Well, they knew she had fallen for someone at work, they just didn't know his name or anything about him. They'd always encouraged her to follow her heart, so she wasn't sure why her mom worried about her doing just that.

"Your dad and I won't be around forever, my darling," Mom continued. "And we don't want you to be alone when we pass."

They had no extended family. Both sets of grandparents had passed when she was a baby, her mom had been an only child, and her dad had one brother who had died as a teenager. There hadn't been aunts and uncles and cousins when she was growing up, it had always just been the three of them, so she could see why her mom was worried about what was going to happen to her after they were gone.

"I'll be fine, Mom. You don't have to worry about me." As she said the words, Chelsea's gaze shifted to the man standing awkwardly in the corner. Josiah hadn't left the room when she answered her mom's call, and he was watching her with longing he wasn't even trying to hide.

Things were complicated between them, but they were improving. While she still gave herself maybe a twenty percent chance of Josiah ever falling in love with her, she did believe he was going to let her in as a friend. Maybe once she knew for sure Josiah would never love her, she could start looking for someone else.

Maybe.

But honestly, her heart already belonged to the man she knew could give her everything if he believed her when she told him that he deserved all the good things the world had to offer.

"Whatever happens, I'll always be okay, Mom," she assured her mother, not wanting her parents to spend a second worrying about her. They should be enjoying every moment of their retirements.

"Oh, my darling, I know you'll always be okay, it's just

who you are. But it's a mother's job to worry about her only daughter."

Chelsea laughed. "You've always been the very best mommy a girl could ever ask for." It was true, her parents had waited a long time to have her, and by the time they were pregnant with her, they'd already given up on the idea of having a child of their own. They had given her everything she needed and wanted, not just material things, but of themselves as well. She was truly blessed to be their daughter.

"We love you more than words can express, my darling."

"Love you bigger than the whole moon, Mama," Chelsea said the words she'd repeated thousands of times over the years. When she was four, the moon had seemed like the biggest thing in the world, and she would always beg to stay up past her bedtime to go outside and stare at it. At four, it seemed fitting to tell her mommy and daddy that her love for them was bigger than the moon. Twenty-three years later, she still felt the same way.

"Love you bigger than the whole sun, my darling."

At her declaration of love for her mom, Josiah had turned and was hurrying out of the room. Knowing that if she didn't go after him, she could lose all the progress she'd made with him these last few days, Chelsea was already standing up.

"I have to go, Mom, I'm sorry, we'll talk later." If she thought Josiah hated the idea of her being in danger like this by going undercover, it was nothing compared to how her mom was going to react when this was over and Chelsea told her everything. But she'd convince her mom she had handled it all just fine, the same way she seemed to have convinced Josiah she could handle it. That she was an asset and not a liability, even if she didn't have the same level of training and experience he did.

"Okay, my darling. I'll talk to you later. Love you."

"Love you, Mom."

Ending the call, Chelsea tossed her phone onto the couch and hurried through the house. She found Josiah opening the door to the basement, and her heart dropped. He was withdrawing again, and she hated it.

"Please don't pull away from me," she begged, and Josiah froze.

"You want that," he said softly. "What your parents have. I can never give you that. Even if I wanted to, I can't be the man that you want. That you need."

"Would you stop telling me what I want and need," she growled in a very un-Chelsea-like voice. Normally, she never yelled at people, it just wasn't her. There were other ways she could stand up for herself without losing her temper, but Josiah had pretty much pushed her right to the edge.

It was so demeaning to imply she didn't even know her own mind.

She was an adult, she'd been in love with this grumpy man for years, she knew how she felt, knew what she wanted, knew what she was prepared to give, and knew that if she got her heart broken, it would be worth it to support Josiah any way she could.

"I know you're hurting. I can't imagine what it's like to lose people you care about the way you did, to watch them die and know you were supposed to die too. I get why you're angry, and I get why you push people away, I really do. But it's no excuse to keep acting like I'm some stupid little girl who doesn't know what she wants. I want you, no amount of wishing on your part is going to change it. If you don't like it, tough. That would be a you problem, not a me problem. Now stop hiding from me and go get your sexy little backside ready for the hot tub while I go change. Please," she added, because while she would stand up for herself whenever she needed to, she didn't like being rude.

For a long moment, Josiah just stood and stared at her, mouth hanging open, like she'd suddenly grown wings and started fluttering around the room.

Then his mouth snapped closed, and he stalked toward her, stopping right in front of her so she had to crane her neck back to meet his gaze.

"Sorry. You're right. I just ..." His fingers raked through his short hair. "I don't get what you see in me."

"You don't have to. You just have to accept that I see it." No one else had to understand what made her fall in love with Josiah, it wasn't anyone's business. Chelsea didn't care if people thought it was weird because Josiah wasn't the most lovable guy around with his surly attitude and perpetual scowl. He was lovable to her, and that was all that mattered.

"You're something else, aren't you," he said. Leaning down, he touched a quick but tender kiss to her forehead before heading out into the small backyard.

Chelsea let out a sigh of relief that he wasn't going to go and hide in the gym again. She wasn't really something else, she was just a girl who fell in love with a boy, knowing he might never love her back, and hoping she wasn't putting misplaced faith in herself when she believed she could handle it if he never fell for her.

# CHAPTER
## *Eleven*

May 16th
  1:35 A.M.

Tonight he felt restless.

Something was going to happen, he could feel it in his bones, he just wasn't sure what.

Josiah was confident that so far their cover had been maintained. They'd been diligent in answering every question the way they'd planned, acting like they were willing to betray their company and step out into the illegal to save Chelsea's life.

Granted, that was mostly Chelsea, but then again, he was playing himself. All he'd had to do was stand around and glare at anyone and everything.

Easy done.

Because they hadn't been able to talk to anyone on this side of things, they weren't sure what to expect. They'd rescued victims of the ring who had been taken to harvest organs, including Ava, so they knew about that side of things. They'd rescued doctors and nurses who had been abducted and forced to work for the ring, including Isabella, so they knew about that side of things.

They'd even managed to take alive some of the doctors and nurses who had willingly signed up to work for the trafficking ring for money and power. Those men and women had been more reluctant to talk, but they'd managed to gather some bits and pieces of information from that side of things as well.

But they hadn't located a single person who had bought an illegal organ from the ring, so they had no idea what the next steps might look like. At some point, they knew they would have a meeting at the clinic Dr. Wood had told them about. From there, he had no idea where things would go and he didn't like that.

Didn't like things being up in the air.

If you couldn't plan for every single contingency, you couldn't ensure things went the way you wanted.

Of course, he knew in life there were no guarantees, but he'd spent six years now doing everything he could to eliminate as much uncertainty from his life as he could manage. Playing things safe, isolating himself from anyone who could wind up hurt, had been the only way to keep his anxiety in check, and now he was stepping away from both of those things.

The woman beside him meant so much more to him than she realized.

Chelsea still believed that he was never going to love her back, but she was wrong. The issue wasn't whether or not he'd fall in love with her because he was pretty sure he already had.

The issue was whether he could accept those feelings.

They terrified him, because allowing himself to care

about another person left him open to losing them. Pushing Chelsea out of his life wouldn't be as logistically easy as cutting off his family had been because they worked together. He could always quit, but he loved his job, it gave him a purpose, a reason to live, and ...

Not seeing Chelsea every day would be losing her anyway.

Beside him, she slept peacefully. Sleeping in the bed together had been her idea, he'd wanted to sleep on the floor again. There was every chance that he'd have another nightmare, wind up hurting her again, but she'd asked and he found it difficult to tell her no.

Another time the soft rise and fall of her chest as she took soft, sleepy breaths, and the way her soft chestnut locks tickled his chin might have been all it took to calm him, soothe him enough he might get real sleep without dreams.

But not tonight.

Tonight, danger seemed to hang in the air.

If Chelsea wasn't with him, he'd be happy to wing it, take things as they happened, it was what his life had been like as a SEAL. But since he did have Chelsea with him, he hated not knowing what to expect next from the trafficking ring.

"Whatever happens, I won't let them hurt you," he whispered to a sleeping Chelsea. Lifting his hand, it hovered above her head for a moment. He wanted to give in to the urge to touch her, but how much more Chelsea could he take before he gave in entirely and told her that her feelings weren't one-sided?

Giving in to the urge, Josiah lowered his hand slowly until it rested against her silky locks. Almost reverently, he smoothed his hand down the side of her head. How could a woman like her ever fall for a guy like him?

She said it didn't have to make sense, and no one had to understand it, but he found himself struggling to accept it because it felt crazy to him. He was about the least lovable man out there, well, for these last several years at least. Before that, he'd just been a regular guy, not really looking for commitment but not against the idea either. It always seemed like if it was going to happen, it would happen in its own time and in its own way.

Now it seemed to have happened, and it felt surreal.

Buzzing had his hand snatching back, his pulse spiking, before he realized it was just his phone that he'd switched to silent when they got into bed, vibrating with a message on the nightstand.

Reluctantly, he rolled over to grab it, trying not to disturb Chelsea. She needed the sleep, and it could be nothing important.

"Hey," he said when he picked it up, noting that Luca "Bear" Jackson's name was on his screen. Bear was the team leader of Prey's Alpha Team and was providing support and surveillance for him and Chelsea while they were under-cover. Alpha Team was set up in a house across the street, but they would only intervene if absolutely necessary.

"Hey, sorry for the wake-up call," Bear said.

"Wasn't asleep."

"Good, because you're about to have visitors. Van just pulled up right outside your house, four men are getting out. We ran the tags, and the vehicle is registered to a Dr. Gant who works at the clinic," Bear told him.

"Guess we know how they make contact now," he said. He'd just been wondering and worrying over what to expect from the clinic, and now he knew. They were going to raid his place in the middle of the night. Not sure what they hoped to achieve by that, but then again, the clinic had to make sure that the people they sold black-market organs to couldn't go to the police. Maybe this was meant to be an intimidation technique.

"We're watching things, but I don't think they're going to hurt you guys. Possibly rough you up a bit to send a message of what will happen if you double-cross them, but I doubt they'll hurt Chelsea, can't if they want their money. You know what to do if you need us."

With that, Bear was gone, and Josiah immediately set his phone down and leaned over to grasp Chelsea's shoulder.

"Wake up, Chels," he murmured.

"Mmm ... go way," she grumbled, batting a hand at him and making him smile.

"Can't. Need you to wake up for me." This time, he shook her a little harder. While she was going to have to act scared, he wanted to give her a head-up and he had minutes at most before those four men would be inside the town-house. There were some cameras set up in the living room and kitchen, providing both video and sound to Alpha Team. He'd activate them as soon as they were taken down there, easy enough done since they were voice-activated, so he wasn't worried about what would happen there tonight, but Chelsea didn't have his experience.

"Sleepin'," she mumbled.

Her cute, little annoyed voice made him laugh. "Sorry, Chels, you have to wake up, we're about to have company."

That got her moving. "Company?"

When she sat up, letting the covers dip enough, he got a glimpse at all that creamy skin he'd touched last night, since her tank top did little to cover much of anything.

*Not the time to get distracted.*

"Bear just called. Four men from the clinic outside the house."

"Here? Now? Why?"

"We're about to find out."

"What do we do?"

"Nothing. We lie here in bed, pretend to be asleep, and do everything they ask of us. Chances are they're going to be careful with you, maybe not so much with me." Josiah wanted her to be as prepared as possible for what was about to happen, and he didn't want her freaking out if they roughed him up a little.

"They're going to hurt you?"

"Maybe. Whatever they do I can take. All you have to do is keep playing the part you've done perfectly so far. You can do this." While he'd initially been skeptical about Chelsea's ability to go undercover, she'd done everything she needed to, and he had no choice but to admit she'd been an asset.

"I won't let you down," she vowed solemnly.

"And I will do whatever it takes to protect you," he promised. This case was important, the ring needed to be dismantled, but Chelsea still came first.

Her hand cupped his cheek, fingers gently stroking his temple. "I know that. I trust you, Josiah. Always."

While he couldn't help but feel that trust was misplaced, he nodded. Then because he was supposed to be her husband, he leaned in and brushed a quick kiss to her lips, before guiding her back down to rest her head on the pillows. "Showtime."

～

May 16<sup>th</sup>
    1:47 A.M.


Lying in bed counting seconds made it almost impossible to pretend she was sleeping.

But what else was she supposed to do?

Josiah's wake-up call that their temporary home was about to be invaded by strangers had her on edge. So far, Chelsea hadn't really had to do anything particularly dangerous. Pretending to be dying in a doctor's office surrounded by people where the doctor couldn't make a move was easy enough. Every time they'd left the hospital, she'd known Alpha Team was keeping watch, same as they were tonight.

They just suddenly felt very far away.

"Relax, Chels." Josiah's warm breath puffed against her forehead, soothing her a little. "You got this."

"Okay," she whispered back. He was right, she had insisted that she was capable of being part of this operation without becoming a liability, and she was going to prove him right. It was just that she didn't like the idea of the men roughing up Josiah. She didn't want him hurt, he'd already been hurt more than enough to last a hundred lifetimes.

Sounds outside the bedroom had her forcing all negative thoughts from her mind, clearing it and allowing deep breaths to relax out the tension in her muscles. All they had to do was play along, and soon they'd make contact with Desiree Tilly, then this would all be over, and all her friends could move on and nurture their fledgling relationships.

"Good girl," Josiah murmured, tucking her tighter against him.

His muscular body beneath hers was strong and sturdy,

dependable, and his promise to protect her filled her mind. Together, they could make this work and bring down the trafficking ring.

Evening out her breathing, she added in a slight snore, none too soon because bright light and loud shouts suddenly filled the bedroom.

If ever there was a time to jump all in to her character, this was it.

"Josiah!" she screamed, jerking upright as he bounded from the bed, placing himself between her and the intruders. In one smooth movement, he'd grabbed his weapon, which he now held pointed at the four men. Chelsea knew he could have dropped all four of them already if he wanted to. Well, he did want to, but he knew he couldn't if they were going to enact their plan, so he simply held the unwavering weapon, three others pointed right back at him.

"It's okay, Mr. Fleet, we're friends not foes." The only man not holding a gun spoke calmly, like he regularly broke into people's bedrooms in the middle of the night.

"You're in my bedroom without an invitation, that makes you a foe," Josiah spoke, his voice low and deadly.

"A little unorthodox perhaps, but due to the nature of our business, I'm sure you can understand why such steps must be taken to ensure all of our safety," the man said.

"Wh-what's going on?" she asked, clutching the blankets tightly around herself, mostly to act afraid, but also partly because she *was* afraid. Instead of letting that fear consume her, Chelsea harnessed it, making it work for her benefit.

"Mrs. Fleet, we were sent by Dr. Wood. He has a potential match for you, which means it's time for you to take the next step." The man nodded at his armed guards, who approached the bed somewhat cautiously, obviously having been briefed on who Josiah was and what he was capable of.

"D-Dr W-Wood sent y-you?" she stammered.

"Yes, Ma'am," the man replied.

"And you h-have a m-match for me?" she asked on a sob, that wasn't really all that hard to fake.

"We're almost positive we do, Ma'am, so please understand that we need your cooperation." Although his voice had never wavered, the man did cast a slight, concerned glance Josiah's way.

He hadn't moved yet, a steady, armed presence between her and the others, and Chelsea knew that acting or not, he wouldn't move until she gave him the okay.

Crawling on the bed, hating that she'd chosen to wear these tiny sleep shorts and tank top that gave these men a pretty good view of her body, Chelsea crawled across the mattress and laid a hand on Josiah's arm.

"We have to listen to them," she murmured, blocking out the way the men's gazes roamed her body, making her feel dirty and violated. "This is what we were hoping for. A chance to save my life."

"No one is going to hurt your wife, Mr. Fleet. Not unless you do something that can't be taken back."

Slowly, Josiah lowered his weapon so it was no longer pointed at the intruders.

"Very good," the man praised. "Now toss the gun onto the floor."

Although she knew it cost him, Josiah did as he was ordered.

The second the weapon was out of his hand, the three armed men were on them. Two grabbed at Josiah, wrangling his much larger body between them, while the third came and gripped her bicep in a punishing hold Chelsea had no doubt would leave bruises.

They were both dragged downstairs to the living room, where the men must have set up two chairs before they came upstairs. Josiah was roughly shoved into one, metal cuffs used to secure his wrists to the chair's arms, and she knew it was only because he let them that the men managed to get them on him.

Likewise, she was shoved down into a chair, metal cuffs locked around her wrists, binding her in place. The way the man who had dragged her down there watched her had her shivering in disgust. As he straightened, the man let his fingers trail unnecessarily along her body, brushing across her breasts, and a warning growl rumbled through Josiah's chest.

"Hurt a hair on her head and I will kill you," he vowed. Not only was that threat absolutely genuine, but it was also the words that would activate the cameras and microphones set up to record everything and allow Alpha Team to watch and intervene if necessary.

The man who had done all the speaking chuckled. "I assure you, Mr. Fleet, your wife is quite safe with us. She is very beautiful though, isn't she." His appreciative gaze roamed her body, and Chelsea tried to shrink into her chair, attempting to hide herself even though there was nowhere for her to go.

"You know who I am, what I was, you also know I'm risking everything to save the woman I love," Josiah told the man, looking him dead in the eye.

It was totally inappropriate given the danger they were currently in, and yet Chelsea couldn't have stopped the flush of warmth at hearing Josiah say he loved her even if she wanted to. The words weren't real, of course, he didn't love her, but she loved hearing them none-theless.

"I can kill all four of you without breaking a sweat, the only reason I'm not is because Chelsea needs to live, and I'll do whatever it takes to make that happen. Touch her like that again, and I'll change my mind," Josiah warned.

"No need for threats," the man said quickly, obviously believing Josiah. "We're simply here to collect the first half of the money. Now that we have a potential match, we need payment. I'm sure Dr. Wood explained how it would work."

"Half up front, half after the surgery," Josiah said.

"Right. Now I'm going to give you your cell phone and you're going to do the transfer," the man said, holding up Josiah's phone, which he must have grabbed while the other men were manhandling her and Josiah downstairs. "I must warn you, if the money doesn't go through, then both of you will be killed, and the scene staged to look like a home invasion."

Josiah snorted at that, and even she had to huff a small chuckle.

There was zero percent chance Josiah would be killed by untrained men in a home invasion. With his training and experience, he was quite capable of killing any intruders.

"No one would believe that," she told the man. "My husband was a SEAL, the only reason you aren't already dead is me. If you try to stage this as a home invasion, then Prey will know something is wrong. Even if they find out what we were going to do, they'll still hunt down our killers."

"A murder suicide then," the man snapped, like the whole thing was irrelevant. "How you die doesn't matter, right now, there are three weapons pointed at you. You will be killed first, Mr. Fleet, then I will allow my men to indulge in your beautiful wife's body before she is also killed. Transfer the money now and don't even think about trying something stupid."

The phone was thrust into Josiah's hand, and he unlocked it and scrolled to the banking app. This was it. Once the money was transferred, she and Josiah would move to the next stage, one step closer to getting eyes on Desiree Tilly. Once they did, this would all be over. The trafficking ring would be dismantled, and she and Josiah would annul their pretend marriage.

That thought was both exhilarating and depressing, all wrapped in one.

# CHAPTER

## *Twelve*

May 16th
  2:01 A.M.

Important undercover operation or not, if one of these men touched Chelsea in an inappropriate way again, he was going to kill them.

Every last one of them.

Mission be damned.

Already scenarios were flying through his mind, different ways he could get out of the cuffs and kill them before they could get a shot off. It definitely helped that one of the men was standing close enough that Josiah could kill him with nothing more than his unrestrained legs, and then take his weapon.

Not putting cuffs on his ankles was a mistake. Even with them on, he still could have taken these ridiculously stupidly trained so-called muscle, but without them he was at a major advantage, and they weren't even smart enough to realize it.

Keeping his muscles tense and ready to spring into action if the need arose, everyone in the room waited in silence for the money to transfer to the other account. Eagle had everything set up so Prey would know exactly when and where the money was going. Already, the rest of Cyber Team would be digging into the account details he'd been given and hopefully tracking them, if not to Desiree Tilly herself, then someone else high up on the ring's food chain.

Beside him, he could feel Chelsea's fear, but she was holding it together perfectly. Everything she'd said and done was completely convincing, and he was pretty sure that if they both got out of this alive and dismantled the ring, he would be trying to convince her to take up a career as an actress. She was Oscar-worthy for sure.

"Done," the man in charge announced as he shot a smile at both Josiah and Chelsea. "That wasn't so bad, was it?"

Since there was no good answer to that question, Josiah merely growled. Good thing his role was really just playing himself because he did not have Chelsea's skill. Enough to survive maybe, but his act was definitely being bolstered by hers.

"S-so what h-happens now?" Chelsea asked. Tears continued to shimmer in her gray eyes, making them look like storm clouds about to send a drenching of rain, but he was pretty sure they were fake.

"Now, my dear, we're going to uncuff you and your husband, take you out to our vehicle, and drive you out to where you'll be staying while you have and recover from your transplant," the man explained. "Allow me to introduce myself, I'm Dr. Gant."

Josiah said nothing, merely glared at the man. Out of the corner of his eye, he saw Chelsea offer up a small smile.

With a nod at the armed muscle, Dr. Gant clearly indicated that they should uncuff him and Chelsea because two of the men pulled out handcuff keys and quickly unlocked them. The second he was free, Josiah grabbed Chelsea and dragged her into his arms.

She was okay, he knew that. Had been by her side the entire time, but he couldn't believe she was okay until he had her body pressed against his own, her sweet lavender scent invading his nostrils. Alive. Safe. Unharmed.

This had gone even better than he could have hoped for. They hadn't even bothered to rough him up. Other than the threats and being a little handsy, the men had done nothing more than drag them downstairs and cuff them to the chairs.

Lifting one of Chelsea's hands, he pressed a kiss to her palm, and then to the faint red marks on her wrist. "You okay?"

"I'm okay," she assured him, a warm smile curling up her lips as she leaned into him, pushed up on her tiptoes, and kissed his lips. "Are you okay?"

"Fine," he assured her. Before he could give his attention to the men standing around them, Josiah reached for Chelsea's other hand. More faint red marks circled that wrist as well, but they would fade quickly.

"Very sweet," Dr. Gant murmured, and in that moment, Josiah knew they were going to be able to do this.

They had everyone convinced that he and Chelsea were in love. While he was sure no one ever doubted that she could convince anyone she loved him, given that he was pretty sure everyone knew she was in love with him, he was also pretty sure that Prey had been worried about his ability to convince people he was in love with this woman enough to break the law.

He didn't blame them for doubting him, after all, no one knew that he had harbored secret feelings for the bubbly brunette. He'd even done a decent job convincing himself that those feelings didn't exist.

But they did, and they were getting harder to ignore.

"Remove the Kevlar, Mr. Fleet, and both of you get dressed, please. We need to get moving," Dr. Gant announced, and when he looked over, Josiah could see one of the men must have gone back up to the bedroom to retrieve clothing for him and Chelsea.

While he was happy to get dressed, happier still for Chelsea to be able to cover up her body so these men stopped leering at her, there was no way in hell that he was taking off the body armor.

"No," he said simply, although he reached out and snatched the bundle of clothing from the man's arms and divided them up, thrusting Chelsea's at her.

"There is no need for the vest, Mr. Fleet, no one is going to harm you or your lovely wife," Dr. Gant assured him.

"The Kevlar stays on," he said firmly as he shoved his legs into the jeans and did up the zipper.

"Please," Chelsea added as she began to get dressed. "The vest doesn't have anything to do with this. He just needs it. He has PTSD after almost dying while he was still an active-duty SEAL, he needs to wear it."

"I will kill anyone who tries to take it off me," he warned. And Josiah was pretty sure he would. While he would never consciously do anything that would put Chelsea's life in any more danger than it was already in, taking off the vest would end his ability to form conscious thoughts.

The vest stayed on.

Always.

For six years now.

It wasn't coming off for any reason.

For a moment it looked like Dr. Gant was going to push the point, and Josiah tensed, ready to spring into action if he needed to. He also cast a glance at where he knew one of the cameras was, ensuring that Alpha Team, who now knew about his need to remain in Kevlar constantly, that he was serious about fighting to the death over this.

But then the doctor nodded. "Fine. Although we do have psychiatrists on staff, if you would like to discuss the issue with a professional. They're usually there to work with our transplant recipients, but I'm sure one of them would be happy to talk with you."

No way in hell was he discussing this with anyone.

If he wanted to work through the issue, he would have talked with Piper Hamilton-Eden, Prey's long-time on-staff psychologist, or Prey's newest psychologist, Susanna Zangari.

Pleased the issue was settled, he threw on the T-shirt, then shoved his feet into sneakers, while Chelsea finished putting on her own jeans and T-shirt. Once they were both dressed, Dr. Gant shot them a mildly apologetic smile as he held up two blindfolds.

"I'm sorry, but I'm sure you can understand our need to consider the safety of all our patients. We don't want anyone to know where our facility is since we step outside the bounds of the law to save lives," Dr. Gant told them. The doctor could put a good spin on it all he wanted, but while yes, he was sure the trafficking ring saved lives, it was also responsible for the deaths of hundreds, possibly even thousands of innocent men and women.

Wearing the blindfold wouldn't be ideal, but he didn't believe these men were going to do anything to harm

Chelsea, so he didn't need to see what was happening around him. Besides, he could kill without needing to see anyway. If he had been able to see, Josiah would have taken note of their route, but both he and Chelsea were wearing the same trackers that Teresa had invented that had saved her life when she was abducted the second time by the trafficking ring.

When the time was right, Prey would know exactly where they were.

Claiming Chelsea's hand, he kept her tugged close to his side as the men put the blindfolds on them, then guided them outside and down to a vehicle. Part of him had been worried they'd be transported in the back of a van, or separated perhaps, but instead, they were both helped into the backseat, buckled in, but not restrained in any other way.

As the engine revved to life, and they started moving, Chelsea leaned in against him, her head resting on his shoulder. "We're really doing this," she whispered.

To anyone else, the words would likely be interpreted as joy that she would receive her supposedly life-saving transplant, but he knew what she really meant.

"We're really doing this," he agreed. The real issue, as far as he was concerned, was what he would do *after* they had dismantled the ring. Could he really annul this marriage to Chelsea and pretend it had never happened, or was he already in too deep?

~

May 16th
   8:36 A.M.

. . .

It felt like they'd been driving forever.

Realistically, Chelsea knew it couldn't have been more than a few hours, but blindfolded like this, with nothing to look at to help keep her distracted, time seemed to go so slowly. She had no idea if they were driving around in circles since she couldn't see. For all she knew, they were only a few miles from the townhouse they'd been renting.

Wherever they were, she knew Prey would be able to locate them thanks to the trackers Teresa had created and trialed just a couple of weeks ago. Although that wasn't really what was helping her remain calm.

It was the man beside her.

Strong and powerful, confident in his abilities, Josiah was everything she needed to feel relatively safe, as safe as she could given what they were walking into.

Their fingers were laced together and resting on Josiah's thigh, and Chelsea wasn't ashamed to admit she was sitting as close to him as she could manage without climbing into his lap. No one had spoken the entire journey, and music played in the car, something classical that she wasn't paying attention to.

Knowing men with guns were sitting all around them, and she had no way of gauging their current state, whether they were relaxed, on edge, eyeing up her and Josiah as threats, or leering at her even though she was mostly covered now, had anxiety constantly churning in her stomach. Each time it felt like it was swelling too big to contain, she'd hold onto Josiah's hand a little tighter, and without fail, his thumb would begin to trace small circles on the inside of her wrist.

By the time the car finally seemed to roll to a stop, Chelsea knew it had to have been hours they'd been driving because the sun was warm on her skin as sunlight poured through the car windows.

"We're here. Your home for the next several weeks," Dr. Gant announced, and she let out a relieved breath knowing they were really there.

Now all they had to do was hope to spot Desiree Tilly or find a way to request a meeting with her without looking too suspicious. Once that was done, they could activate their trackers, and Prey would come to shut things down and take everyone involved into custody.

They were so close, and it filled her with a rush of pride to know she was going to be a part of taking down this dangerous ring.

Fresh air washed over them as someone opened the door beside Josiah, and he slid out, keeping hold of her hand as he did so. When they were both standing, someone undid the blindfold tied around her head, and she hated the way the man let his fingers linger on her skin. She'd been sitting in the middle of the row, and she was glad that no one had sat on her other side, because she wasn't sure she could have kept her cool with one of these men looking for opportunities to touch her, which she was sure they would have done.

Bright light flooded her eyes as the blindfold fell away, and she had to scrunch them shut against it. Too long stuck in the dark made her eyes uncooperative, and she was glad she still had Josiah to cling to. He had quickly become her rock, and she wasn't sure how she was going to go back to the way things had been before once this was over.

That was a worry for another day, though.

Blinking her eyes open tentatively, Chelsea took in her surroundings. Despite knowing what happened here, she couldn't help a small gasp of approval falling out at the sight of the stunning mansion before them and the perfectly manicured grounds.

"Beautiful, isn't it?" Dr. Gant asked, and she nodded in agreement.

"Is this the clinic? I was under the impression that's where we were headed. I know you said we were going to a house where we'd stay until I was well again, but I didn't realize you meant a house like this," she said.

"This is separate from the clinic. The clinic is where we mostly focus on testing, treatments, appointments, that sort of thing. But since Dr. Wood has already found you a match, we thought we may as well bring you right out here. Think of this place as a cross between a hospital and a rehabilitation facility. We have operating rooms and state-of-the-art rehab equipment. But we also have beautiful rooms you'll stay in before your transplant, and then once you're past the first several days or possibly weeks after surgery, depending on how you feel. There are tennis courts, swimming pools, libraries, games rooms, and spa facilities. We have vegetable gardens and orchards, if you're interested in cooking your own food we have kitchen facilities, otherwise we can provide all meals. Basically, this is a luxury resort you'll recover in after your surgery."

So while the people with enough money to buy themselves a black-market organ were enjoying a luxury spa resort, those abducted and cut open were left tied to beds in rooms on ships or hidden, rundown clinics in countries scattered across the globe.

The injustice of it all had her fuming, but she tamped down her rage and instead shifted her gaze from the impressive mansion and grounds, to the man standing beside her. "How long until I have my surgery?"

"We're hoping within the next couple of days," Dr. Gant replied.

That meant they only had days to confirm a sighting of Desiree Tilly or get access to her, because there was no way to fake a dying kidney once a surgeon cut her open. It didn't give them long, but she believed they could do this. At worst, they'd have to call in Prey without a Desiree Tilly sighting and hope that one of the doctors here would cough up her contact information for a plea deal.

At least this place seemed like a headquarters of sorts. The old cruise ships were clearly being used to try to circumvent being caught by mostly keeping to international waters. The smaller clinics that had been raided a couple of months ago were also not the kind of place you could imagine the head of the ring hiding out.

But this place ...

If she were Desiree Tilly, she'd make this her home.

"We'd like to go to our room now so my wife can rest. As I'm sure you can imagine, pulling her out of bed in the middle of the night has taken a toll on her health, and she needs to rest," Josiah said firmly.

"Of course, of course." Dr. Gant hurried them toward the front steps of the mansion. "I'll have you taken to your rooms. You'll find the closet fully stocked, fresh sheets on the bed, you'll have your own bathroom, which should have everything you need, but if you find you're missing anything at all, please don't hesitate to ask. I'm sorry that we needed to handle things this way, but I'm sure you understand, after all, we aren't the only ones taking risks here. Soon it will all be worth it, you'll have your new kidney, and you'll be able to return to your life healthier than you've been in a long time."

A young woman met them at the front door, and from

the way she kept her gaze on the floor, Chelsea immediately got the feeling that the transplant donors weren't the only ones not here by choice.

This was one giant mess, all started by one woman desperate enough to break the law to ensure her daughter's survival. Now there were so many lives impacted, and even though she believed Prey would destroy the trafficking ring, nothing could ever be made right for all those affected.

The young maid didn't speak as she led them upstairs and down hallways before stopping outside a room. And neither she nor Josiah spoke as they nodded their thanks and stepped inside their home for the next few days. The room was as gorgeous as the rest of the mansion. A four-poster bed sat under the window, through an open door on the adjacent wall, she could see a bathroom, there was a small seating area with a loveseat, two armchairs, and a table. All the furnishings looked expensive, and Chelsea hated that Desiree was able to afford them at the cost of other people's lives.

When Josiah opened his arms, she didn't hesitate to walk straight into them, snuggling closer when they closed around her.

"We have to be on now, every second, there could be cameras everywhere," Josiah whispered, his lips against her ear.

"I know." If they slipped up now, they'd be killed, possibly before they could activate the trackers, as activating the trackers was the signal to Prey that their target had been sighted and for them to move in.

"You can do this."

"Together we can do this," she corrected.

# CHAPTER

## *Thirteen*

May 16th
4:17 P.M.

With all the things he'd done in his life, this should be one of the easier ones.

From what he'd seen so far, and they hadn't been able to explore much yet, Josiah hadn't seen many guards hanging around. He was sure there were some, probably around the perimeter, but the mansion itself really did seem to be a luxury spa hotel.

Something which set him on edge almost as much as having Chelsea here with him.

Not only were luxury hotels not his scene, but he hated knowing that those with enough money to buy their shot at living through an illegally acquired organ were treated like royalty, while those supplying those organs suffered slow, agonizing, horrific deaths.

But as much as that bothered him, it couldn't compare to his fear for the woman beside him.

Even though he knew she was as angry at the injustices as he was, and she was scared she wouldn't be able to pull off her role, she was doing this as well as he could ever have hoped for. Better than he'd expected. He was ashamed to admit now that he'd ever doubted her.

"You don't leave my sight for any reason," he warned as they approached the doctor's office. They had been summoned for an appointment with Dr. Gant after spending the last few hours in bed feigning sleep so Chelsea could "recover" from the ordeal of being snatched out of bed in the middle of the night.

Maybe she hadn't needed sleep to recover, but he had a feeling she had needed the reassurance of lying in his arms for a few hours to settle her nerves. Despite her fears, she was facing this head-on, with a confidence that amazed him.

If he'd had trouble ignoring his feelings for Chelsea before they undertook this operation, it was going to be a million times worse when they went back home. Back then he'd known she was smart and funny, kind and generous, but he hadn't grasped the depths of her compassion, her strength, her determination to be true to herself, her courage to assert her wants and needs, and her ability to take risks knowing she might be hurt.

She sure as hell had more courage, strength, and determination than he had.

"I won't," she assured him with a soft smile as they reached the doctor's door.

No more than two seconds after he'd knocked, the door was flung open by Dr. Gant, and Josiah had to wonder if the man had been watching their progress on the cameras he could feel capturing their every move. They were hidden well, and he couldn't obviously search for them, but he knew they were there, nonetheless.

"Good afternoon, Mr. Fleet, Mrs. Fleet. I trust you were able to get some rest?"

"Yes, thank you," Chelsea replied.

"Your room is to your liking?"

"Very much so, it's beautiful," Chelsea answered.

"Good, good, come in then, take a seat." The doctor stood back to allow them into his opulent office then closed the door behind them. They were ushered over to the two leather chairs on one side of the desk, while the doctor strolled around it and took the other.

For a moment, Dr. Gant studied them, his eyes assessing, and Josiah had to fight the urge to squirm.

He never squirmed.

Ever.

Never felt the need.

But this was different. This wasn't about him or about his team. It was about the woman he had fallen for despite his best efforts not to.

His instincts were screaming at him to wrap her up in Kevlar, offer her his own vest if he had to, to lock her away somewhere nothing and no one could touch her. Keep her safe at all costs, even if that cost was his own life.

If it weren't for Chelsea's steady hold on his hand, he might very well have let the rage boiling inside him for six long years, out on Dr. Gant and every single other person working for the ring he could get his hands on. But her hold steadied him, soothed the roughest edges of his fury, kept him grounded enough that he merely glared at the doctor.

"Let's be honest with each other, shall we?" Dr. Gant asked, and Josiah stiffened.

It would take him a mere second to launch himself across the desk if it came down to it. He could kill the doctor before the man could react in any way, and he readied himself to do it if the next words out of Dr. Gant's mouth were an accusation.

"You know who we are and what we do, and we know who you are and what you were trying to do," Dr. Gant continued. "But I'm sure you understand that by being here, by paying us half the money already, you're as guilty as we are now."

Chelsea dropped her gaze in mock remorse. Josiah merely continued to glare at the man.

"We understand," Chelsea whispered forlornly.

"I hope now you understand that we are merely providing a service to those like yourself who are able to afford it. While there are some unfortunate losses, this is all for the greater good. Do you have any idea how many lives can be changed by just one donor? We're saving lives here. We're doing the right thing even if you don't agree with it."

A growl rumbled through his chest, and Chelsea's hand smoothed down his arm.

"We're here because we're desperate, not because we agree with what you're doing," Chelsea said.

"Nothing is more important than Chelsea's life," he snarled, it was the absolute truth.

Dr. Gant grinned at them. "They say love makes one do crazy things, and I guess it's true. We're hoping that once Chelsea is well and you return to your lives, you will, of course, dissuade your team from continuing to pursue us. It would be unfortunate if Ms. Hendricks or Ms. Dash were to end up back on our tables. And Ms. Baker was a delightful spitfire of a nurse, wasn't she? Would be a shame if she and her baby had to find themselves on the other side of the bed, wouldn't it?"

The threat stoked the fires of his rage, and he clenched his teeth together before he started spewing venom at the despicable man sitting smugly in his leather chair, dressed in a designer suit, with a Rolex on his wrist.

"We'll do what we can to turn them away from you," Chelsea agreed softly.

"Perfect." Dr. Gant clapped his hands together. "This appointment is not a medical one, no poking and prodding today, Mrs. Fleet, I'm sure you're sick of all that by now."

"I am." Chelsea nodded.

"I wanted to check with you whether you'd like to do your dialysis today in one of our medical rooms or in your own room."

"Josiah can do it, he learned how," she said. "When I was first diagnosed, Prey had a nurse brought in especially to do my treatments, but they know my diagnosis now, know I'm in kidney failure. They think Josiah and I have gone away on a vacation to spend what could be our last weeks together. When they found out we were a couple, they were shocked, but supportive, and Josiah asked to learn how to do my dialysis so we could be alone together."

"I'm not at all surprised to hear they were shocked. Given what we know about Mr. Fleet, I'm surprised he was open to a relationship. But not surprised at the lengths he would go to in order to save your life," Dr. Gant said that like it was a compliment. "I'll organize to have everything sent to your room then, and I do have some good news."

"Good news?" Chelsea asked.

"While you were resting, I was organizing with our team, and your donor is on their way here as we speak. Tomorrow we'll run some final tests, and then I'm hopeful that the day after that we'll do your transplant," Dr. Gant informed them.

Tears brimmed in Chelsea's eyes, and she leaned into him. Josiah immediately engulfed her in an embrace, knowing that her tears weren't ones of joy or relief like the doctor probably interpreted them, but of anguish, knowing that the man or woman who had been matched as her donor was suffering right this very second.

"It's overwhelming, I know," Dr. Gant said in a tone that dripped with false sincerity. "But just remember what you're gaining. A new kidney doesn't just save your life, it gives you the life you dreamed of. You and your husband can go on to live a long and happy life together, grow old and gray side by side. You can raise children, enjoy grand-children, travel the world, and share many special moments together. This is the beginning of something wonderful. That's what you focus on, Mrs. Fleet."

The man's words only made Chelsea cry, and Josiah knew it was because she was thinking that it was exactly what she wanted with him, but thought she could never have. And it made his heart ache to know he wasn't brave enough, strong enough, or courageous enough to take that leap of faith and give it to her.

~

May 17th
    12:28 A.M.

The slight shift in the mattress beside her had Chelsea springing awake.

Unlike last night when Josiah had woken her from a dead sleep with the news that their townhouse was about to be broken into, tonight her sleep had been restless. She was unable to settle enough to let her mind drift off. Even her body felt tightly coiled, like a spring ready to be let free.

Not even Josiah's warm, strong body beside her was enough to calm her.

How could anything let her relax when she knew right now there was some young man or woman, scared and alone, possibly in pain, maybe having already lost some of their organs, being brought to this luxurious mansion because of her? While she was sleeping on thousand-thread-count Egyptian cotton sheets, they were tied to a hospital bed.

That person would soon be rescued, but they didn't know that, and that was eating her alive.

Lifting her head, she saw Josiah attempting to ease out of the bed carefully, obviously trying not to disturb her.

"What're you doing?" she whispered. They weren't sure if this room was bugged, or if it was just the common areas, so they had to play things safe and assume that every single thing they did was being watched at the very least, possibly every word they said being listened to as well.

"Go back to sleep, Chels," he ordered in that way that told her he was up to something and trying to protect her from it.

"Nuh-uh," she said quickly. "We're a team for as long as we're here, whatever you have planned, I want in."

Crying yesterday in Dr. Gant's office because she craved every single thing he'd mentioned with Josiah and yet knew she was never going to get had been silly. There were bigger problems right now, more important issues to deal with than her not getting the fairytale ending with the man of her dreams.

Lives depended on them pulling this off, so she had to stay on target.

Which was exactly why she wanted in on whatever he was up to.

"This is too dangerous. I want you to stay in bed, try to get some sleep."

"I'm supposed to look like I'm not getting enough sleep," she reminded him. "And this whole thing is dangerous. We're safer if we stick together."

"Not for this."

"What exactly is *this*?"

When he didn't answer, merely tucked the covers back up around her and reached for his pants, she realized what he intended to do.

"You're going snooping," she accused. Given they knew cameras were dotted throughout the mansion, that was more than just dangerous, it was pretty close to suicidal.

"And you're going back to sleep."

"I wasn't sleeping, I was tossing and turning, and at best fitfully dozing," she informed him as she threw back the covers and swung her legs over the side of the bed.

"I'll take fitfully dozing over this," Josiah snarled, but she knew it wasn't from anger, he was just afraid for her.

"We go together or I go on my own," she informed him, hurrying to the closet to grab some clothes.

"Chelsea." Josiah huffed in annoyance.

"Josiah." She huffed right back at him, and she was pretty sure she saw one side of his mouth curve up into the smallest of smiles. "We have free run of the house, we can pretend we just got lost if we get caught."

"Given who we are, they're not going to believe that."

"Then we make them believe it. We'll pretend we were looking for a doctor because I wasn't feeling well."

"No."

Rolling her eyes at him, she crossed the room, clothes in hand, to stand before him. "I'll sell it enough that we have a reasonable explanation for being there without making it so

I'm so sick I need tests. Besides, there's a simple way to not have to worry about any of that."

"Yeah?"

"We don't get caught." Laughing mostly to ease the tension in the room, not really because she thought her joke was funny, Chelsea quickly got dressed.

While he didn't say another word about it, she knew he wasn't pleased to have her with him as they both slipped out of the room and into the quiet hall. They hadn't had much of a chance to look around yet, but they knew the basic overview of the mansion's layout.

The ground floor was the common areas, living spaces, libraries, media rooms, the kitchen, games room, and spa rooms. The second floor, which is where they were right now, was the rooms used by the paying guests who were here to receive their illegally bought black-market organs. The third floor was where all the medical suites and offices were, they'd only been up there to Dr. Gant's office.

"Where are we going first?" she whispered as they walked down the hall.

"Third floor. Best chance at finding anything."

She agreed. There would be no need to have any sensitive documentation lying around in the areas used by the people who were paying you for organs. Later, they would try to strike up conversations with as many of the guests as possible, hoping that someone would have spotted Desiree Tilly, but after midnight, most people would be in bed.

No one stopped them as they wound their way through the quiet halls, and although she tried to spot the cameras she knew had to be there, she couldn't see any of them.

"You sure there are cameras?" she asked quietly.

"Positive."

"Aren't they going to see us then? Or are you hoping no one is monitoring the cameras this late?"

"They won't see us."

Josiah said it so confidently that she paused, wondering what trick he had up his sleeve. "How do you know?"

"Because I disrupted their Wi-Fi. I suspect no one is watching them right now, and by the time they check in tomorrow, if they even notice that the cameras were down for a couple of hours overnight, it'll be too late to do anything about it. We're not going to take anything or disrupt anything, we're not going into any of the rooms up there where we know they're keeping their prisoners. No one will be able to say they saw us, even if they do suspect us."

"I don't think they do. I think they buy I'm dying, and they think you're some sort of psychotic, dangerous, almost animal-like man waiting for a chance to rip them to pieces if they don't save me."

"They're not wrong," Josiah muttered, and despite her fear of getting caught, heat flushed through her body.

Maybe she shouldn't love Josiah's possessiveness so much, but she did.

It gave her hope.

"When you say things like that, it's really hard not to kiss you," Chelsea murmured, finding her body drifting closer to Josiah's without any conscious thought on her part.

Instead of answering, he merely dipped his head and feathered his lips across hers, then abruptly straightened, grabbed her hand, and started walking again.

Talk about giving her whiplash.

Sometimes Josiah was so protective that she would have sworn he must truly care about her, then he did sweet things like kiss her or hold her. But he never said anything about wanting more, about having feelings for her, about seeing her as a life partner and not just for the duration of this operation.

Reaching the stairs, they found no one guarding them, so they hurried right up them and headed for the room near the top that was Dr. Gant's office. Chelsea really wanted to keep heading down the halls, find the poor people trapped in the rooms up there, and assure them that they just had to hold on a little longer and then they'd be going home.

But they couldn't do that.

Couldn't risk getting caught or chance anyone letting their plans slip too early.

Josiah picked the lock to Dr. Gant's office in about three seconds flat, and they both slipped inside. They didn't turn on the light, but Josiah had a tiny penlight with him that he used to light the way and hurry over to the desk.

"I'm guessing you have a specific plan on being in here?" she asked, staying closer to the door.

"Plant a virus on his computer, we need access to his contacts," Josiah said, already booting up the computer on the desk.

"How long will it take?" They had no idea if this floor was patrolled, and if it was, then how regularly.

"Less than a minute. Which is why you could have easily waited in bed for me."

"And miss out on all this fun?" she teased, making him huff, a sound that could have been a chuckle or just an expression of annoyance, she wasn't sure which.

Just as Josiah was pocketing the small USB and shutting off the computer, Chelsea's head whipped around. That sounded like ...

"Footsteps," she said, spinning to face Josiah. Whoever

was out there might not open the door to check the room, but then again, maybe they would.

"Hide," he said.

"Where?" The only place in the office where they could possibly hide was under the desk, and that was like the equivalent of hiding under the bed, it would be the first place anyone looked for them.

He didn't argue with her, just rounded the desk, grabbed her hand, and pulled her back with him, shoving her down and under the heavy wooden desktop, then joined her.

They huddled together, and Chelsea held her breath, praying whoever was out there just kept on walking by. But then she heard the door handle rattle. A moment later, the door swung open and light swept across the room.

# CHAPTER
## *Fourteen*

May 17th
    12:57 A.M.

His worst fears were coming true.

He should have insisted that Chelsea remain in their room.

As the beam of light danced across Dr. Gant's office, Josiah knew he should have gone with his gut, which was to take Chelsea into their bathroom, which was less likely to have a camera in it, then tie her to the bath, and leave her there. That way if he was caught, he could have pretended Chelsea was ill and he was looking for some painkillers or something.

Even if she'd hated him for it, at least she wouldn't be here right now.

If they were caught like this, hiding under a desk, there would be no logical way to explain their presence in the doctor's office. They'd be found out and quickly find themselves tied to hospital beds awaiting tests and then organ removals.

Josiah's finger hovered above the tracking device.

Worst comes to worst, he'd activate it.

It was too early, they hadn't had a chance to find out if Desiree Tilly was here, but at least he'd uploaded the virus so that Prey could gain control of Dr. Gant's computer. Given it was kept here at a secure location, he doubted the man would be as careful with it as he would with whatever computer he used at the clinic.

Beside him, Chelsea was holding her breath, her body rigid, and he saw she also had her finger poised above the tracker. At least they were on the same page about that.

"Damn doctor, how many times have I told him to check his damn office door is locked?" a deep male voice muttered.

Then the light disappeared, and a moment later, the sound of the door closing and locking seemed to echo through the small space.

Safe.

By some miracle the guard hadn't searched the office.

Thank goodness for Dr. Gant's inability to remember to lock his own office. If it wasn't for that, the guard would have known something was wrong and come looking to see what. Under the desk would be the first place the man would have looked, and it would have been all over for them.

"Breathe, Chels," he ordered as he grabbed her hand and dragged her out along with him.

"We almost got caught," she said on a shuddering breath.

Anger surged inside him. Mostly, it was a shield for his

fear, but he was so angry with Chelsea for putting her life on the line when she didn't have to that he could barely look at her.

Since here and now was not the time or the place to let loose, he kept his hold on her hand and pulled her along with him to the door. After waiting a full couple of minutes so he was confident the guard had well and truly continued with his route, Josiah eased open the door.

Confirming that everything was clear, he quickly stepped into the hall, bringing Chelsea with him, then locked the office door from the inside and pulled it closed.

It shut with a clunk that was much too loud for his liking, so he started moving quickly back the way they'd come, heading for their room. Once he got there, he was going to leave Chelsea and head to the gym. He needed to blow off this anger before he did or said something he'd regret.

With each silent step he took, his anger grew.

Raging inside him like a wounded bull.

Seemingly sensing his fury, Chelsea didn't speak a word, just hurried to keep up with his much longer strides.

When they finally reached their room, he stepped inside with her then gestured at the bed. "Get some sleep."

"Wait, where are you going?" she demanded, with no self-preservation whatsoever. Did she not remember how he'd put his hands around her throat the other night? The lingering red marks were a constant reminder that he was a physical danger to this woman, who was too sweet for her own good.

"Gym."

"You mean you're running away again, hiding."

Yep, Chelsea didn't have a shred of self-preservation

hiding beneath all that creamy soft skin. How could someone be so smart and yet so dense, all at the same time? He'd told her he would protect her, that nothing would happen to her, and yet he'd let his desire to make her happy cloud his judgment.

He was as angry with himself as he was with her.

"Go to bed, Chelsea," he ground out.

"No. Not unless you come with me." The damn woman actually jutted out her chin, daring him to disagree, and planted her hands on her hips. It would be a whole lot easier to maintain his level of terrified rage if she didn't look so adorably sexy.

"Go to bed," he ordered again. If she kept pushing, then the tight control he had on his emotions was going to snap.

"Talk to me, I'm right here. I know we almost got caught, but we didn't. Everything worked out okay."

Her cavalier attitude to her own safety, her own life, was the final straw. All that rage he'd been holding back, not just since they left Dr. Gant's office a couple of minutes ago, but every drop of anger that had bubbled and boiled inside him for six years, suddenly exploded out.

Grabbing her shoulders, he backed her up until she was pressed against the closest wall. "You could have been killed," he snarled. "Do you know what that would do to me? Do you understand that? Do you really think I don't fight my feelings for you every single second of every single day? I can't let anyone get close to me, Chelsea, don't you understand that?"

Somehow recognizing he was gripping her too tightly, he abruptly released his hold on Chelsea's shoulders and stormed across the room. He couldn't be that close to her and not touch her, and dragging her into his arms and kissing her senseless would be a stupid thing to do when the walls he'd built around himself were wobbling precariously.

"I should have died. I wanted to die. My place was with my team. I never should have walked away alive that day. But I did. I've done everything I can for the last six years to try to honor their memories, to do something that would give meaning to what we were all trying to do. Work. That's all I want. All I need."

His fingers dug into his scalp, yanking on his short hair until his skin stung. He needed the pain to feel grounded.

Whether she cared or not, they'd come precariously close to dying tonight.

Okay, maybe those deaths would have taken weeks as they were disassembled piece by piece, and sure, Prey would have arrived to stop that from happening, but it was the principle of the thing.

Losing Chelsea would shatter his last remaining sliver of sanity.

Have him devolving into the angry monster he already feared he was.

Like he wasn't the biggest threat to her in this entire mansion, Chelsea crept toward him. While her eyes were wide, he didn't detect a hint of fear in them, only the usual compassion and love he always saw.

"Stay away from me," he growled, backing up. "I don't want to hurt you, but I'm not in control of myself right now."

"Oh, Josiah, I think for the first time in six years you finally *are* in control," she said softly.

"Ridiculous." He scoffed. "Don't you see? I wear this vest. I keep my family locked out of my life. I don't let myself acknowledge my feelings for you because it's what I need to do to survive. What I need to do to make sure the anger doesn't consume me."

"But it does consume you. The anger and the fear keep you locked in a sort of stasis where you're unable to move forward. But tonight, you're standing right on that precipice. You can do what you've been doing, hiding away, letting the anger and fear control you. Or you can take that very first step and realize I'm right here waiting for you. Your team wouldn't want you to live the rest of your life like this. They'd want you to keep living, to find happiness and joy, that's what honoring their memory looks like. Not working yourself to death and isolating from everyone."

While she spoke, Chelsea had continued to take slow steps toward him until now she had him backed up against a wall, his fingers curled into fists hanging at his sides. It was the only way he could stop himself from reaching for her.

"If you had died that day but one of your teammates had lived, is this what you'd want for them? Loneliness? Anger? Fear?"

"No." He said the word he knew to be true even if he wanted to deny it.

"What would you want for them?"

"What you said. Happiness, joy, for them to keep living."

"Why?"

"It wouldn't have been their fault I died." The words came out as the natural answer even though he'd spent six years twisting himself into mental knots trying to make their deaths his fault.

"Right. You had your vest on, they didn't. It's tragic, and it's a massive loss, one you'll always feel. There's no magic answer, Josiah. The anger isn't just going to magically disappear. The fear will linger even after you learn to live without wearing the Kevlar. But you don't have to get to the end of the journey in one step, there can be a million tiny steps along the way."

Lifting her hands, she placed them on his chest. Their warmth seemed to sink deep inside him, even though he knew that with the body armor between them it wasn't physically possible.

"Take that first step, please. Trust that while you lost a team, you still have another one. Me, the rest of Prey. Your mom. Your dad. Your brothers. We're still your team, whether you want us to be or not, and teammates don't give up on each other. Ever."

It felt like there was nothing solid beneath him, that he was in free fall, but his fingers uncurled one by one, and then they did the only logical thing they could do.

They reached for Chelsea.

~

May 17th
1:11 A.M.

The second he reached for her, she knew.

Chelsea let out a breath of relief, knowing that not only had Josiah taken a step back from the ledge he'd been balancing way too precariously on for her liking, but he had also taken the first step in reclaiming his life.

His hands circled her waist, lifting her off the floor, and it was the most natural thing in the world to wrap her legs around his hips and hold onto his shoulders. Something she couldn't quite name danced in his dark eyes, or maybe it was an amalgamation of so many different emotions that they all blurred together.

"Don't like you being in danger," he murmured as he tipped his head forward so his forehead rested against hers.

"I know." Her fingers began to massage his tense muscles. "But I'm okay, and I'm here as your partner, to watch your back. Trust me just a little."

"I do," he muttered, clearly displeased with the concept.

She giggled. "Good. I know you're trying, Josiah. And I don't want to push you too hard too fast, but try to accept I'm here and I'm not going anywhere. You know I love you, and you ..." she paused to take a breath hardly daring to believe he'd actually said it, "you said you fight your feelings for me, so you care about me too, even if it's not love. That means you know I'll always put your needs first. I'm not asking for any commitment, I'm not asking you to fall in love with me, to date me or marry me, or anything more than trusting me to be there for you."

"It's not about trust, it's trying to control the fear and anger," he admitted softly, almost like he was ashamed of the words. But there was nothing for him to be ashamed of. Josiah was a hero, one who was struggling, who thought he had to do it all alone.

*Please let me in.*

The whispered thought ran through her mind as she pulled her head back. "Then stop trying."

"Pretty sure I'll fall apart if I do that."

"Then fall apart."

"Can't. I might ..." One of his hands remained on her waist, his other lifted to brush calloused fingertips across the mostly faded marks on her neck from when she'd woken him out of a nightmare the other night. "I might hurt you again."

"I'm tougher than I look." Not wanting to force him to do anything he wasn't comfortable with, she let her lips hover millimeters from his.

For some reason she couldn't explain, Chelsea felt like he had to make this first move.

Not because she wanted to push him into something he wasn't ready for, but because she needed to know it was what he wanted.

Right now, his emotions were all over the place. He was terrified because they'd almost been caught, angry that she'd been in danger, but more than that, he was battling against himself as he tried to shake off the shackles of his past and find his way through all that fear and anger to a better place.

When his lips brushed across hers, it felt like her second victory in as many minutes. Or really, the victories were Josiah's. He was the one fighting as hard as he could right now.

"Make love to me, Josiah," she whispered against his lips.

"Not sure I can do soft and sweet for you this time any more than I could last time."

His warning was adorable. "Who said I wanted soft and sweet? Don't you know by now I want you any way you'll let me have you?"

Despite his warning, as he carried her to the bed, there was a tenderness to the kisses he kept peppering to her lips, and he laid her down with a reverence that made her feel like a queen. With quick, deft movements, he stripped her of her clothing, stopping regularly to dot more kisses to her lips, then as he bared them her already pebbled nipples, her stomach, and the inside of each thigh, mere inches from where she really wanted those sexy lips of his.

"You need to be a little more naked a little more quickly," she said with a pout when he stood beside the bed looking down at her.

One of those extremely rare smiles of his graced his lips, and when he let go like that, he quite literally stole her breath.

"Breathe, Chels," he said with a small chuckle as he leaned down and kissed her again.

Sucking in a shuddering breath, she watched with rapt fascination as Josiah stripped out of his clothes. His movements were almost graceful, and his body was such a work of art that she could quite happily stare at it forever.

"You should be in a museum," she said dreamily, making him laugh again. Two in quick succession, she was one lucky girl. Even though this was their second time having sex, last time she hadn't expected there to be a repeat, and while she was still reminding herself not to get her hopes up, that he was here with her again had to mean something. At the very least, she stood a chance.

"You're the one who should be in the museum," he corrected as his hands began to skim her body, seemingly everywhere at once. They tweaked her nipples, kneaded her breasts, then trailed up her sides, making her break out in a mass of goosebumps.

When he moved to settle between her legs, she grabbed at his shoulders. As much as she craved the feel of his tongue on her most sensitive flesh, there was something else she craved even more.

"Need you inside me," she said urgently, trying to maneuver his much larger body where she wanted it.

With the third chuckle of the evening, he grabbed her hips at the same time he flung himself down beside her, somehow rolling her so she came up straddling his hips. "Take me how you want me then, babe."

"You should be careful making that kind of proposition," she warned as she settled her knees on either side of his hips, his hard length jutting up to meet her.

"I should," he agreed, and yet from the way his fingers dug into her hips, she concluded he wasn't all that worried about it at all.

Lowering her hips until his tip rested right against her opening, Chelsea warred with herself. She wanted to just sink down, take him inside her, let the pleasure already simmering inside her boil over, but she also wanted to take her time and savor the moment.

Making progress with Josiah or not, she knew this could be the last time she made love to him.

Placing her hands on the Kevlar vest, hoping one day she might be lucky enough to run her fingers over every inch of delectable muscle beneath it, she sank down just an inch, enjoying the small sting as his impressive length stretched her.

"Going to torture us both, Chels?"

"You're the one who said you couldn't do soft and sweet, but I don't see you complaining."

"No complaints," he said, his voice softer than she'd ever heard it.

Sinking down a little more, taking another inch of him, her heart swelled with so much love for this man that her eyes got all watery.

The pad of Josiah's thumb touched her cheek, catching a stray tear. "You okay, Chels?"

"Perfect," she assured him. "I'm perfect."

Inch by inch she took him. Josiah's fingers dug into her hips a little more with each passing inch, and she knew he'd leave behind bruises. Not that she cared. She'd wear those marks with pride for as long as they lasted.

By the time he was buried deep, she could already feel the first flutterings of pleasure. This really was perfect. The two of them together, nothing between them, the way she wished it could always be.

"Not sure I can hold back much longer, Chels," Josiah warned, and she could see how tautly wound he was.

"Then don't."

"Touch yourself," he ordered as he used his grip on her hips to thrust into her.

Keeping one hand on his chest, above his heart, her other moved quickly to where their bodies were joined, circling her needy little bud. Inside her, Josiah seemed to grow bigger, although she knew that wasn't really a thing. Maybe it was just that the sensations he was creating were bigger than anything she'd felt before.

Her fingers worked faster.

Josiah's dug harder into her skin.

His thrusts were almost desperate.

"Come. Now," he ordered, and just like that, the command detonated an explosive of ecstasy inside her.

The most perfect pleasure licked along her veins, touching every part of her body, seeping down into her very soul. Josiah roared out his own pleasure, continuing to thrust into her even as her orgasm began to fade.

When it disappeared into nothing more than a few delightful aftershocks, Chelsea sank down to rest against Josiah's chest, suddenly exhausted.

"Need to go clean you up, babe," he said softly, trying to move her.

"No," she protested, sleep already tugging at her mind. "Want to stay like this, with you inside me, not ready to let you go yet."

"Okay, Chels," he agreed, reaching for the blankets and

tugging them up and over them, keeping her on his chest, his softening length snug inside her.

"Never going to be ready to let you go," she mumbled as she tumbled into sleep, praying Josiah would keep fighting his demons.

# CHAPTER

## Fifteen

May 17th
9:41 A.M.

The desire to keep Chelsea in the room where she was at least partially safe still thrummed through his body.

It chanted to him in his head on a near-continuous loop.

But so far Josiah was managing to control the impulse.

Last night, he'd almost lost control, falling off the brink, and there was every chance he wouldn't have been able to find his way out of that dark hole. Only somehow, Chelsea had managed to pull him back up.

She was so damn sure of everything. Not just herself and her feelings and desires, but so confident when it came to him as well. She believed in him, and because of that, he was doing his very best to believe in her.

Not just believe in her ability to play out this undercover operation to completion, but also that maybe he could find a way to live again. Maybe honoring his fallen teammates wasn't working himself to death but taking the chance he'd been given and living his life to the fullest.

Now was not the time to examine that too closely, though. For as long as they were there, his focus needed to be on keeping Chelsea safe and finding what they needed to end this trafficking ring once and for all.

Which is why he was fighting against his protective instincts, and Chelsea was with him as they wandered out of the dining room. She hadn't gotten nearly enough sleep last night, and he knew the black smudges under her eyes were completely genuine. He hadn't slept much either, but how was he supposed to just drift off after hearing Chelsea's barely conscious declaration that she never wanted to let him go?

"There are more people here than I thought there would be," Chelsea said softly as they made their way through to one of the living rooms.

She was right. The dining room had been like one you'd find in a hotel, with at least four dozen tables, and almost all of them had been occupied. That meant there were at least fifty people here who were buying organs. Possibly more.

A lot of lives were about to come tumbling down.

Every one of those couples would be prosecuted for the part they had played in the suffering of the ring's victims. Marriages would be torn apart, children would lose parents, so many lives destroyed, all because some people thought that if they had enough money, they could treat others like objects instead of fellow human beings.

"We'll try to talk to as many as we can, but we're going to have to give up a large portion of the day to pretending you're undergoing dialysis," he murmured, dipping his head to nuzzle against her neck so no one else would hear his words.

"There's a couple over there, they look about our age, let's start with them," Chelsea suggested, taking his hand and leading him in that direction.

While he was good at observing, taking mental notes, and picking up on the tiniest of details, Chelsea was good at talking, putting people at ease, and getting them to open up. Their strengths would definitely complement one another.

"Hi," Chelsea said as they approached the couple.

"Hi," the man said back.

From the way the couple sat, with the woman lounging in an overstuffed armchair and the man with his own chair pulled close, hovering protectively over her, Josiah assumed that it was the woman who had received the lifesaving transplant, or was about to.

"You guys mind if we sit?" Chelsea asked, indicating the couch opposite the two chairs.

"Not at all," the woman said, offering them a smile. "You two new here?"

"Just arrived yesterday," Chelsea replied, as both of them sat down on the couch. "I'm Chelsea, and this is my husband, Josiah."

"Amy and Gavin," the woman supplied. "That middle of the night wake-up call is terrifying, isn't it?"

At her words, the man, Gavin, bristled, and it was clear that he was protective of his wife. It was also good to know that the break-in hadn't been just for them, which meant the ring really did believe they were there to buy an organ.

"Terrifying," Chelsea agreed. "You guys have been here for a while?"

"We're almost ready to leave," Amy said with a grin.

"My wife is almost back to her old self," Gavin added, a tender smile on his face as he brushed his knuckles across his wife's cheek.

"I'm so glad your surgery was successful," Chelsea said, smiling at the couple even though he knew she was as upset as he was about the way these wealthy people were fine with knowing their donor had suffered horribly. "And you were ... okay ... with how everything went down?"

Immediately they both had the grace to look embarrassed. At least that was something.

"It wasn't easy," Amy said, shifting uncomfortably in her seat. "But knowing that the donors they use are at least criminals helped. Money to get their lives restarted seems a good trade off for giving up an organ."

Interesting.

They hadn't known that's what the ring was spouting out.

"We try not to think about it too much, it makes Amy upset," Gavin inserted.

Yeah, Heaven forbid that the people paying to disassemble another living, breathing human being's body, should have to feel upset about it. Upset was nothing compared to the pain and terror the victims were suffering.

Chelsea nodded. "Yeah, I'm a little ... upset ... about it too. But, I mean, it's that or die, so ... I can see why you just try not to think about it."

Just because the trafficking ring knew who they really were didn't mean anyone else here needed to. Besides, he wasn't even sure Amy and Gavin, or anyone else here, would care if they learned the donors weren't criminals but everyday people just like them, who had been snatched off the streets and imprisoned by the ring.

"Can I ask what transplant you needed?" Chelsea asked.

"Skin," Gavin replied. "My wife was in a terrible accident, and her legs were so badly burned she almost lost them. The doctors weren't able to find us a donor, and my wife didn't have enough good skin left to transplant, plus she was still weak and recovering. When we were contacted by the clinic, we jumped at the chance to get Amy her life back."

"Of course," Chelsea tutted understandingly. "You guys are still young, you have your whole lives ahead of you, of course, you wanted to grab that chance and run with it. We're the same way."

"Gavin would do anything for me," Amy said, staring lovingly up at her husband.

The other man's gaze met his, and Josiah realized that at least they had this in common. Because he would do anything for Chelsea. Including, he realized with somewhat shocked horror, attempt to face his demons.

"Same way you're here doing this for your wife," Gavin said.

Josiah nodded. Suddenly, needing to touch more of Chelsea than just her hand, he hauled her into his lap, uncaring of what anyone watching, either the couple they were talking with or anyone watching surveillance footage, thought.

"We want to have kids, grow old together, play with grandbabies, and travel the world," Chelsea said as she snuggled into him.

"Same," Amy said, leaning into her husband's touch when he palmed her cheek.

"You guys want kids?" Chelsea asked, the question sounding completely innocent, even though Josiah knew where she was going with it.

"Definitely. You too?" Amy asked.

"For sure," Chelsea answered. "Have you seen any kids here? I can't think of much worse than having to bring your precious baby here, knowing this is probably your last chance at saving them."

"Couldn't agree more," Amy said. "We haven't seen any kids, and we've been here for months. Skin transplants are tricky. Oh, wait, there is one kid here sometimes. A little girl."

A little girl.

Desiree Tilly's daughter?

If the kid had been spotted here, there was every chance that Desiree was either living here or at least visited from time to time.

"Is she a patient?" Chelsea asked.

"I'm not sure," Amy replied. "She doesn't look well, so I'm guessing she's sick, but she's the only kid I've ever seen here, and she loves playing outside in the gardens. Maybe she's just the daughter of someone who works here."

Looked like they would be spending the majority of the day in the gardens.

They were running out of time. They were meeting with their "donor" at some time this afternoon, and then tomorrow, Dr. Gant was planning on doing Chelsea's surgery. Obviously, they couldn't let things get that far, which only gave them approximately twenty-four hours to find out if Desiree was here.

Either way, Prey would raid this building sometime today or tomorrow, and in doing so would effectively shut down the trafficking ring. This was clearly their main base, and there was no way they could maintain their operation without it. At least it would take them a while to rebuild.

But Desiree Tilly wasn't just in this for the money and power, she was also in this to save her daughter's life. Which meant she was never giving up. She'd find a way to rebuild no matter how long it took her.

While he understood that level of desperation, he would do anything within his power for Chelsea, especially if it was to save her life. The woman couldn't be allowed to keep doing what she was doing.

~

May 17<sup>th</sup>

    10:22 A.M.

"This is ridiculous, we can't just wander around out here all morning."

"Why not?" Chelsea asked, tilting her head up to glance at Josiah. There was something different about him today, something changed last night. It wasn't like he was a completely different man or anything, but there was a softening to him. The way he looked at her, there was a tender affection that hadn't been there before.

Wishful thinking, maybe, but she didn't believe so.

He was trying, doing the best he could to battle his demons while simultaneously working this operation and keeping her safe.

That he was trying meant everything to her. She was so proud of him, and she found herself falling deeper in love with her grumpy SEAL.

"Because we'll look suspicious."

"Nah." Chelsea shook her head, then swept an arm around the gardens. "We're not the only ones out here. Other couples are wandering about, too. It's why they have the grounds. If they were onto us, they would have killed us when they broke into the townhouse."

"Unless they suspect we were the reason Dr. Gant's office was unlocked last night."

Josiah was certainly being Mr. Worrywart this morning. "I doubt the guard even mentioned it to the doctor. You heard him, the door is often left unlocked, and he's annoyed about it. Annoyed but accepting. I don't think he would have said anything. Even if he did, I'm sure Dr. Gant would just assume he'd forgotten like he usually does."

"And if he doesn't assume that? If he decides to go check the security footage and realizes the cameras were down for a short time, who do you think he's going to suspect?"

Well, the answer to that was easy.

Them, of course.

But still she couldn't help but feel that Josiah was fixating on the what-ifs without any evidence. "Stop borrowing trouble."

"Need to be prepared for all scenarios."

"You are. We are. We have the trackers. They aren't going to kill us right away. Prey will be here within hours of us activating them."

"They know about the trackers."

"No, they know Teresa was rescued after they took her from her apartment," Chelsea corrected. "They might suspect there was something with a tracker, that it's how Teresa was found, but that's it."

Resting her cheek against his bicep, she nuzzled closer, trying to will some of her calm into Josiah. She doubted very much that he was this much of a worrier when he was still an active duty SEAL.

Didn't take a genius to figure out what was different this time around.

Her.

It was nice he cared so much, but she didn't want him twisting himself up in knots about everything that could possibly go wrong. For now, everything was going perfectly to plan, and that was something to be celebrated.

As she gazed out across the garden from the small, vine-covered pergola on a little hill, she saw something that had her straightening.

"Did you see that?" she asked, pointing to the moving figure she'd spotted moving faster than the others.

"See what?"

"In the maze. I saw something. A single something, not a couple. Smaller than the others." While, of course, anyone could walk around out here on their own, and she was sure there were people who had come to the mansion for surgery without a loved one accompanying them, almost everyone they'd seen had been a pair.

"A kid?"

"Maybe," Chelsea hedged. She was pretty sure it was a child, but the figure had moved quickly, then disappeared behind the tall hedges of the maze again. "Only one way to find out."

With a curt nod, Josiah started walking, keeping his steps easy and measured even though she could sense the tension in him, the desire to go running after the figure she had seen. Together, they wandered their way back down the hill, past gorgeous displays of colorful flowers, as they headed for the maze.

Chelsea likewise wanted to go running off to check it out, but they couldn't draw undue attention to themselves. They had no idea how many cameras were set up, but they were both confident that almost every move they made in any of the common areas, including the gardens, was monitored.

When they reached the maze, they were met with two possibilities.

Left or right.

"Let's split up," she suggested, already knowing Josiah would hate the idea.

"No."

"Don't be ridiculous. We have to. If the kid is in here, we need to find her. I swear I won't leave the maze. If I don't find her, I'll come back to the start and wait for you right here. Nothing is going to happen to me," she added, giving his hand a reassuring squeeze.

"You leave this maze without me and I'll ..." Josiah trailed off, but he didn't have to finish the sentence, the answer was written all over his face. He wouldn't just be angry with her, he'd be terrified. He was trying to fight his demons, and her betraying him like that would set him back, maybe even turn him off the whole idea.

"Promise." It was an easy one to make because she loved this man with everything she had and would never intentionally do anything to cause him pain.

Grabbing her shoulders, he dragged her in for a hot, hard kiss that left her panting, then he stalked off to the right.

For a moment, Chelsea couldn't move, all she could do was stand and watch Josiah disappear around the corner. Her fingers brushed across her lips, still tingling from the bruising kiss, and she silently begged the universe to throw all the help it could Josiah's way.

Turning to the left, she started walking. The hedges were high, probably around eight feet tall, and neatly trimmed. It was peaceful in there, quiet, the rest of the world seemed to fade away as she ambled along. She could see why someone had designed the maze, it was so tranquil, it was like stepping into a different universe.

As she walked, Chelsea listened for signs that someone else was in there with her. She really wasn't afraid of anything bad happening to either her or Josiah, but she wanted to be careful because she knew it would be important to him.

The maze was more difficult than it had looked from up above it, but Chelsea had a good sense of direction, and she was sure she could find her way back with relative ease. Besides, she was there with a retired Navy SEAL. Josiah wouldn't have any trouble finding his way through the maze, out of the maze, and locating her if she got lost.

After about ten minutes, she spotted movement up ahead. A flash of white, gone almost before she'd seen it.

"Hello?" Chelsea called out, picking up her pace.

There was no answer, but as she took the next turn, she spotted the same flash of white. Breaking out into a jog, she turned another corner, and then another, and there she came face to face with a little girl of about six. The child had chestnut brown locks tied in two pigtails, vivid blue eyes, and a dimple in her left cheek. Exactly like Desiree Tilly's daughter, Bridget.

"Oh, hi, honey," she said, offering her most reassuring smile to the child who was looking at her shyly. While she liked kids, she hadn't spent a whole lot of time around them, so she wasn't quite sure what to do or say to put the little girl at ease. "I didn't realize anyone else was in the maze. I'm trying to beat my husband to the middle. Is this the right way?"

The child nodded. "It's that way," she said, pointing to their right.

"You play in the maze a lot?"

"Yeah, I like the tall, tall, tall leaves," she replied, gesturing to the hedges.

"It's so fun in here, a great place to play. Do you live here?"

"I'm not 'sposed to talk to strangers," the child said, making Chelsea grin.

"Absolutely true, I'm glad your mom taught you that. She knows you're out here, doesn't she?"

"She's always working, so I always play in the garden. Sometimes I even play out here when it's raining. Mommy gets mad, but if she doesn't want me to play outside, then she should play with me inside."

"Can't argue with that, sweetie. Sometimes moms and dads need to work, though. Your mom works here?"

The little girl looked around as though someone was going to pop out of the hedges at any second and scold her. Then she took a step closer and curled her finger, beckoning Chelsea in with a conspiratorial smile. "My mommy is the boss, everybody here got to do what she says, 'cept me, cos mommy always says I'm the boss of her cos she don't ever want to see me sad. My mommy gets sad lots cos my daddy and my brothers died. She always tells me she's never gonna let me die."

"I'm sure your mommy loves you more than anything else in the world," Chelsea said softly, her heart breaking because she could absolutely understand Desiree Tilly's desperation to save this adorable child.

But the cost of saving Bridget's life was too high. She would never wish the little girl a single second of pain and suffering, but nor could she allow Bridget's mother to keep killing people.

"Keep going that way, left, and left, and left," Bridget said, holding up her left hand and making an L. "Then you can win."

With a giggle, the little girl skipped off, and Chelsea couldn't help but wonder what was going to happen to her once her mother was imprisoned. Which, now that she had confirmation Bridget was here and so was Desiree, was going to happen sometime in the next twenty-four hours.

# CHAPTER
## *Sixteen*

May 17th
3:36 P.M.

"We should do it now," Josiah insisted, not sure why they were still having this argument several hours later.

"After we get a visual," Chelsea insisted just as strongly from where she was sitting by the window. It was the same spot she'd been in since she spoke with the little girl they both believed was Bridget Tilly in the maze this morning.

After meeting the child, Chelsea quickly made her way back to the entrance, and after he'd walked the entire distance of the maze, or at least as far into it as he could get, he headed back to the entrance and met up with her. She'd been so excited to tell him about talking with the girl, and how certain she was both by the fact that the child matched their physical description of Bridget Tilly, and by what the girl said about her mother being the boss, and the loss of her father and siblings.

There was no way that little girl wasn't Bridget Tilly,

and he doubted that Desiree would be far away, but Chelsea wanted to wait until they spotted the woman. So they'd come back inside, ordered lunch to be delivered to their room, and then gone up there to pretend to do her dialysis.

Chelsea had sat by the window, occasionally spotting glimpses of the child playing in the gardens, getting more annoyed when no adult went to check on the little girl, even as the hours ticked by. They'd spent most of the time arguing about whether or not they should set off their trackers and bring Prey in.

If there was a way he could pass on intel to them, he'd have agreed with waiting, at least until their visit with Chelsea's "donor" because spending more time in the medical suites would have told him how many victims were there, and how many doctors, and if any appeared to not be there by choice. But they had no way to communicate, didn't even have their cell phones since the people who took them there had left them behind at the townhouse.

Waiting increased the risk for no good reason.

While he was pretty sure that they were within a couple of hours of the townhouse, even though they'd driven for longer than that, so they technically had enough time for Prey to get there and plan their entrance, he couldn't help but be antsy with Chelsea in the mix.

They had yet to discuss their plan for when the raid happened, although he had discussed a signal with Alpha Team, so at least he'd know when it was time to get her to hide somewhere. But they needed to come up with more details than that. Where would she hide? What signal would he give her that it was safe to come out?

Once the raid started Desiree, Dr. Gant, and the others would all know he and Chelsea were responsible. There was no way they wouldn't. Which meant she would have a huge target on her back.

The thought made his chest tighten painfully, making it difficult to draw a full breath.

"Look!" Chelsea suddenly squealed from the window, darting to her feet and pointing. "Josiah, look. I see her. Desiree Tilly, by the maze, holding Bridget's hand."

Joining her by the window, he followed her line of sight and spotted the same thing she had seen. A small girl of around six, skipping along, holding a woman's hand. The woman had the same chestnut brown locks, pulled back into a bun, and while it was impossible to accurately identify her from this distance, he was comfortable agreeing that the woman was the head of the trafficking ring.

About to activate his tracker right here and now, without any more discussion on the matter, since Chelsea's only objection had been trying to get a visual on Desiree Tilly, before he could press his finger to where the small tracker had been placed under his skin, there was a knock at the door.

"Mr. Fleet, Mrs. Fleet, I've been told to come and collect you for your meeting," a somewhat timid voice called out.

"After we get back," Chelsea whispered. "This shouldn't take too long, and then we can set them off. Prey isn't going to move in until dark anyway, and we're not at risk until tomorrow morning."

Instinct had him wanting to argue.

Protective instincts.

The kind that went crazy at the thought of keeping Chelsea in danger any longer than he had to, but she was right. Prey would wait until the early hours of the morning when things would be the quietest before raiding the estate.

Glaring at her because that tightness in his chest kicked up another few notches, she merely smiled and stood on tiptoes to give his short hair an affectionate ruffle.

"Don't borrow trouble, Josiah. We're safe for now. We have until tomorrow morning at least. A couple more hours and this will all be over," she murmured, a note of wistfulness seeping into her voice.

There was no need to ask to know why.

As much as she wanted this ring shut down, she was sad that it meant their fake relationship and marriage would be over.

Only it wasn't all that fake, not with the intensity of the emotions burning inside him.

"Mr. Fleet? Mrs. Fleet?" the voice from the other side of the door called out.

"It's going to be okay," Chelsea whispered, pressing a kiss to his cheek. "Sorry, we're coming," she called out louder as she tugged him along with her toward the door. "Sorry," she repeated once she unlocked and opened it. "Didn't mean to keep you waiting, we were just ... enjoying each other's company."

The young woman, who was the same one who had guided them to their room yesterday morning, blushed a deep red as her gaze darted between them and then dropped to the floor. But before it had dropped, Josiah caught the disapproval in it, pretty much confirming his suspicions that the woman wasn't there by choice. If she knew what was going on there, and thought they were being cavalier about the many innocents suffering beneath this roof, then she hadn't taken this job willingly.

"This way please," the woman mumbled, and they both followed her through the halls and down to the stairs. "Dr. Gant said to meet him in the patient's room. Turn right at the top of the stairs, head straight down, take a left, and it's room 304."

With a polite nod, the young woman disappeared, and hand in hand he and Chelsea ascended the stairs. They followed the directions they had been given, and the mansion started to look less like a luxury spa hotel and more like a hospital. Most of the doors were closed, but there were a couple of nurses and a doctor wandering about.

When they reached room 304, he knocked once and then opened the door.

It took every ounce of control he possessed not to immediately tear into the doctor.

Even then, it was probably more Chelsea's hand tightening around his that kept him still.

In the room's only bed lay a woman around Chelsea's age. She had long brown locks that fanned out in a tangled mess on the white pillow. A white sheet covered the woman's body, but he could see the leather straps protruding down the bottom, binding her ankles to the bed's metal frame. Likewise, her wrists were bound, both of which he and Chelsea had been expecting to see.

The ball gag in the woman's mouth, they had not.

Both the woman's gaze and Dr. Gant's snapped to them as they entered the room, the woman's shooting daggers as she eyed them defiantly. Good. She was still furious about what was being done to her, which meant she stood a good chance of recovering once she went back home.

"Mr. and Mrs. Fleet, meet your donor," Dr. Gant said as he indicated the woman, who turned those angry eyes on him. "Unfortunately, she has a bit of a problem keeping her teeth to herself. She's bitten three nurses already, and managed to chew through our first attempt at restraining her. So far, the ball gag seems to be doing its job."

Dr. Gant's cavalier attitude came dangerously close to snapping his control. That the woman also had a feeding tube threaded down through her nose, and he could only imagine how horrible that must feel with the restriction of the ball gag making it difficult enough for her to breathe, pushed him further.

Chelsea's nails dug into his skin, giving away the horror she was feeling even as she stood still as a statue beside him, and that was it.

Killing the doctor would only make things worse, but he wasn't going to stand for this. "Take it out," he snarled.

The doctor merely laughed. "Mr. Fleet, you knew what we do, that's why you reached out to us. You prioritized saving the life of your wife over the lives of these people." Waving a dismissive hand at the woman in the bed. "Too late to back out now."

Oh, it was too late all right.

Too late for the doctor to do anything to change his fate. As soon as Prey got there, Josiah was going to rip the man apart with his bare hands.

~

May 17th
    4:09 P.M.

By the time they stepped back into their room, Chelsea was shaking all over.

She wasn't sure if it was rage, or guilt, or grief, or maybe a combination of all three, but she'd barely made it through that meeting with Dr. Gant and the poor woman bound to the bed.

Of course, she'd known how the victims of the trafficking ring were kept. She'd heard firsthand accounts from Ava and Teresa, heard it from Isabella about what things were like on the other side of the bed for medical personnel who weren't there by choice. As part of her work with Cyber Team, she'd also read through every statement given by the men and women who had been rescued.

If you'd asked her, she would have said she was prepared for what she was going to see while she was there, but nothing could have prepared her for the reality of that. Knowing it, reading it, and hearing about it were very different than actually seeing it with her own two eyes.

"Shh, Chels, it's okay." Josiah's large hands closed over her shoulders, dipping down to her wrists and back up to her shoulders, down and up, down and up, with firm strokes.

"It's not okay," she shot back, wriggling out of his hold so she could turn around and bury her face in his chest. She didn't even care that the Kevlar made it hard and uncomfortable, blocked her from absorbing his heat, at least she was in his arms, safe, while that poor woman lay up there suffering.

"It will be," he reminded her.

"She hates us." There was no mistaking the venom in the woman's gaze as they'd stood beside her bed listening to Dr. Gant drone on about the transplant, and what to expect, how it would go, details of the surgery.

"For now. But soon she'll know the truth."

"What if they decide to do the surgery on her now?"

"They can't." Josiah's hand rubbed circles on her back, but the motion wasn't soothing her. She was too riled up. "We know what Dr. Gant said, both surgeries will happen at the same time tomorrow. A team will remove your damaged kidney and prepare you for the transplant while another team will remove hers. We know that's not really going to happen, but it's what he just explained, so while that woman will be uncomfortable and angry for another few hours, no one is going to be operating on her."

Hours felt too long.

She wanted this over now.

Maybe they should have activated their trackers this morning when Josiah wanted to. Chelsea had been so focused on getting a visual on Desiree Tilly that she hadn't thought of the suffering of the victims. If they'd set off the trackers hours ago, maybe Prey would have already been there.

Even though she knew they likely would have waited until dark before storming the mansion, it felt like they'd wasted so many precious hours.

Desperate for an outlet for her raging emotions, Chelsea didn't even think, just reached for the zipper on Josiah's jeans. "Need you inside me," she pleaded as she unzipped him.

"Chels." Josiah said her name slowly, and there was clear conflict in his voice, like he wasn't sure this was what she really wanted.

Only it was.

More than that it was what she needed.

"You know you keep promising me hard and fast, but really, if you think about it, what you've really been giving me has been pretty sweet." Reaching a hand inside his boxers, she grasped his already hardening length and ran her hand along it before palming his tip and circling her hand on his sensitive flesh. "I want my hard and fast. Here. Now. Take me. I'm yours."

To emphasize her point, Chelsea pulled her hand free, and leaned down to grab the hem of her ankle-length skirt. Before she could, Josiah growled, and gripped her wrists, holding her still.

"You should be careful talking like that," he warned, his lips just above the pulse point in her neck, the warm puff of air against her skin making her shiver with need.

A raw, desperate kind of need she'd never felt before.

This was more than attraction, more than love, it was something deep and almost animalistic. Something primitive that she couldn't even explain. All she knew was that she had to have him inside her right now.

Hands still circling her wrists, Josiah suddenly yanked her off her feet. The motion startled her, and she squeaked at the sudden pain in her shoulders, and quickly wrapped her legs around his hips.

Bunching up her skirt, Josiah dipped his fingers under the soft cotton of her panties, and with no hesitation, he plunged two inside her.

Chelsea cried out at the beautiful intrusion, and the sting as he stretched her, the second of pain quickly morphing into pleasure as he curled his fingers so they brushed across the special spot inside her. His thumb found her bundle of nerves, pressing against it hard and fast, just like she'd asked for.

Shoving his jeans and boxers down enough that his length could spring free, Chelsea stroked it with greedy fingers. This was hers, and she felt pretty possessive of it.

Another squeak fell from her lips when Josiah suddenly withdrew his fingers, and in one smooth move did something she hadn't even realized was actually possible to do in real life. He ripped her panties off her body. The skin where the material had pulled against as it tore stung, but the sensation only seemed to add to her growing need.

Guiding him to her entrance, Josiah thrust his hips once and buried himself deep inside her. Filled with him, she moaned as everything around her seemed to click into place. This was where she belonged, and she prayed he felt it too.

"Damn, Chels, how do you feel so ...?" Josiah trailed off as he pulled back and then slammed into her again.

Clutching at his shoulders, she rocked her hips forward, enjoying the friction. "So right," she finished for him.

"Right," he agreed, somewhat awestruck.

With that declaration, he spun them around so her back was pressed up against the door, shoved her tank top up so he could get to her bra-covered breasts, which he promptly claimed with his hot mouth, grabbed hold of her backside, and began to thrust into her.

Hard and fast, just like she'd asked for.

Each one sent her back ramming into the wooden door, likely hard enough to leave bruises, and she loved it.

Higher and higher she rose. The combination of his lips and tongue teasing first one pebbled nipple and then the other, with his hard and fast thrusts, had pleasure rushing toward her. All she could do was clutch at his shoulders and hold on for the wild ride he was giving her.

When one of his hands shifted to take her bud, tweaking it between his thumb and forefinger, that was it.

She combusted into a fiery ball of pleasure as ecstasy ripped along her veins, consuming her.

Maybe she cried out his name.

Maybe he cried out hers as she felt him come inside her.

It was impossible to know because she was too wrapped

up in the orgasm that seemed to go on and on. As it finally subsided, she leaned forward to bury her face in Josiah's neck, breathing in his comforting woodsy scent, her body so convinced it was all hers that she didn't even have the energy to remind her brain and her heart that Josiah might have feelings for her, but he'd also put in a lot of effort to fighting against them.

"Thank you for giving me what I needed," she whispered as tears stung her eyes. Happy tears, grateful tears, maybe a bit of sadness that Josiah might choose to keep fighting his battle instead of surrendering.

His arms wrapped around her, holding her tight against him, his face burying itself in her hair, and she felt him do what she'd just done to him, breathe in her scent as though committing it to memory. She hoped that wasn't because he didn't think he'd be doing this again.

She prayed it was because he was reminding himself of what would always be his, even if he chose not to let himself be hers.

Their fake marriage was about to come to an end.

With a last deep breath, Josiah grasped her hips again and pulled out of her, setting her back down on her feet. Taking her hand, he guided her into the bathroom, grabbed a washcloth, ran it under warm water, then kneeling before her, cleaned her up.

There was no need for words when he tossed the washcloth into the sink and stood. They both knew it was time.

The look on his face as they both activated their trackers felt far too much like a goodbye for her liking, and her heart filled with an ache she knew would never completely heal.

# CHAPTER

## Seventeen

May 18th
1:03 A.M.

Neither of them could sleep.

Although Josiah lay in bed, his arms wrapped around Chelsea, his body was tense, as was hers.

After setting off their trackers, it had been a long afternoon and evening. They'd made the rounds, gathering intel, and also classifying every couple they spoke with into categories of how much of a risk they believed them to be.

When this went down, he wanted to know that the only threats inside were the guards.

Knowing he was going to have to leave Chelsea somewhere killed him.

He literally had a ball of terror lodged in his chest, pressing against his heart, making every breath he took painful.

But there was no other choice.

Neither of them was armed, and while he knew Chelsea

could shoot a gun with reasonable accuracy and had trained in self-defense ever since she started working at Prey, since Eagle insisted on mandatory lessons for all employees with no prior military experience, she wasn't trained enough to come with him. He could kill with his bare hands without batting an eye, and as soon as he got his hands on a weapon, it would make things even easier.

Not that he planned on using one when he found Dr. Gant.

The doctor deserved a longer, slower, more painful death.

Keeping Chelsea with him would put her in greater danger, so as they'd walked the mansion today, they'd also kept an eye out for good hiding places.

Their room was out, because once Prey breached the estate's perimeter, Desiree Tilly and Dr. Gant would suspect that it was him and Chelsea who had led them there. That meant he either had to stay in there and guard Chelsea or get her out of the room.

The anger that raged inside him insisted that he take an active role in bringing down the ring. He needed to shed blood, get his hands dirty.

Maybe he hadn't been able to get justice—or revenge—for his teammates, but he could get it for Ava, Isabella, Teresa, the woman slated to be Chelsea's donor, and every other innocent victim the organ trafficking ring had claimed.

"How much longer do you think?" Chelsea whispered into the dark.

"Not much," he assured her, unable to resist skimming a hand the length of her spine. In truth, he didn't know. There was every chance the trafficking ring was using some sort of jammer, and their signal hadn't been picked up, but he didn't believe that to be the case.

If it was and Prey hadn't arrived by morning, then he would take Chelsea and they'd run. He'd cut out his tracker and leave it close to the perimeter of the estate, and then they'd bring Prey back with them.

Whatever happened, protecting his girl was his number one priority.

And he wasn't even going to consider the fact that he'd just called Chelsea his.

Thankfully, he didn't have time to examine it because the hoot of an owl flitted through the open windows.

"Is that them?" Chelsea asked, already sitting up.

Another hoot followed the first, and then a third. Three in quick succession, the signal he and Alpha Team had discussed.

"Showtime," he told her, the same words he'd uttered when they were lying in their bed at the townhouse waiting for this all to begin. Now it was almost over, and he wouldn't have any excuses left.

He would have to confront his future and decide what it was going to look like.

For now, though, he had a trafficking ring to destroy.

Both of them threw back the covers and climbed out of the bed. Josiah grabbed a pair of dark colored jeans and a black T-shirt from the clothing that had been provided for them. Not as good as the usual tactical gear he'd wear if he'd been with his SEAL team, but it would at least help him blend a little better into the darkness, and he had his Kevlar vest on.

Safe.

So long as he had that on, he was safe.

Too bad he didn't have one for Chelsea. Still, at least

she'd be hiding away and not out where any bullets would be flying.

"You remember what to do?" he asked as he shoved his feet into shoes.

Chelsea was half dressed, but she paused to roll her eyes at him. "After we've gone over it at least four dozen times before we lay down in bed to pretend to go to sleep, do you really think there is any chance at all that I might have forgotten?"

"What do you do?" he asked, enunciating each word, because while Chelsea was obviously feeling good enough to be all sassy, he was not. There had not been a single mission he'd embarked on with his SEAL team, not even his very first, that he'd been this on edge, this afraid. There was always a bit of nerves, the knowledge he might not come home, but there wasn't this full-on fear that made it difficult to function.

"I wait fifteen minutes, because that was your plan with Alpha Team, and then I go and find the linen closet at the far end of the hall and hide in there until you or someone else I recognize comes to get me." She parroted back what they'd gone over, amusement in her tone. There was a bit of trepidation there, too, and he knew she was trying to lighten both their moods with a little bit of humor.

"Smart Alec," he muttered, but as soon as he was dressed and ready to go, he strode over to her, grabbed her shoulders, and dragged her closer so he could crush his mouth to hers.

The future was uncertain, but nothing could change the fact that he cared deeply for this woman.

Might even love her.

Whether he confronted and accepted those feelings or not, they were there.

Something he'd have to remind himself of later.

For now, he just needed her to be safe.

"Don't get distracted," he murmured into her hair when he was able to drag his lips from hers.

"Hey!" she exclaimed. "I don't get distracted."

"You care about everybody, a little too much some-times," he told her, palming her cheek. "Stay safe. That's your only job."

Even though she nodded her assent, Josiah knew there was every chance she would do something to put herself in danger. Having a big heart was a good thing, but it could also be a dangerous thing.

"Your job is to stay safe, too," she told him, fisting his T-shirt, a tremor in her bottom lip letting him know most of the sass she'd been giving him was bravado.

He gave her a single dip of his head, because he didn't want his last words to her to be a lie if things didn't work out the way they hoped, and he didn't make it back to her. As far as he was concerned, his job was to ensure she lived. His life was optional.

Because Josiah knew if he didn't go now he might not be able to make himself walk away from her, he touched one last kiss to her forehead before turning and heading out the door.

It was quiet in the hall. While he would have liked to be able to lock all the couples in their rooms so he knew where they all were, from what they'd gathered, none of them had any military or law enforcement training, so none should present a threat. Likely they'd all just panic and hide in their rooms once the shooting started.

Before it did, he needed to take care of Dr. Gant.

The horror in Chelsea's eyes when they came back from that meeting with her "donor" would forever be etched in his mind, and that growing anger fueled him as he strode silently through the halls.

From what he could gather yesterday, when they were up on the third floor, the medical personnel had rooms in the opposite wing from the medical suites. That was where he headed now. Prey would enter as quietly as they could, avoid as much of a firefight as was possible, but sooner or later, someone would realize what was happening and he wanted the doctor dead by then.

There was no way to know which room belonged to the head doctor, but he was able to count out any of the rooms that were locked. They'd belong to whatever doctors and nurses weren't there of their own volition.

Double doors at the end of a corridor caught his attention. Whatever was on the other side of them would be grand, exactly the kind of room a man like Dr. Gant would commandeer as his own.

Stealthily, he hurried down the hall. Easing the doors open, he spotted an enormous four-poster bed in between two floor-to-ceiling windows. The curtains hadn't been fully drawn, and enough light filtered in to illuminate the figure in the bed.

Dr. Gant.

Revenge had been something he'd dreamed about for six years. That revenge had been intended for the men who killed his team, but now it would come to another man who liked to play God for his own amusement, for his own power and money.

Bloodlust set his body on fire as he crossed the room and wrapped a hand around the man's neck. When terrified blue eyes popped open, he grinned.

"Hello, doctor."

May 18<sup>th</sup>
  1:13 A.M.

Watching Josiah walk out the door had so many emotions swirling inside her.

Too many.

They tangled together, getting clogged, stopping the words she wanted to say from coming out, not even letting the tears that burned the backs of her eyes fall.

It felt wrong to let him go alone.

Of course, she understood that he had way more training and experience than she did. She also got that she would be a liability, that having her with him would divide Josiah's attention between her and the guards who would be swarming inside the house as soon as the first gunshots were fired.

But she didn't want him to go out there alone.

What if there were too many guards for him to fight against?

Just because Josiah had more training and experience than all the guards put together, it didn't mean they couldn't still kill him.

After all, they were armed and Josiah wasn't.

Killing one on one with his bare hands was easy for him. Maybe even two on one, or possibly three on one. But what if there were four of them? Five? Ten?

Before she even realized it, Chelsea was taking steps toward the door, unable to let him go alone. She might not be as good as he was, but she could do something, she wasn't completely helpless.

"No," she rebuked herself aloud. "You can't. You promised. Well, you agreed at least. If Josiah thinks you followed him, he won't be able to concentrate, and you don't want to be the reason he dies."

Although ...

There had been something in his eyes she hadn't liked when she'd told him his job was to stay safe, too. Something that said he didn't completely agree with her.

"Don't do anything stupid, please," she whispered into the empty room as though her plea had the power to travel through the mansion to wherever Josiah was and convince him that his life mattered.

Did he know that?

She feared he didn't. Feared that for him, this was the revenge mission he never got to go on, and that surviving it wasn't as high on his priority list as it was on hers. He hadn't been able to get justice for his SEAL team, but he could get it for Cyber Team.

"You have to trust him," she reminded herself as she deliberately turned her back on the door. She was supposed to wait fifteen minutes, then go to the linen closet at the end of the hall. Hiding felt cowardly, and if she'd had access to a weapon, she would have insisted on going with Josiah regardless of his arguments.

Wandering to the window, she looked out into the dark night. Prey was out there somewhere, she knew that, but she just wanted them here. Wanted Desiree Tilly in handcuffs, Dr. Gant and the rest of the staff here by choice as well. Wanted all these innocent victims like the poor woman tied and gagged upstairs, dreading a surgery that wasn't coming to be safe, back home with their families and recovering from their ordeal.

She stared out the window, desperate for a glimpse of

the men she knew were coming. Of course, she couldn't see them, they were too good for that. They wouldn't be seen until they wanted to be, but it didn't stop her from looking.

"Huh," she said, a small smile quirking her lips up as she did indeed notice a small movement in the gardens. "Guess they aren't as good as they think they are, or I'm just better than I think—"

The rambled words she was speaking aloud to herself so she didn't lose her mind broke off when she realized what she'd just seen.

It wasn't a member of Prey.

Too small.

Childlike.

"Bridget." She gasped.

What was Desiree's little girl doing out there? And all alone, too, because there were no other moving shadows nearby.

Did Desiree know about Prey? Had something tipped her off, and she was readying her guards to attack?

Without even considering what she was doing, Chelsea spun around and hurried toward the door.

Easing it open, she glanced down the hall and spotted no one.

As far as she was concerned, her promise was void. Bridget was out there, and she wasn't going to let the little girl get caught in the crossfire. She'd get the child, and they'd hide somewhere together until it was safe.

Tiptoeing down the hall toward the stairs, Chelsea made it to the first turn when she saw the dancing of flashlights.

Ducking back out of sight, she weighed up her options. It hadn't been enough time yet for Prey to get inside. Maybe it was one of the couples wandering around in the early hours of the morning? Or maybe it was the guards.

A muffled pop had her freezing.

She knew that sound.

It was a gun with a silencer being fired.

Darting her head back around the corner, she saw a shadowed figure closing a door, then moving down to the next one and opening it.

They were killing the couples here who had come to buy organs. That meant they knew Prey was there. They were cleaning house like they'd done on the boat after Ava escaped.

Panicking right now would get her killed, but Chelsea couldn't seem to stop her breath sawing in and out of her chest, or slow her wildly hammering heart.

The linen closet.

She had to get to it.

It was still a valid hiding place, and once the men had fired into her and Josiah's room, she could get outside to Bridget. She wouldn't put it past these people to kill the child even if Bridget was the reason Desiree had started the trafficking ring to begin with.

More muffled pops echoed through the otherwise quiet mansion as she ran for the linen closet.

Once inside, she pulled out a stack of blankets and crammed herself into the back of the shelf before stacking them in front of her like an incredibly useless barrier. If she was spotted in there, the blankets would do absolutely nothing to stop a bullet.

Seconds felt like hours, and she tried to be logical about it, count out each step the guards would take, the opening of the doors, the firing of the weapons. Chelsea tried not to miss how many rooms were between her and where she'd spotted the guards. If she miscalculated, she'd leave her hiding place too soon and be spotted and likely shot on sight.

Only once she was almost positive that the guards must be gone did she slowly push away the blankets. No one had opened the linen closet looking for her, so the guards either believed she'd been in her bed when they'd fired their shots, or they knew she hadn't been there and were now searching for her.

Knowing that Josiah would be furious with her for not staying put, Chelsea also knew that if she did, she could easily be found. Getting out of the house was her best bet, and Bridget was still out there alone.

Bad idea or not, she was getting to that child.

Each step she took through the house, her nerves ramped up another notch. The metallic stench of blood was beginning to permeate the hall, and it made nausea churn in her stomach.

Death.

It was the smell of death.

While she wanted the people who had gone there to buy an organ to be punished for their choices, choices they'd known were wrong, they didn't deserve to be shot in their beds. They'd made these choices out of desperation, she got that, and they believed the donors were all criminals, she got that, too, but prison would have been a more fitting punishment.

By the time she reached the top of the stairs, Chelsea was physically shaking. She was definitely not cut out for this. Being undercover was one thing, but the constant waiting for a shot to hit you in the back—or the front—was quite another.

At the bottom of the stairs, she heard voices.

Positive she was about to be spotted, she took off at a dead run.

With her pulse pounding in her ears, she couldn't hear anything else as she darted across the gardens, doing her best to hide behind things as she went, and keeping low to make herself less visible.

By some miracle, she made it all the way to the maze. Bridget was out here somewhere, and she was positive this was where the child would hide.

Taking the same route she'd used the other day, only this time running full speed, she spotted the little girl right around where she had first met her.

"Bridget?"

At the sound of her name, the child squeaked and began to crawl under the hedges.

"Wait!" Chelsea shouted. "It's me, remember? We met here before, you told me how to get to the middle so I could beat my husband."

The girl froze then slowly crept backward, looking up at her with big, round eyes.

"Do you remember me?"

Bridget nodded slowly.

"What are you doing out here all alone, sweetie?"

"Bad men are coming. My mommy was angry, and I got scared," Bridget whispered.

"So you came to your favorite place?"

Another nod from the child.

Cautiously moving closer, Chelsea dropped down to sit on the ground beside the little girl. "Those men that are coming, they're not bad men, I promise you they're not," she assured the child. It wasn't like she wanted to tell the girl who her mom really was, and if she tried, she'd lose whatever tentative trust they'd built. One day, Bridget would find out the truth, that day might even be today, but it wouldn't be here and now.

For now, she had to keep the girl safe until this played out.

The bob of a light announced that someone was coming before she heard the footsteps. Reaching out, Chelsea grabbed the little girl, pulling Bridget into her lap and angling them so her body was between the child and whoever was coming.

A shadowy figure appeared in the maze, and she heard the last voice she'd been expecting.

"Step away from my daughter."

# CHAPTER
## *Eighteen*

May 18<sup>th</sup>
1:18 A.M.

Hand still wrapped around the other man's throat, Josiah dragged Dr. Gant out of the bed and slammed him up against the nearest wall.

Right as he did so, a small alarm began to sound in the room.

There was no need to ask what it meant, he could figure that out all on his own. The guards knew that Prey was there.

Like he thought the alarm was going to change anything, Dr. Gant's terrified expression morphed into a smug one. If he thought that guards were going to come running to his rescue, the doctor was sorely mistaken.

Tightening his hold on Dr. Gant's neck, completely cutting off his air supply, Josiah slammed the man's head into the wall hard enough to leave behind a small smear of blood. Then he threw the body on the floor at his feet.

As he stared down at the quivering man, the doctor's face morphed slowly into those of the men who had killed his team. Justice hadn't been served that day, but today it would be. This man would pay for his sins, pay for the pain and suffering he'd inflicted on others, pay for every tear that Chelsea had shed.

Ramming his foot forward, he connected with the doctor's ribs, and the man let out a howl of pain that didn't come anywhere close to satisfying his need for blood.

"Too late to stop it," the doctor wheezed, trying to push himself up.

"Too late for you," he agreed, staring down at his prey, blinded by his rage, his need to let out the fury that had consumed him for the last six years. It had been slowly eating away at him, destroying him from the inside out, and if he didn't let it loose, it would steal whatever goodness was left in his life.

Chelsea.

That's what he'd lose.

"Too late for your wife," Dr. Gant shot back. "Protocol says to shoot all guests so they can't talk to the cops. As we speak, your wife is probably lying dead in her bed."

"Good thing she's not in her bed then, isn't it?" There was no way Chelsea wouldn't have followed their plan, she'd promised, which meant right now she was safely tucked away in the linen closet. The guards could shoot at the bed, but they wouldn't hit their target because there was no target there to hit.

If they realized that, it would still take them a while to find her, and by then Prey would already have control of the situation, he was sure of it.

"You brought them here," Dr. Gant snarled, the words coming out as an accusation, but honestly, how could the man have expected anything else? He'd taken a huge gamble in agreeing to sell a kidney to Chelsea, and he'd lost, big time.

"You should have known trusting us was stupid."

"I wasn't going to," the doctor admitted. "But you love her. You weren't faking that. It was the only reason Dr. Wood approved you."

There was nothing Josiah could say to argue that point.

When he walked away and left Chelsea in their bedroom, he'd been willing to admit to himself that he had feelings for her. But they weren't just feelings, he was in love with her.

How could he not be?

She was perfection, she was everything good and right with the world, she was light in the dark, and for some reason, she actually loved him.

Miracle.

There wasn't another word to describe it.

"She's everything I'll never deserve," he whispered aloud, more to himself than the doctor.

If he did this, if he let all the rage inside him flood out, and kill the man before him, it would be killing in cold blood. It wouldn't be following orders like when he'd been a SEAL, it wouldn't be for any noble reason like making the world a safer place and saving lives. The doctor was going to prison for the rest of his life. Prey were already there, it was a done deal. The trafficking ring would be demolished, but if he did this, there would be no coming back.

All he'd be doing was proving he wasn't good enough for Chelsea.

His fears that the anger inside him was too dangerous would be proven true, and he would have been right to keep everyone at a distance these last several years.

Right this very second, he stood at the precipice, what he chose to do would shape the rest of his life. These last few days, he'd thought that his future depended on whether or not he could let Chelsea in, but he'd been wrong.

Instead, his entire future depended on what kind of man he wanted to be. Someone who was ruled by anger, who killed in some misguided need for revenge, or someone who valued the life they'd been gifted.

"Get up," he growled, grabbing hold of the doctor and yanking him to his feet.

"You'll never deserve her," Dr. Gant sneered.

"I know. But I want to try to be even half the man she deserves." With that, he slammed his fist into the doctor's head and watched with great satisfaction as his eyes rolled back and he passed out.

Making quick work of tying the man up, he hurried to the door, aware of growing commotion in the medical suites. There were no guards in the hall, but a few of the doctors and nurses were coming out of their rooms.

Most gave him wary looks, but they didn't try anything, and he didn't stop to take care of them. He needed to get downstairs again, check on Chelsea, and meet up with Prey.

On the stairs, he came face to face with one of the guards.

The man startled when he saw Josiah striding toward him, and when the guard lifted his weapon, Josiah launched himself at him.

Thankfully, the staircase wasn't particularly long, and he knew how to take a fall and work with gravity, not against it, to minimize injury. Tackling the man, he took him down with him, and together they tumbled down the steps, landing in a tangled heap at the bottom.

Without giving the guard a chance to come up swinging, Josiah slammed a fist into the side of the man's head, just like he'd done with the doctor upstairs. Sensing movement behind him, he commandeered the now unconscious guard's weapon and came up ready to shoot.

"Whoa there," a familiar voice spoke. "Guess you won't be needing this."

A weapon was held up as the figure moved forward. Not one, but three of them, and while they weren't who he'd been expecting to see, he was equally as glad to see them as he would have been Prey.

Blake "Rocco" Wise was the one who had spoken, who was now grinning at him as he stepped forward. The man led the SEAL team that had been involved in rescuing Ava and Nathaniel Trevino in Mexico, who Tobias had joined when they raided the small South Pacific clinic where Isabella had been working, and then had helped rescue Teresa.

They knew the ins and outs of this operation, but they still shouldn't be there.

"SEALs don't operate on US soil," he said as he relaxed a little.

"Guess we better not tell anyone then," Rocco said with a wink.

"No way we weren't joining this one, not after everything we've already done to bring down these traffickers," Forest "Phantom" Dalton added. The man had also broken the rules when Kalee, the woman he'd fallen in love with, needed him.

"No one will ever know we were here," Beckett "Ace" Morgan said confidently.

"Someone will if Rex gets near Chelsea," Decker "Gumby" Kincade snickered, coming up to join them.

Everyone laughed at that, and even Josiah huffed out a

small chuckle. So far, Rex had managed to get attacked by Ava, Isabella, and Teresa, although none of them knew it was him at the time. The SEAL had taken all the ribbing his team had given him good-naturedly and praised the women for defending themselves.

But he didn't want Chelsea in a position where she had to defend herself, even from someone who wasn't really a threat.

The thought was enough to get him moving, and the guys fell into step behind him as he headed for the linen closet where Chelsea should be hiding and waiting for him.

"Have you got Desiree yet?" he asked.

"No, but we're hoping she's here," Rocco replied.

"She is. We saw her yesterday afternoon. Her kid, too."

Rocco quickly relayed that intel to the rest of his team and Alpha Team, and Josiah wished he had a comms unit too so he could be in the loop.

As though reading his mind, Ace held one out to him. "We've got one for Chelsea too."

The closer they got to Chelsea's hiding place, the stronger the smell of blood became. "One of the doctors told me protocol was to kill as many of the buyers as they could, shoot them in their beds," he told the others.

"Chelsea?" Gumby asked.

"We had a plan, she was leaving the room a few minutes after me and hiding," he assured them. So long as she'd followed through, she should be safe.

Still, nerves danced inside him as he reached the linen closet and opened the door, a tingling told him something wasn't right.

"Chels?" he called out.

There was no response, and his nerves amped up to panic.

"Chelsea," he demanded, reaching into the closet and beginning to rip out everything that was in there.

But the thing he was searching for was nowhere to be found.

Where the hell had Chelsea gone, and why had she broken her promise to him to hide until he came for her?

≈

May 18th
    1:29 A.M.

"Mommy!"

The little girl Chelsea was clutching tight, began to struggle in her grip, and she didn't know what she should do.

While she was reasonably certain that under normal circumstances Desiree Tilly wouldn't do anything to hurt her daughter, these weren't normal circumstances. Just because the woman has started this entire trafficking ring with the goal of saving her daughter's life, with it all crumbling around her, it was anyone's guess how she'd react.

What if she decided she wasn't going to spend the rest of her life in a prison cell? Lose access to her daughter, the same way she would if the child had died. Was this woman unbalanced enough to decide that her best course of action was for her and her daughter to be together in death?

"Shh, sweetie, stay here a moment," she soothed the child, maintaining her grip even as the girl wriggled, trying to break free.

"But it's my mommy," Bridget whimpered.

"Let my daughter go now, or I'll shoot you," Desiree said, and at her mother's harsh words, Bridget finally stilled.

"No," Chelsea said with more confidence than she felt. "I don't think you will. Not with Bridget here."

"Mommy, why would you shoot her? She's not one of the bad men. We played in the maze together before, I told her how to get to the middle so she could beat her husband and win."

This poor, sweet little girl had no idea who her mother truly was. Bridget was too young, too innocent to understand what was happening around her. All she likely knew was that her mother loved her and provided the medical care she needed to manage her condition.

"Come, Bridget, now," Desiree barked, but this time the little girl burrowed into Chelsea's hold.

"Stop it, Desiree, you're scaring her, and I know that's not what you want," she told the other woman.

"What would you know?" Desiree sneered. "You got what you wanted, you've destroyed everything I've built. It's all falling down, all coming apart, and ..." The woman broke off in a sob. "You just gave my daughter a death sentence."

Shifting slightly so she had Bridget tucked more securely in her grasp, but could also get a better look at Desiree, Chelsea shook her head. "No. No death sentence for this precious child. She's completely innocent in all of this, and the last thing anyone wants is for her to suffer any more than she already has. Put your weapon down, Desiree, surrender, and Prey will make sure that Bridget always has access to the medical care she needs."

"But only if I surrender, right?" Desiree's mocking snarl looked particularly eerie in the beam of the flashlight.

"No. Regardless of what you do here tonight, I will

personally ensure that Bridget is always well taken care of and is seen by the best doctors in the world." It was an easy vow to make because there was no reason for this innocent little girl to suffer. It didn't matter who Bridget's mother was, or the pain and suffering she had inflicted on hundreds of people, this child had nothing to do with any of that.

"It won't be enough, it wasn't before," Desiree wailed.

"I know. What happened to your husband and your sons was awful. No one should have to go through all those losses. I understand why you did this, how desperate you must have been. That loss … it was crushing you, and you thought losing Bridget would be the final blow. But just because I understand the whys doesn't make any of this okay, you know that, Desiree. How would you have felt if someone had taken your husband, cut him open, and taken his organs to save someone else?"

This woman was unstable at best, completely deluded at worst.

There was no chance that Chelsea was going to be able to talk Desiree Tilly into turning herself in, no matter how hard she tried.

The woman could only see things one way.

Hers.

Saving Bridget was the only thing she cared about, and she saw her trafficking ring as the only possible way to do that.

With it all burning down around her, she was quickly unravelling, and Chelsea was pretty sure that at the end of that rope would be bullets for all three of them.

The problem was, out here in the maze, nobody knew where she was. Sooner or later, Josiah would realize she wasn't in the linen closet where she had promised to hide. When he found that out, he was going to be so angry with her, but he'd be scared too. Honestly, she'd rather take the anger than his fear, because the last thing she'd wanted to do was scare him.

Despite the terror she knew he'd feel, she also knew he'd come looking for her. Could she at least keep Desiree Tilly talking long enough for him to find her?

It was a gamble, but it was all she had.

If she tried to rush the woman, she had no doubt that Desiree would fire before she could tackle her and try to get control of the weapon. Chelsea had no weapon of her own so it wasn't like she could fire an incapacitating shot and then go looking for Josiah.

Plus, she had Bridget to think about.

The little girl trembled in her arms, obviously upset about her mother's behavior. Should she try to get the girl to run? Even if Desiree was planning a murder suicide rather than be caught and imprisoned, she didn't think the woman would just randomly fire on her own daughter if Chelsea told the girl to run.

But if she did that, she left Desiree with no deterrent from just shooting her and running after the little girl. Chelsea was under no doubt that the only reason she wasn't already shot and bleeding out was the fact that she'd been so close to Bridget when Desiree showed up. The woman wasn't going to risk a shot hitting her child, at least not yet anyway.

"Where are they?" she asked softly.

"Where are who?" Desiree asked.

"Your husband, your sons. Where are they buried?" If there was one thing Chelsea was sure of it was that Desiree Tilly loved her family. It was the compounded losses of her parents, then her sons, then her husband, that had tipped her over the edge, and now they might be the only thing to bring her back.

The gun aimed at her wavered a little. "They're not. I had them cremated," Desiree whispered. "So they could always be a part of our lives."

"Daddy and my brothers watch over me from the necklace," Bridget whispered, and when Chelsea glanced down, she saw the little girl had pulled out a heart hanging on a chain around her neck. It was about two inches wide, and there seemed to be words engraved on it, although it was too dark to read what they were.

"That's nice," Chelsea whispered back. "Your daddy and your brothers love you very much, and you get to have a piece of them with you everywhere you go, so they never have to leave you."

"Mommy has one too. When I'm sick and I have to have another operation, Mommy and I always hold our hearts in our hands right before the doctors take me away, and we ask Daddy and my brothers to watch over me."

"Family is everything," Desiree murmured.

"And you did all of this to try to save all you had left of yours," Chelsea said. The gun had lowered a little more, and she was trying to figure out what her best move was. Telling Bridget to run and then rushing Desiree might be the only way to end this, but if she went that route, she would have to pray that she was quicker than a bullet.

Even more than she didn't want to die today, she didn't want Josiah to have to find her body, dead from a gunshot wound, the same way his team had been taken from him. They were a team right now, and to lose her would destroy him, she was positive of that.

But what was the alternative?

Wait there and hope that Josiah found her before it was too late?

Just because Desiree was wavering didn't mean that she wasn't still going to kill all three of them before they could be found.

Risky or not, she had to make a move.

Bunching her muscles in preparation for what she was about to do, Chelsea shifted her hold on Bridget enough that she could both push the girl away from her mother and fling herself toward Desiree all at the same time.

"Family really is everything, and I don't think there's a person alive who can know for certain what lengths they would go to in order to save the people they love," she said softly, and when Desiree's shocked gaze met hers, Chelsea sprang into action. "Bridget, run!" she shouted as she launched herself forward.

Right as she moved, a deafening shot cracked through the night.

# CHAPTER
## Nineteen

May 18<sup>th</sup>
    1:31 A.M.

Where the hell was she?

Josiah stared from the empty closet to the scattered piles of sheets, blankets, pillows, and towels. There was nowhere else she could be and yet his mind seemed to refuse to accept that.

She was supposed to be there.

She'd promised she'd be there.

It was practically the last words he'd spoken to her.

Yet she was nowhere to be seen.

A horrifying thought seeped into his mind, and barely aware of the shouting voices of the SEAL team, he took off at a dead run to the room he'd shared with Chelsea. Just an hour ago he was lying in bed, her warm, soft body snuggled against his side, not hating the idea of being married to her anywhere near as much as he should.

She could have been ...

No.

He couldn't allow himself to think it.

And yet ... the alarm in Dr. Gant's room had gone off less than fifteen minutes after he'd left their room. Fifteen minutes was the agreed-upon time for Chelsea to sneak out and hide in the linen closet.

Which meant she could have still been in the room when the guards had fired those shots.

If she were dead, he was going to rain down punishment on this ring the likes they couldn't even comprehend.

Flinging open the door, his gaze drove straight toward the bed. She couldn't be lying dead there, bleeding out like his team had. He couldn't lose another person he cared about.

Couldn't.

Was as simple as that.

There was no lump in the bed that indicated a body beneath the covers. He scanned the room because Chelsea shouldn't have been in the bed anyway when the door was opened and a shot fired.

But there was no body anywhere in the room.

No puddles of blood.

Nothing.

It appeared empty.

If Chelsea had heard the shots, maybe she'd had time to hide before they'd come into the room. Running for the bathroom, he threw on the lights, scanned the room, but it was empty too.

Unable to stop, the need to find Chelsea so strong he could barely breathe, he turned back to the bedroom and began tearing it apart. Every cover stripped off the bed, he checked under it and in the closet, but Chelsea wasn't anywhere to be found.

"Don't think she's here, brother," Rocco said, his voice far too calm for Josiah's liking.

"Then where the hell is she?" he roared again.

"She wasn't in here when the shots were fired," Gumby said from the bed. The man had picked up some of the covers Josiah had thrown on the ground, and he was sticking his fingers through two holes.

Bullet holes.

Ace knelt and picked up one of the pillows, pulling out some of the stuffing through another bullet hole. "Two shots. They thought you were both in here."

"Means your cover wasn't broken," Phantom added. "If they knew it was you two specifically, they would have made sure you were both dead. Instead, it looks like they just opened the door and fired head shots and chest shots, then moved on to the next room."

"No signs of a struggle either," Gumby added, dropping the blanket back onto the bed. "So I don't think they shot, realized she wasn't in the bed, saw her, and then tried to grab her. If they tried, she would have gone down swinging. Besides, if she hadn't been in the bed, they likely would have just shot her."

"I don't think Chelsea was in this room when they fired the shots," Ace agreed.

"She was supposed to hide in the linen closet, that was the plan," he muttered as though repeating it might make it more true. It was obvious that Chelsea had disregarded the plan, but that didn't help him figure out where she was.

"What would make her change her mind?" Rocco asked.

Josiah just shrugged as he paced anxiously around the room. The fear brewing inside him was too much, and add in anger that Chelsea might have decided to just walk out of there, knowing the risks, knowing it would kill him to lose her, and he was pretty close to losing his tentative grip on control.

"There has to be something," Rocco pushed. "Chelsea is a smart woman. She's not reckless, and she cares about you. If you two had worked out your plan, she wouldn't have done something different unless she had to."

"What would she have done if she realized what the guards were doing?" Ace asked.

"Hidden," he said immediately. She had no weapon, so it was really her only option. "If they were going room to room, they had to have used a silencer, though. Otherwise, they would have set off a panic, had frantic couples running everywhere. Unless Chelsea was already in the hall when the shots were fired, I doubt she would have realized anything was wrong. Even if she'd hidden when the door opened, she wouldn't have just gone running off. If she was looking for a place to hide, then she had one. The linen closet. Only we all saw she wasn't in it."

They were going in circles and not doing anything to find Chelsea.

She had to be somewhere.

"Has Desiree Tilly been located yet?" Josiah asked.

"No," Rocco replied. "Alpha Team is rounding up all the medical personnel. We took out the guards on the way in. They might have been able to shoot sleeping people, but give them people who shoot back and they were useless."

"Could Chelsea have gone looking for you?" Gumby asked.

"She knew to hide until I came to her," he answered. "I know she wanted to do more, but she understood that without a weapon there wasn't much she could do. She didn't like the plan, but she wouldn't have just thrown it away for no reason."

"Yet she's not in the room or the closet," Ace said, stating the obvious and holding up his hands, palms out in a placating gesture when Josiah growled at him. "I know, dude. You're scared. But she has to be here somewhere. Like Rocco said, Chelsea is smart, whatever she did, she did for a reason. All we have to do is figure out what that reason is."

Dragging his fingers through his hair, Josiah stormed over to the window, trying to rack his brain to figure out something that would have been so important to Chelsea that she would abandon their plans, knowing he'd be terrified for her when he got to the closet and didn't find her waiting in it.

"You said that so far Desiree Tilly hasn't been found," he said.

"Right," Rocco agreed.

"But you took out the guards, and Alpha Team is dealing with the medical personnel," he said, more to himself this time than the others.

"Guards started shooting at us as soon as we approached the mansion. Rex and Bubba are still clearing rooms, but we haven't had a chance to check every single place someone could hide. If Chelsea felt the linen closet had been compromised, she could be anywhere in here," Gumby said.

Actually, he wasn't so sure Chelsea was anywhere in the mansion.

The guys were right, something had Chelsea change course tonight.

While Chelsea was smart, she had one pretty big weakness. Her heart. She loved too much sometimes, cared too much.

Desiree Tilly couldn't be in the mansion because if she was, the guys would already have her in custody. That meant she had to be in another property on the estate because both he and Chelsea had seen her with their own eyes.

There was only one thing he could think of that would draw Chelsea out of the relative safety of the mansion and the linen closet.

"The little girl," he murmured, his gaze landing on the maze.

"What girl?" Ace asked.

"Bridget Tilly. Chelsea would leave for the kid," he explained. He'd told Chelsea that one day her big heart could get her into trouble, and he'd been right. Instead of being safe with him right now, surrounded by an entire team of SEALs, she was out there somewhere. "That doesn't help us find her, though."

Chelsea would absolutely have risked her safety for the little girl, but how would she know where to look for the kid? What would have made her think that the child needed her?

It was only because he was still staring out the window at the maze down below, trying to figure out what could have led Chelsea to think that Bridget needed her, that he saw it.

Light.

In the maze.

Yesterday, Chelsea had spent hours staring down at that maze, hoping for a glimpse of Bridget's mother. If she'd been staring out the window tonight, she might have spotted the little girl looking for a safe place to hide when the shooting started.

"I know where she is," he announced, already running

for the door, desperate to get to his girl, because the head of the trafficking ring was still out there and Chelsea had gone after the woman's daughter.

~

May 18<sup>th</sup>
    1:35 A.M.

Chelsea waited for the burning pain.

While she'd never been shot before, that's what she imagined it would feel like. Like someone had sent a flaming projectile searing through your flesh. Well, that basically was what was happening, the bullet might not be on fire, but its temperature after being shot simulated that same sort of heat.

Only no white-hot agony ever came.

Glancing down at herself, Chelsea didn't see any dark red blood glistening in the beam of the flashlight, and …

The flashlight.

It was now on the ground, and so was Desiree Tilly.

That made no sense. She didn't have a gun, she hadn't fired any shots, the only one with a weapon was Desiree. Had the woman shot herself?

About to take a step forward, Chelsea froze when she saw it.

Another shadowy figure.

Harsh breathing and a borderline hysterical giggle cut through the deathly silence.

"That felt really good," a scratchy voice spoke, and the figure stepped closer into the beam of the flashlight now lying on the ground by Desiree's presumably dead body.

With the light illuminating the other person, Chelsea sucked in a breath when she recognized them. It was the woman. The one who had been chosen as her donor. The woman they'd seen tied to the bed, with the ball gag in her mouth, shooting daggers at them with her eyes.

She had no idea how the woman had gotten free, how she'd managed to track them to the maze, or how she'd procured herself a weapon, but none of that mattered. Desiree Tilly was dead, the trafficking ring was dismantled, and it was all finally over.

Relief had her sagging, and she swayed a little as her adrenaline began to crash, already running through in her mind all the things she had to do next. Call back Bridget, but ensure the child didn't see her dead mother, that was the last image the little girl would need in her mind. Then she'd have to make her way back to the mansion and hope Josiah wasn't too angry with her for running after Bridget when she saw the girl alone out here.

"Don't move," the woman's voice, a little stronger this time, a little less hysterical, ordered, and Chelsea looked over to see the weapon now pointed at her.

"It's okay," she soothed, "I'm not a threat to you."

A hard, cold laugh sounded. "Sure. Of course you're not. You only came here to buy an organ. Came here to buy *my* organ," the woman hissed.

"No, I didn't."

"Why are you lying? You were there. In the room they took me to. You stood there with your husband and talked about me with that disgusting doctor, like I was nothing more than a piece of meat. You did nothing to help me, even though you knew I wasn't there because I wanted to be," the woman raged.

She'd gone from trying to talk down one unbalanced

woman to another. Chelsea absolutely understood where this woman was coming from. She believed she was fighting for her life, and that Chelsea was a threat to her, as much a threat as Desiree, and the doctors and nurses. Trying to convince her otherwise could be challenging.

"We weren't here to hurt you, and we weren't here to buy an organ," Chelsea said, keeping her voice as calm and soothing as she could manage while her heart hammered in her chest. "My name is Chelsea, and I work for a security company called Prey Security. I don't know if you've ever heard of us, but we're definitely the good guys."

In the thin beam of the flashlight, the woman didn't move. The weapon was still trained on her, and Chelsea tried to make herself look as non-threatening as possible and prayed she could do this. She didn't want to survive the head of the trafficking ring only to be taken out by one of its victims.

"The man who was my husband, his name is Josiah, and he works with Prey too. He was a SEAL for a while before coming to work for Prey. We work for the Cyber Team, and we've been tracking this organ trafficking ring for months. They abducted one of my colleagues and very best friend in the whole entire world, and they stole her kidney. When she managed to escape and was then rescued by a SEAL, we were determined to bring the ring down."

Was it her imagination, or did the gun lower just a little?

"You must have escaped as well. Your hand, it looks broken," Chelsea said, nodding at the hand hanging limply at the woman's side. The thumb looked like it was at an awkward angle, and she wondered if the woman had broken her own hand to escape. "The trafficking ring started coming after us when we wouldn't back down from trying to shut them down. They went after my friend

Isabella, and then another of my colleagues and best friends, Teresa. After that, we knew we had to do something drastic to get them to stop, so Josiah and I came undercover."

"Undercover?"

"Pretending I was dying and needed a transplant, but I don't, I'm healthy. We just needed a visual on Desiree Tilly, the head of the ring, the woman you just shot, then we called in our team. They're here now. You're safe. You're going home."

"Y-you're lying," the woman stammered.

"No, I'm not. You are safe now, but I need you to lower your weapon." When the woman still hesitated, Chelsea took a cautious step forward. "Can you tell me your name?"

The woman shook her head, but even in the thin light, Chelsea could see that her cheeks were wet with tears. With a shaking hand, the woman clung to the only thing that felt solid to her, that made her feel safe.

"Please. I swear to you that this is over. My people are already here, they probably already have the guards and everyone else involved in handcuffs. If you just put the weapon down, I'll take you to them and show you. Please, I know I'm asking you for a lot, but I need you to trust me."

It was working, she was sure it was. The woman's arm wobbled a little more before dropping so the weapon pointed at the ground.

"Maple," she whispered so softly that Chelsea almost didn't hear the sound.

"Chelsea!" Josiah's voice shouted her name a split second later, and Maple swung around, her weapon lifted again as Josiah and several other men dressed in tactical gear rounded the corner.

"Don't shoot," she shouted, not sure if she was talking

to Maple, Josiah, the others, or everyone all at once. "Don't shoot."

"Y-you said it was o-over," Maple shouted, fear and anger warring in her tone.

"It is," Chelsea rushed to assure the woman. "Josiah, don't shoot. This is Maple. She's the woman Dr. Gant introduced us to, the one in the bed." The last thing they needed was for Josiah or one of the others to mistake Maple for Desiree or another person involved in the ring. "Maple, this is Josiah. Remember, I told you that he works with me. I told you that we called in our team to help, to end this. That's who they are."

"What if you're lying to me?" Maple wailed, clearly conflicted.

"Nobody here wants to hurt you, I swear to you, but you're also holding a loaded gun pointed at good men, men who have dedicated their entire lives to saving others. If they wanted to hurt you, Maple, if they wanted to kill you or disarm you, then believe me, you'd already be on the ground, either dead or in cuffs. But they don't want to hurt you," she pleaded, willing the woman to believe her.

"Put the weapon on the ground, Ma'am," a voice she recognized as belonging to Navy SEAL Rocco spoke calmly, but with an air of authority. "Hands where we can see them."

"Don't cuff her, Rocco," Chelsea warned. "She broke her own hand to get herself free."

"Damn, if Rex were here, we can pretty much guarantee Maple would have clocked him," Ace said with amusement.

"Remember I told you about Ava, Isabella, and Teresa? They all managed to get in a hit to Rex before they realized who he was," Chelsea supplied for Maple's benefit.

When the woman glanced over her shoulder, Chelsea gave an encouraging nod.

With slow, shaky movements, Maple set the weapon down and then held up her hands like Rocco had instructed. Immediately, the tension left the group. One of the guys stepped forward to help Maple sit down, no doubt to administer first aid.

Chelsea felt herself grow shaky as the second shot of adrenaline drained out of her system, and Josiah stepped toward her.

About to tell him it was over, that Maple had been the one to kill Desiree Tilly, she glanced at where the other woman had fallen only to gasp when the spot lay empty save for a puddle of blood.

"Josiah, Desiree was shot. I thought she was dead, but now she's gone."

# CHAPTER
## *Twenty*

May 18th
   1:42 A.M.

At Chelsea's words, he and Rocco's SEAL team sprang into action.

Josiah closed the last of the distance between himself and Chelsea, Gumby and Phantom moved in closer to Maple, and Rocco moved around them to block one side of the maze, while Ace moved back a little further down the way they'd come to block the other.

"Are you sure?" he asked Chelsea.

"That Desiree was shot? Absolutely. Don't be mad, but I saw Bridget alone out here and I had to come to her, she's just a little girl. I was going to take her somewhere to hide, but then Desiree came. She was armed. I was talking her down as best I could to buy time. When she lowered the weapon, I told Bridget to run, and I was going to tackle her."

"You were going to do what?" he demanded, his voice low and dangerous as a new bout of fear flooded his system.

One of her slim hands stroked his arm. "It's okay, Josiah. A shot went out, and for one second I thought I was hit, but it was Maple shooting Desiree. I saw her go down. Maple did too. Ask her. I thought Desiree was dead. If I'd realized she wasn't, I would have told you immediately."

"I believe you, Chels," he assured her. He was still furious she'd put herself in danger to go after Desiree Tilly's daughter, knowing the woman would also be looking for the child, but in the end, he could hardly ask Chelsea to stop being who she was.

She was a strong woman who knew what she wanted, who cared for others, who looked for good in everyone around her. It was those exact qualities that made him fall in love with her, so he really couldn't be angry at her for just doing what Chelsea did.

The problem was, a dangerous woman was still out there.

As long as Desiree Tilly was free, this would never really be over.

"We need to lock down this place, we can't let her escape," he said to Rocco, who nodded his agreement.

"Let's get Chelsea and Maple back to the house, then we can search for Desiree," Gumby said.

"And Bridget. She's out here, too," Chelsea reminded them all. "Josiah, she's scared. Not just of what's happening, the shooting, and everything. Desiree told her you guys are bad men. I tried to convince her it wasn't true, but she won't just be scared of you guys, she's scared of her mom, too. She heard Desiree ranting at me, I don't know who she's going to trust right now."

Actually, they all knew one person the little girl would trust.

Chelsea.

But he couldn't allow her to remain out there after she'd almost been shot by two different women in the space of thirty minutes. Chelsea couldn't die. Damn, even the thought of her hurt had him breaking out into a cold sweat.

"I'll tell her I'm your husband," he said to Chelsea before she could offer to help search for the missing child and the girl's deranged mother.

For a second, he was sure she was going to argue, but then she nodded. "That should work.

"Gumby and I will get Chelsea and Maple to the house," Phantom said, and Josiah had to force himself not to argue.

As badly as he didn't want to leave Chelsea's side, he had the best chance of gaining the little girl's trust when they found her.

"Wait." He grabbed Chelsea when she went to brush past him. This might just be the hardest thing he'd ever have to do in his life, but he wasn't going to allow his girl to walk out there without the best protection he could give her.

"What?" Chelsea asked.

Shoving his weapon into her hands, he grabbed the hem of his T-shirt and yanked it up and over his head. When he reached for the straps of his Kevlar vest, she gasped, her hands darting out to cover his, trying to stop him.

"You don't have to do that," she whispered, under-standing better than anyone here what this would cost him.

The thing was, though, he did have to do this.

More than that, he *wanted* to do this. No matter how much the idea of taking off his vest terrified him beyond words, the thought of losing Chelsea scared him more.

Since he wasn't sure he could talk without his voice trembling, Josiah just stripped off the vest, then tugged it over Chelsea's head. It was a little big for her, but it would still do the job, affording her more protection as she left the relative safety of the maze for the large expanse of garden she'd have to cross to get to the house.

"Josiah," she whispered his name, her voice heavy with emotion. "Thank you."

Those words ran deeper than just a thanks for the vest. She was thanking him for fighting against his past, for trying to beat his demons, for giving her a chance.

Nodding in acknowledgment, he leaned in, touched his forehead to hers, and then slipped his T-shirt back on.

There was no coming back from this, no pretending that he hadn't made this sacrifice because he was prioritizing her over himself, over his past, over his fears and guilt and anger. Giving her the place in his life she always should have had because he finally accepted that not having Chelsea was worse than being scared of losing her.

"I love you," she murmured, pushing up onto tiptoes to press a kiss to the corner of his mouth as she pushed his weapon back into his hands.

She started toward Phantom and Gumby, and he had to clench his fingers around the cold steel of his weapon to stop himself from reaching for her. There would be time later to talk things through when there wasn't a scared child, and a desperate criminal mastermind hiding in the maze.

"Chelsea!" A little voice called out at the same time a small child wriggled out from under the hedges and bolted toward Chelsea.

"Bridget." Chelsea breathed in relief as she took a step toward the girl.

"She's all I have left, no one is taking her from me. You keep trying. You keep trying to stop me, to shut down what I've built, but doing that will kill my baby girl. I tried to make you stop, I tried to make you back off, I warned you, and when you kept coming after me, I knew you all had to die. Everyone who gets in the way of me saving my daughter's life has to be punished, they have to die," another voice screamed, as a figure barreled through the hedges.

Reaching for the child, Chelsea shoved Bridget behind her right as the shot rang out.

As Chelsea cried out in pain, Josiah was already flinging himself toward her.

With the second shot came a wave of white-hot agony blasting through his body.

More shots tore through the night. Someone was sobbing, someone was screaming, all he cared about was getting to Chelsea.

He had to know that she was okay.

Ignoring the fiery pain pulsing inside him, Josiah crawled the short distance to where Chelsea lay on her back. Her eyes were open, staring up at the sky, and for a second, he thought it was too late.

She was dead.

He'd already lost her.

But then she took in a ragged breath, and his fingers began to skim her body in search of the injury.

A hole in the Kevlar right above her heart told him exactly how close to losing her he'd come.

If she hadn't been wearing the body armor, she'd be dead.

No ifs, ands, or buts about it.

Dead.

That bullet would have pierced her heart instead of being stopped by Kevlar, and he would have lost her.

His decision to prioritize light over darkness had saved her life.

Dizzy with relief, he sank down onto the ground beside her, vaguely aware of voices shouting around him. What they were saying didn't matter, the only thing that did was that Chelsea was alive.

A muffled grunt of pain caught his attention, and he turned his head to see Chelsea struggling to sit up, a man beside her rubbing a hand over his jaw.

Not any man.

Cole "Rex" Kingston.

Apparently, the SEAL had shown up just in time to get a blow in from a desperate Chelsea.

"Tried to keep you out of the thick of things, dude, so you didn't go home with yet another injury," Mark "Bubba" Wright snickered, but there was a tenseness to his tone.

"Sorry, but I have to get to him," Chelsea said, her tone heavy with despair.

"You need to stay still, Chelsea, you were just shot," Rex reminded her.

"Don't care," she wheezed. "He saved my life."

With a small sigh, Rex looped his arm around her shoulders and helped her move so she was on her knees beside him. Josiah tried to move, too, but his body refused to cooperate.

"Why did you do that?" Chelsea whispered as her gentle fingers stroked along his cheek.

"Because I couldn't lose you," he answered simply.

"But I don't want to lose *you*," she shot back.

Badly as he wanted to assure her that she wasn't going

to lose him, that he'd just taken a pretty major leap to leaving the past in the past and looking to the future, the heaviness weighing down upon him told him he might not have much choice in the matter.

If this was it, if he was about to die, then he couldn't leave this world without uttering the most important words he'd ever speak.

"Had to save you, Chels, because I love you," he murmured before he lost his battle with consciousness and was whisked away into an all-consuming darkness.

~

May 18th
    2:54 P.M.

Pain thudded through her chest with every breath she took.

Chelsea knew it wasn't all because of the broken ribs.

Some of it was the ache in her heart.

For years, she had been dreaming of hearing Josiah say those words to her. For years, she had known the chances of him ever reciprocating her feelings were virtually non-existent. For years, she'd endured the pity of her friends as they watched her, unable to let go of the unrequited love she had for a man that most would look at and likely find unlovable.

Now he'd finally said those words she'd hardly dared to hope for, but it was nothing like she'd imagined it would be.

If Josiah had ever fallen for her, she thought that every-thing would be perfect. All her dreams would have come true, and after telling her he loved her, he would have whisked her up into his arms and carried her to bed, where he would have made love to her for hours.

Well, the bed part had kind of turned out to be true.

After Josiah had passed out, she'd been unable to hold back her tears, all her fear about losing him coming out in huge gut-wrenching sobs. Not ideal since a bullet had literally plowed into her chest.

Okay, so it had been stopped by the Kevlar, but she'd never spent much time thinking about how a bulletproof vest worked in real life. Just because it could stop a bullet from piercing flesh didn't mean it could prevent injury.

And it hadn't.

The pitch-black bruise spiraling out around her heart was proof of that.

Several of her ribs had been broken by the bullet, and it literally hurt to do everything. To breathe, to move, even lying completely still, taking the tiniest breaths she could imagine was utter agony.

In the end, as she'd been lying in Rex's arms, sobbing as she watched the rest of the SEALs work on Josiah, keeping him from bleeding out, switching from apologizing to Rex for hitting him to begging Josiah not to die, someone had sedated her.

When she finally woke up, she was in the hospital.

Of course, her first words had been asking about Josiah, and the relief she felt when she heard he was also in the hospital would remain with her forever.

"You know, they told me that the bullet didn't do any damage. That it went straight through and didn't touch any of your internal organs. They said that you're going to be okay, that your body is just resting after surgery, but you should know that I'm not going to believe it until you wake up and tell me yourself," she murmured to the man in the bed.

Her doctor had forbidden her from leaving her bed, but she'd thrown a most un-Chelsea-like fit until the older woman relented and agreed to let her go to Josiah's room. For that, she was grateful because she was pretty sure the woman could have just had her sedated again and not had to put up with her begging and pleading.

Maybe the doctor was a romantic at heart.

Like she'd always been.

This couldn't be the end of her and Josiah's story, it was supposed to be the beginning.

"Hey, how're you doing?" Rex asked as he strode into the room. At over six feet tall, the SEAL was only a little shorter than Josiah, and with his black hair and dark eyes, and the tattoo peeking out from his T-shirt sleeve, he could be an intimidating presence if you didn't look past that to the softness in his gaze. His touch had been gentle when she'd been sobbing in his arms, and he'd kept assuring her that Josiah wasn't going to die.

At the time, she hadn't believed him.

Even now she had doubts.

It was more than twelve hours later, and Josiah was still asleep.

Totally normal the doctor assured her, but what if they were just lying to her? What if he was a lot worse off than they were pretending, and they just didn't want to upset her by telling her the truth?

"You're panicking again," Rex said as he came up behind her chair and began to massage her tense shoulders.

"You sure you want to be that close to me, given I almost broke your jaw last time?" It was hard to make the joke, but she was trying her best not to fall into a full-blown panic.

Rex chuckled. "Not quite a strong enough hit to break my jaw. When you're all healed, we'll work on it."

"You want me to be better at hitting someone?"

"Want you to be safe," Rex corrected. "Although Eagle is definitely doing a good job at teaching all his employees self-defense."

"Guess his nagging paid off," she agreed. Her gaze was still fixed on Josiah's sleeping face. For once in all the years she'd known him, he finally looked at peace. There were no furrows in his forehead, no lips pulled into a tense line. She wished he could always be this peaceful, but more than that, she wished he would wake up. Just for a moment. Just to tell her he was okay.

"He *is* going to be okay. The bullet didn't do much damage. He lost a bit of blood, but it was nothing life-threatening. Once his body recovers a bit, he'll wake up. When he does, he's going to be pretty angry to find out you're injured and not giving your body the rest it needs."

"Then he can be angry. I'm not leaving."

"I'm glad he has you, you're good for him."

"I hope I am, I try to be," she said, looking over her shoulder at the SEAL and wincing at the piercing pain in her chest.

"Special ops world is pretty small, you know that, so we all know what happened to his team, what he lost, and how it affected him. He told you he loved you. He took off that vest that none of us even knew he was obsessed with, but now all understand why he was. He did that for you because he loves you. I'd say you're doing better than try, you're giving him everything he didn't even know he need-ed." After one last squeeze of her shoulders, he headed for the door. "Try to get some rest, and call if you need anything."

"Thank you, Rex, for everything you and your team did for me and Josiah, for Ava, for Isabella, for Teresa, for helping us bring down that ring so they can't hurt anyone else."

"Our pleasure."

Alone again with Josiah, she reached over and trailed her fingertips across his brow. "Everyone keeps saying you're going to be okay, but I need you to wake up and say it. Please."

Tears blurred her vision, and she thought that's all it was at first, but then it happened again. A twitch in his eyes. Then his lashes were fluttering on his cheeks.

Next thing she knew, she was looking down into Josiah's dark eyes.

Relief had the floodgates opening, and Chelsea didn't even care that crying made it feel like her chest was on fire.

"You can't take it back," she told him.

"Take it back?" he croaked, sounding totally confused.

"You said you love me, and I won't let you take it back."

A slow smile curled up his lips. "Not going to take it back."

More relief flooded her system, and she cried even harder as she reached for the glass of water with the straw that was sitting on the small table beside his bed. Holding the straw to his lips, she let him take a few mouthfuls before setting it down.

Josiah's dark gaze traveled her body. "You were hurt. Should be resting."

"Had to be here with you," she answered simply.

After studying her for a long moment, his forehead crinkled into the familiar Josiah frown. "You're in pain."

"Some broken ribs," she explained. "But I'm going to be okay. You saved my life."

"Broken ribs suck. You're going to take longer to heal than I am," Josiah said, tutting in dissatisfaction. Shifting slightly, moving the tubes and wires connected to his body out of the way enough that he could lift the sheet, he fixed her with one of his don't bother arguing with me stares. "Hop in."

"Don't think I'm supposed to do that. You were shot, you need to rest, and I don't want to hurt you."

"The only way I'm resting is if I know you are." When she still hesitated, he reached over and took her hand, wincing as he did so. "Get in the bed, Chelsea. Now."

Because there really wasn't any other place she'd rather be anyway, she stood slowly, gasping at the excruciating pain that spiraled out from her chest. Josiah grumbled, and she almost smiled at his typical annoyed sound.

Sighing in relief when she settled onto the mattress beside him, she didn't even care if the bed wasn't really big enough for two adults. Josiah was alive, she was alive, Desiree Tilly was dead, the organ trafficking ring was dismantled, little Bridget was somewhere safe where she could receive the medical care she needed and be well looked after, pain aside, life was pretty good.

Exhaustion took hold, and she drifted off with a smile on her face.

# CHAPTER
## Twenty-One

May 19th
10:38 A.M.

"You shouldn't have done that, Chelsea," Josiah growled.

"Sorry," she said for probably the hundredth time in the last few minutes. Since she looked so guilty and apologetic, he let out a sigh and toned down his anger.

After all, he wasn't really angry, he was afraid.

"Don't be sorry," he muttered, dragging his fingers through his short hair and enjoying the slight sting on his scalp because it was something to focus on that wasn't the nausea swirling in his stomach.

"I am, you're clearly stressed, and you should be resting, and I definitely should have learned my lesson after last time," Chelsea rambled, watching him with worried eyes and a nervous expression that he didn't like one bit.

She was in pain, he knew that, likely a whole lot more pain than he was in. All he had was a small hole in his side that had already been stitched up and would heal quickly, while Chelsea had broken ribs that would cause her pain with every breath she took.

Instead of getting her all stressed out and anxious, he should be doing everything within his power to keep her calm and relaxed so she was in as little pain as possible.

He hadn't just come close to losing her, if he had let his old fears take precedence over his feelings for Chelsea, she would quite literally be dead right now.

When Desiree Tilly started firing at them, or more specifically at her own daughter, then the bullet that hit Chelsea's chest, right over her heart, wouldn't have been stopped by the Kevlar because he would have been wearing it. His wound had never been life-threatening but Chelsea's had been a death sentence.

"Come here." Even though she was merely inches away from him, sitting beside him on the bed they'd shared all night, it wasn't close enough. He needed to be able to feel her, hold her, know she was close and safe in his arms. "Sorry."

"I'm really the one who should be sorry," she said, even as she let him tug her against his chest. "You freaked out when I answered your mom's call when we were at the townhouse, and then you explained to me how you'd been keeping your distance from them. It was just when I saw how she'd blown up your phone with calls and messages, I could see how much she was worrying about you. You're her baby boy and she loves you no matter what. I just didn't want her to worry anymore. I didn't know she was going to hop on a plane and fly over here."

"It's okay."

"It's not."

Letting out a breath, Josiah forced himself to let go of

the fear. If he could take off the body armor and give it to Chelsea, an act that saved her life, then he could face his parents.

"No, it really is okay," he assured her.

Pulling her head back enough that she could look up at him, she studied him carefully with her gorgeous gray eyes. "It is?"

Dragging in a breath, trying to steady his nerves, he nodded. "I don't want to let fear and guilt rule my life anymore. Part of me is always going to feel like I should have died in that desert along with the rest of my team, but I have to accept that I didn't. Everything you've said to me these last few weeks is true. My team would want me to live. Honoring them is moving on, being happy, living my life, falling in love."

A smile immediately curled her lips up. "I told you already that you can't take that back. You said it, it's out there, and there's nothing you can do about it."

"And I told you that I don't want to take it back." Josiah wasn't going to lie, it was utterly terrifying having that declaration of love out there. It felt like tempting the universe to snatch Chelsea away from him. But it had had its chance to do that, had given him the option of hiding behind the vest or letting go, and he'd chosen letting go, saving Chelsea's life in the process.

"I am never going to tire of hearing you say that." Chelsea's smile was so bright that he found himself wanting to do anything to keep it that way, even saying words that, while true, still felt weird coming out of his mouth.

"Love you, Chelsea."

That smile of hers brightened further. "And I love you. So much. For so long now. I know everything isn't going to be perfect and magical from here on out, you still have a lot to work through, but I'm going to be right there, loving you every step of the way."

Which was the only way he could face this.

Especially what was going to happen any second now.

This second it appeared when the door to the hospital room was flung open.

Six years had passed since he'd last laid eyes on his parents in person, and they both looked older. His mom's hair had still had a smattering of chestnut in it back then, but now it was completely gray. She'd put on a few pounds, and there were a few new wrinkles in her face, but nothing had changed the love in her eyes.

She was still his mom.

Despite the way she'd burst into the room, once her gaze landed on him, his mom froze. Standing there, like a deer caught in the headlights, seemingly unsure what she should do or say.

Behind her stood his dad. Like his wife, his dad had aged, his belly hanging slightly over the waistband of his jeans, a little less hair than had been there before, and definitely more wrinkles. But still his dad.

"I'm just going to go and get something to drink," Chelsea murmured, trying to tug herself gently from his arms.

Instinct had him tightening his hold. He could do this, was doing it whether he was ready or not, but it would be so much easier with her by his side.

"Stay," he ordered.

"I don't want to intrude."

"Stay," his mom echoed, and Chelsea nodded and sank back into his arms.

Then like the dam had burst wide open, his mother was crying. She hurried to the bed, wrapped her arms around him, and alternated between telling him how much she loved him and how angry she was that he'd shut her out. His dad was there, too, patting his shoulder, holding his wife, not saying anything, but tears shimmered in his eyes.

"I'm sorry, Mom," Josiah whispered, his face pressed against his mother's neck, feeling very much like a little boy again.

"You should be," his mom shot back, but there was no heat to her tone. "I should put you over my knee and give you the spanking of a lifetime, like you were a little boy again."

"Mom, you never spanked me when I was a little boy," he reminded her. Back then, his mom had been an expert at the long-winded, I'm so disappointed in you lecture. A skill he was sure she was going to resurrect, because he definitely deserved a lecture.

"Because I loved you too much to hit you." His mom's hands framed his face, and there was so much love in her gaze that his eyes grew misty. "I always loved you, my sweet son. I wish you hadn't shut us out, but it doesn't mean I stopped loving you. Ever. Not for one single second."

Same way Chelsea had never stopped loving him even when he gave her no reason to like him let alone love him. Automatically, his hand reached for Chelsea's, and it didn't go unnoticed by his mom.

"And this must be your lovely Chelsea. It's an absolute pleasure to meet you, dear," his mom said, turning her warm smile to the woman at his side.

"It's nice to meet you, too, Ma'am."

"Pfft, we don't do ma'ams in our family, dear."

"Mrs. Fleet then," Chelsea corrected.

"So polite, dear. You can call me Melanie, and maybe

one day, Mom, when you're part of the family," she added with a sly smile that slid between the two of them.

Chelsea laughed. "We can't tell you much about what we were doing undercover, but technically, I am part of the family since Josiah and I haven't gotten our marriage annulled yet."

A growl rippled through him at the very thought of ending their marriage. It might not have started out real, at least on his part, but it had grown into the most real relationship he'd ever had. Chelsea was right, he had a lot of emotional work still to do to even come close to being the kind of man she deserved, but he'd do that work, no matter how hard it was because he wanted to be a man worthy of her.

A husband worthy of her.

"Married?" His mom clapped her hands in delight. "Thank you, dear. For bringing my son back to life. I thought I'd lost him, but now I have him back, and a new daughter-in-law as well." Placing a hand over his and Chelsea's joined ones, she squeezed. "Now do I get to help you both plan a wedding celebration?"

Josiah groaned, Chelsea laughed, and his dad clapped him on the back.

"I think you'd better go along with this one, son," his dad said. "You owe it to your mom and your girl."

Truer words had never been spoken. He had a lot to make up for. He'd let grief and guilt turn him into someone who had pushed everyone else away to survive. But for the people he loved, who loved him back, he was going to do his best to disassemble those walls.

~

May 20th
    5:16 P.M.

"You going to tell me where we're going?" Chelsea asked, eyeing Josiah somewhat suspiciously.

After they'd finally been discharged from the hospital— well after they'd insisted they were leaving either way, so a doctor may as well sign them out—he'd had someone bring his truck to the hospital and bundled her into it.

Although she'd asked him at least two dozen times in the last thirty minutes where they were heading, he was yet to crack.

Sneaky little thing.

He was up to something, she knew it, and she hated being left out of secrets. Well, this kind anyway. A surprise birthday was totally different, but she wanted to know why Josiah was all tickled pink.

It was so amazing seeing him this way. There was a spark of life in his eyes that hadn't been there before, a flicker of peace that she was praying continued to grow over the next days, weeks, months, and years.

Like she'd told him already, she didn't think that everything was going to be perfect from here on out. He still had major issues to work through, she had some unresolved trauma from their time undercover as well, coming that up close and personal with evil had changed her, but they had time. There was no rush, it was clear Josiah didn't want them to annul their marriage, and of course, she didn't either, but that didn't mean they had to act married until he was ready.

"Nope." Josiah popped the p, and she tossed him a glare.

"I want to know where we're going," she told him. Not that she thought the answer would be anything bad, but she was dying of curiosity here.

"You pouting at me, Chels?" Josiah asked, amusement in his tone.

Tears stung the backs of her eyes. Seeing him this light and free made her so happy that she could hardly breathe. Which was a nice change of pace from the throbbing agony in her chest from her broken ribs making it so she hardly wanted to breathe. In fact, if she didn't have Josiah right beside her, and the hope of a happy future together, she might just give up on the whole breathing thing since it sucked to have to do it every couple of seconds and endure the worst pain she'd ever felt.

Okay, that was a lie. Chelsea wouldn't want to be dead either way, but this really did suck pretty majorly.

"Damn, Chels, are you crying? I can tell you where we're going," Josiah said, panic in his tone.

"No!" she yelled quickly. It was bringing him joy to keep this little secret of his, and she wanted that for him. "Happy tears, I promise."

"Sure?" He cast his gaze away from the road, and it roamed her face, searching for the truth. He must have seen it because he nodded, and one of his hands moved from the wheel to rest on her thigh. "If this is too much we can go to your place, or Prey, or back to the hospital. Whatever you need."

"Yuck for the hospital," she said quickly. There was nothing they could do for her anyway, her broken ribs would have to heal on their own. Her place no longer felt like a home after everything that had happened to Ava and Teresa there. The apartments at Prey were fine, modern and spacious, equipped with everything anyone would need, but they weren't homey. Besides, she was intrigued to see what Josiah wanted to show her.

Josiah chuckled, and the sound had a few tears tumbling free. Which he noticed and his gaze quickly grew panicked again.

"Happy tears," she reminded him. Honestly, she couldn't even remember a time in her life when she'd been this happy. She'd had a great life, parents who loved her, good friends, her dream job, but something had always been missing.

This man right here.

He was the other half of her soul, and she'd recognized that the moment she met him even if it had taken him a whole lot longer to see the truth.

"I don't want to go anywhere but wherever you're taking me," she assured him. "I guess I'm just a bit of a pouter when I'm left out of things."

"Noted."

"How long are your parents staying?" she asked after a couple of minutes of silent driving. Thankfully, Josiah hadn't been angry with her for telling his mom he'd been hurt and was in the hospital. She knew she shouldn't have because he'd told her they were estranged, but his mom had been so worried, and she didn't want the woman worrying any longer.

"They're going to stay for a while," Josiah replied, his hand tightening on the wheel so much his knuckles blanched white. "Apparently, my brothers and their families are going to fly up here, too."

"You okay with that?" Placing her hand over the one hand he still had on her thigh, she squeezed lightly, reminding him he wasn't facing this alone. She was right here, and she wasn't going anywhere. She would support him however he wanted to face his family, but she hoped he was willing to give them a chance and stop shutting them out when it was clear they loved him very much.

Letting out a long, slow breath, he finally nodded. "Yeah. I'm terrified because I know my brothers are going to be a lot harder on me than my parents were. Well deserved. I hurt everyone by pushing them away. It wasn't intentional, I was just trying to survive, but nonetheless the outcome was the same."

"They get that because they love you," she reminded him. Bottom line was neither she nor his family had lived through the hell Josiah had, so who were they to judge him for how he'd handled his trauma? "I'm glad you're letting them back in. I'm glad you're letting me in."

The fingers on her thigh squeezed almost to the point of pain. "Me too, Chels. Thank you for standing by me. For not giving up on me. I'd already given up on myself and if you hadn't been there ... I don't know what would have happened to me."

Thankfully, that was not something they needed to worry about finding out. "I'll always be there for you, Josiah. Because I love you."

"Love you back." She could tell the words felt a little rusty coming from his mouth, but she didn't care, he was saying them and that was all that mattered.

Lapsing into silence, a comfortable one, they drove for another fifteen minutes or so before Josiah pulled up outside a luxury apartment building right in the middle of the city.

"What are we doing here?" she asked, totally confused.

"You'll see." Climbing out, he rounded the car and opened her door for her. Taking her hand, he helped her down. While she tried to hide her wince, she was pretty sure he noticed it anyway. She certainly noticed his, and she did her best not to lean on him too much because she didn't want to cause him extra pain.

Apparently, he didn't like that, because he huffed and pulled her close against his side. After handing the keys to his truck to a valet, they headed into the building. Curiosity was bubbling inside her, and a million questions wanted to come pouring out, but she held them back. This was Josiah's moment, and she wanted him to have it and enjoy it.

He led her to the elevator and scanned a card before pushing the button for one of the top floors. Neither of them spoke as the elevator took them up, and Chelsea reveled in the warm, comforting, strong presence of the man holding her. This was everything she'd ever wanted, and it was so hard to believe that it was real.

But it was real.

And she wanted to soak up every second of it.

When the elevator opened, Josiah guided her out and down a hall, stopping outside one of the apartment doors and pulling out a key. Once he opened the door, Chelsea's gaze was immediately drawn to the stunning view from the floor-to-ceiling windows on the other side of an airy living room.

"Through there is the kitchen dining room," Josiah said, pointing to a door in the wall to their right. "And that way is three bedrooms and two bathrooms," he added, pointing to the left. "The master suite has the same views as the living room."

Unable to resist wandering over to the windows and staring out at the city below them, Chelsea knew her mouth was hanging open in shock as she took it all in. The apartment was gorgeous, and she'd had no idea that Josiah lived there. Although from the slightly musty smell, it didn't really seem like anyone had been there for a very long time. Had he rented it? Did it belong to a friend of his? A family member?

"What is this place?" she asked, glancing over her shoulder to find him watching her with a tender expression.

"This place is mine. Well, I hope it's going to be ours."

May 20th
5:55 P.M.

The shocked look on Chelsea's face when he told her he owned this place made keeping the secret on the way here more than worth it.

Plus, she was cute when she pouted.

It also made this moment more bittersweet than just bitter.

"You own it?" Chelsea asked incredulously. Then her eyes narrowed. "Are you some sort of secret millionaire? Or billionaire? Because I have to tell you that would be super romantic and a perfect plot twist for our romantic storyline."

Laughter burst out of him at the absurdity of her statement. "No, Chels, I'm not a secret millionaire or billionaire. Sorry to burst your bubble."

She shrugged and crossed over to him. "I don't care even a little bit. Our story has already been pretty perfect."

"It would also turn out to be a pretty cool plot twist if *you* were the secret millionaire or billionaire," he teased, wondering how it was even possible to feel this level of lightness and hope after so many years trapped in the dark.

Her eyes lit up and she giggled. "Reverse secret millionaire or billionaire, you're right that would be cool. Alas, I am not. Not even close. Although, as my parents' only kid, I will inherit a bit when they die. They're good with money and they don't like extravagant things so I will get a lot, but quite honestly, I'd rather have them forever than their money."

Which was exactly the way it was supposed to be. And the same way he was with his parents, although his inheritance would be split four ways.

If he'd had his choice, he would have eased his way back into a relationship with his parents rather than them just turning up the way they had. Maybe started with some texting, then when he felt up to it, some phone calls, then some video calls, before he was finally ready to meet face to face.

Instead, he'd had to jump into the deep end. Which had turned out to be what he really needed anyway.

"So if you're not a millionaire or a billionaire, how did you afford a place like this? These views are magnificent, and we're right in the middle of the city, plus there are three bedrooms and two bathrooms."

For a moment, the bitter threatened to outweigh the bittersweet, and as though she somehow sensed that his mood was dropping, Chelsea leaned into him, wrapping her arms snuggly around his waist and resting her cheek against his chest. There was a slight tug on his wound as he likewise wrapped his arms around hers, but the physical pain helped to anchor him. Stopped him from giving into the emotional pain and letting it drag him back down.

"My team and I pooled our money to buy it. It was our retreat, our place to hang out when we were on leave. When we were shipped out, we rented the place out to give us extra income. We spent some fun times here. Laughing, talking, just hanging out." Memories flashed through his mind, images of his friends lounging around the living room, pizza boxes scattered about and empty cans. "Good times."

"I'm glad you have those memories of them," Chelsea whispered. "When the bad ones try to choke them out, hold onto them. Remember your friends the way they would want you to remember them. Alive, strong, healthy, and happy."

"Happy," he echoed. For so long that word had been foreign to him, so far out of reach he had completely given up on it. Until one stubborn brunette with storm gray eyes and the biggest of hearts set her sights on him. "We always planned that if something happened to one of us, the rest of the guys could decide what to do with the place. Some of them had already gotten married, and were starting families, so at some point we probably would have sold it and split the cash. For the last six years it's been rented out, I sent the money to the widows left behind. Wanted to help ease their burden however I could."

It hadn't been enough. Josiah knew he should have been man enough to face them himself, express his sorrow that he hadn't done enough to save their loved ones, and apologize for still being alive when the men they loved weren't.

"Of course you did. You may have hidden this big heart of yours, but I always saw it." Chelsea's hand pressed on his chest against his heart, and warmth seemed to seep deep down inside him, thawing that heart he'd hidden even from himself.

"If you don't want to live here, then we can still sell it, split the money with the guys' families, and then buy something else, but ... I'm hoping you might want to build our future here. I'll buy out the other's partners for fair market value." This place was full of happy memories, and he wanted to add to them with Chelsea. Wanted to build a lifetime of joy in a home that had meaning to him. A way to honor his fallen teammates in the right way, by remembering them as the vibrant people they'd been and not dead bodies with empty eyes lying in the hot desert sand.

"I can't think of anywhere I'd rather build our future than right here, surrounded by the memories of the people you loved and lost." Chelsea beamed up at him, tears shimmering in her eyes, but this time he didn't have to ask to know they were happy tears.

"It was pure luck that the last rental contract ended right before we went undercover. I'd intended to talk to the real estate agent about looking for new tenants when we got back."

"Not luck, the universe giving you what you needed, a safe place to start over."

Josiah was never going to think of the world in the same romantic ways that Chelsea did, but he knew having her around would always mean his world was full of love and light, of joy and peace.

"I know we were told that sex was absolutely off the table for at least a couple of weeks, but if you don't make love to me now, I'm pretty sure I'm going to die," Chelsea said, and the complete and utter seriousness of her words made him laugh.

"No one ever died from lack of sex before, Chels."

Arching a brow at him, she planted her hands on her hips. "You really want to risk it?"

More laughter tumbled from his lips, and he couldn't remember the last time he'd laughed so many times in such a short space of time. Years. Before he lost his team and his world became cloaked in darkness.

Now light was trickling in. It wasn't flooding in yet, there had been too much damage done, and he'd need to work hard to clear away the darkness, but for now, there was enough light for him to see not only his surroundings but what lay ahead.

A lifetime of happiness with this woman who was daring him to deny her sex.

Sex he had no intention of denying, because he needed her more than he needed to breathe.

"Are you going to be a good girl and let me do all the work?"

"Not a chance, you're hurt too."

"Hmm." Backing her up until she bumped into the closest wall, Josiah planted one hand on the wall beside her head and leaned in until his lips were millimeters from hers. "That's a shame," he murmured as his free hand dipped down the waistband of the ankle-length, floaty white skirt she wore. "Because if you don't agree to let me do all the work, I'm not sure I can give you what you want." Nudging a finger between her legs, he dragged it along her already soaked panties.

Hips bucking of their own accord, seeking more, Chelsea gave him her best puppy dog eyes. "Wouldn't be fair to let you do all the work when we're both hurt. I don't want you to break open all your stitches."

"Such a shame." Keeping his touch featherlight, he

continued to sweep his fingertip across her center, brushing against her bud with each soft caress.

"So your plan is to torture me instead?" she asked with one of those adorable pouts.

Nipping at that plump bottom lip of hers, he shook his head. "You're the one being unreasonable here. I'm offering you as many orgasms as I can ring out of you, and you're arguing with me."

Sex really was a bad idea for both of them, but in this moment he just didn't care. What was a little physical pain when he could sink inside Chelsea's tight heat, joining his body to hers, and finding the peace he'd thought was unattainable?

Teasing her entrance by slipping his finger in as deep as he could with the cotton of her panties still in the way, he pressed his thumb against her bundle of nerves and circled it a couple of times.

"You really going to argue with me, Chels?"

Hips rocking against his fingers, her hands came up to grab onto his shoulders, and he knew from the arousal burning brightly in her eyes what she was going to say before she even opened her mouth.

May 20<sup>th</sup>
    6:08 P.M.

How could she possibly say no when Josiah was touching her like that?

How could she do anything but whimper and lean into his touch, try to get more of it?

A low chuckle rumbled through his chest, and his breath was warm against her lips. "So what's it going to be, Chels?" he asked, his thumb pressed harder against her bud, and she moaned, her hips pressing forward, silently begging him for more.

As badly as she craved sex, after all, she'd been the one to ask for it, she didn't want him trying to do all the work, didn't want him trying to prioritize her lack of pain over his.

But he wasn't budging, and he was currently trying to drive her crazy with these featherlight touches. They weren't enough to get her off, just to make her desperate for him. Not that he needed to work very hard for that because she was always desperate for his touch.

"Be careful," she murmured, her fingers tightening on his shoulders.

"You'll tell me if the pain gets to be too much," he shot back, an order not a question, and she nodded only because she knew if she didn't, he wasn't going to take things any further than this.

And that was unacceptable.

"Say it," he commanded as he pressed the finger just inside her deeper, and she was surprised he didn't rip her panties.

A shiver rocketed through her as she remembered how he'd ripped them off her when they were back at the mansion, the day they'd seen Maple bound and gagged. That had been surprisingly sexy, even if it had left her with a few red marks.

Marks faded, but memories lasted forever.

"I'll tell you," she agreed, all but writhing against him now. Magic fingers. It was the only way she could describe them, and they weren't even directly touching her. Darn panties.

Grabbing her hips, he lifted her. She expected him to let her hook her legs around his hips, maybe grind herself against the bulge in his pants, definitely press her lips to his and kiss him until she couldn't breathe.

But he didn't hold her like that. Instead, he shifted her until she was cradled in his arms. There was desire in his eyes as he looked down at her, there absolutely was, but there was so much more than that. Tenderness, affection, love.

This wasn't going to be sex, it was going to be making love.

Carrying her through the apartment and into the master bedroom, she couldn't stop a gasp as she took in the stunning room. The furnishings were a little less modern than the living room had been, and the giant, king-size four-poster bed positioned so it got the best of the view from the floor-to-ceiling, wall-to-wall windows was the perfect place to christen their new home.

Setting her down on her feet, Josiah's fingertips left a trail of fire everywhere they touched, and that seemed to be everywhere at once. Her tank top disappeared, and since wearing a bra had been too painful for her broken ribs, her breasts were bared to him. Dark black and blue bruises marred her left breast, and the desire in his eyes dimmed a little as he touched the softest of kisses to her damaged skin.

Then he took her other breast into his mouth, sucking hard and making her shiver.

He dragged his teeth along her pebbled nipple before releasing it and shooting her the sexiest smile she'd ever seen. It quite literally made her weak at the knees, but his hands were there, guiding her skirt and panties down her legs, then helping her step out of them.

Scooping her up once again, he laid her out on the bed, his gaze devouring her as it scanned her from head to toe. Then he was stripped out of his own clothes, leaving them scattered about on the polished wooden floorboards, and joined her on the bed.

Instead of stretching out above her, he lay beside her, his fingers skimming her stomach, drifting ever lower. It took all her control not to rush him, grab his hand, and put it where she wanted it, but this was about enjoying one another, not just getting an earth-shattering orgasm.

Not that she didn't want that earth-shattering orgasm, but it came when it came.

Almost idly, she palmed his thick length, began to stroke it, enjoying the way it twitched in her hand.

Eventually, Josiah's hand found its way between her legs, and she parted them to give him better access. His exploration was slow but steady, his fingers traced along the insides of her thighs, so close to where she wanted him, that she couldn't think of anything else.

By the time one of his fingers circled her entrance, she was pretty close to begging. The cocky smirk on his lips told her he knew how close she was to pleading for more, so she did the only thing she could do, she loosened her hold on his erection and instead began to trail her fingertips up and down it.

He gave her one of those sexy chuckles, then touched a line of kisses down the column of her neck as he slipped a finger inside her. Not nearly deep enough for her liking, but at least it was something. As he edged his finger in deeper, a teeny tiny bit at a time, his thumb traced lazy circles on her bundle of nerves.

"You're going to kill me, aren't you?" she asked, watching Josiah through heavy-lidded eyes. He was so handsome, and this wouldn't be the worst way to die, not by a long shot.

"So impatient, Chels," he teased, pressing his finger in the rest of the way. Instead of starting to thrust it, he just left it there, stroking the tip against that spot inside her that immediately had her hips coming off the bed.

"Nuh-uh, Chels. You're not supposed to be doing anything," he reminded her as he placed one of his hands on her stomach. Josiah had large hands, and it basically swallowed her stomach whole. Pressing just hard enough to keep her in place, he ever so slowly added a second finger.

"Killing me, it's totally your goal," she murmured as his thumb began to move against her bud.

Since she still had his length in her hand even though he'd twisted a little, she began to stroke him harder, faster. She was going to come soon, and she wanted him to come too. Wanted to unravel him the same way he was unraveling her.

A third finger joined the two already seated inside her, and Chelsea felt her internal muscles begin to quiver. Sensing that, Josiah stroked more firmly, his thumb relentless on her bundle of nerves, pushing her closer and closer to her release.

When it came rushing up to meet her, it tore through her with the power of a hurricane. Pleasure danced along her nerves, and she squeezed Josiah's fingers, which never faltered in stroking her, not even for a single second. Like her own hand never stopped stroking his length and she felt it jerk in her hand as he reached his own peak, painting her chest with the evidence of his release.

Breathing hard as she floated down from her high, she

saw Josiah watching her with a hint of worry in his expression.

"Too much?" he asked.

"Just the right amount," she corrected. And now she was ready for the next round.

"Sorry, Chels." Josiah caught her hand when she reached for his length, knowing he needed a little while to be ready for round two, but wanting to speed things up a little bit. "You're hurting, and I'm calling it for today."

"You promised me multiple orgasms," she reminded him.

"You're adorable when you pout." Touching a kiss to the tip of her nose, he climbed off the bed and gathered her into his arms. "Going to go and clean you up, then you need some rest."

"What about all the orgasms you said I could have?"

"You'll get those, as many as you can take, more than you can take, so many that you'll beg for a break."

"Yes," she breathed, heat already pooling between her legs.

Josiah chuckled. "Not today, though. I'm cleaning you up, then we're going to take our meds, order dinner, and get into bed. We have the entire rest of our lives to have as many orgasms as we want."

That was true. And she was hurting. Tired too. That kind of bone-deep exhaustion that came with high emotional stress. Maybe bed wasn't such a bad idea, especially since Josiah would be coming to bed with her.

"I love when you talk about the rest of our lives," she told him as he set her on the counter beside the sink in the master bath and began to run a cloth under warm water.

For a moment, he stilled, but then he turned off the faucet, squeezed out the cloth, and began to clean up her chest. "Me too. It terrifies me, but because it's you, I love it more than it scares me," he admitted as he moved the cloth to between her legs and cleaned her there.

Grabbing his shoulders, she pulled him close. "Thank you for fighting your demons, for you, for me, for your family."

"Thank you for never giving up on me."

"Never. Not possible. I love you too much to imagine my life without you in it."

The most breathtaking smile graced his face. "I love you too much to keep letting my demons drag me down. I want a life with you, and I'm going to fight as hard as I can to get it."

"Just remember, you are never fighting alone. I am always here, right beside you, I'm not going anywhere."

"I know. It's the only thing that led me out of the dark. You, your light, it saved me."

While Chelsea felt Josiah was giving her too much credit, she was so grateful that her happy ever after was finally here. Drawing him into a kiss, she let her romantic little heart sing with joy.

# CHAPTER

## Twenty-Three

May 21st
11:46 A.M.

When the doorbell rang and he had to pull his lips away from Chelsea's, Josiah started rethinking this whole Cyber Team celebration thing.

It had actually been his idea. Shocking though that was. Chelsea had been talking about making time to visit Ava and Teresa, Isabella too, and since she was still in a whole lot more pain than he knew she was trying not to let on, he told her they should come here.

The way her face lit up at the suggestion had him blurting out his next one.

Everyone should come. Ava and Nathaniel, Isabella and Tobias, Teresa and Micah. It was only a few extra people, and while he didn't know Nathaniel and Micah well, the two were in the same SEAL team, and he'd been a SEAL, so surely they had enough in common to make small talk about.

He hoped.

Because small talk had never really been his thing, and in the last six years he hadn't done it at all. Merely glared at anyone who tried to instigate a conversation with him that wasn't directly related to something they were working on for Prey.

Unless that someone was Chelsea.

While he might have sent her the same glares and angry vibes as he gave off to everybody else, it had never been the same. Not on his end anyway. There had always been something about her that drew him in, and he was so glad he was no longer fighting against those feelings.

Not fighting against them and dealing with six people were still different things in his mind, and he felt his palms grow clammy. How the hell was he supposed to deal with six people all at the same time? The very thought of it terrified him.

"If you don't want to do this, we can ask them to leave," Chelsea offered him, and when he glanced down at her and saw the sincerity in her expression, he knew he absolutely was not going to do that.

"This is important to you."

"But not more important than you."

Nodding his acknowledgement of the truth of those words, he still knew they were doing this no matter how anxious it made him. "I want to do this, Chels, it's just ... so many people all at once."

Josiah didn't have to hope that Chelsea would understand it wasn't just the number of people but the context, he knew she did. This same number of people in a briefing wouldn't have fazed him at all, but this wasn't a briefing, it wasn't work, it was just casual, friends hanging out, and that's what had him breaking out in a cold sweat.

"You can change your mind at any time. If you want them gone, just let me know," Chelsea told him.

"Stay put," he told her when she went to move off the couch to let their guests in. His wound hurt, but it wasn't on the same level as broken ribs. He knew because he'd broken his ribs twice before. The pain was like nothing else because there was literally no way to avoid it. Breathing wasn't optional.

With Chelsea's warm smile in his mind, he hurried over to the front door.

The second he did, he was met by six more warm smiles. They didn't hit the same way that Chelsea's did, but nonetheless, these were people who could become friends if he could take a step out of his own way and let them in.

For now, the future of Cyber Team felt uncertain. Or at least the future of the way the team looked right now. Both Ava and Teresa were dating men who were active-duty SEALs and still had a couple of years left before they could retire. They had major choices about what their lives were going to look like, and he knew Chelsea believed they were both going to move to the West Coast to be closer to their guys, maybe even take jobs with the West Coast Cyber Team Olivia Oswald had been prepping for.

"We brought enough pizza to feed an army," Ava told him, indicating the stacks that the guys were carrying.

"And some of basically every snack known to man," Teresa added with an amused smile and glance Isabella's way.

The tiny blonde noticed immediately and rolled her eyes. "Are you implying that's my fault?"

"It *is* your fault, firecracker," Tobias told her.

"Well, excuse me for being pregnant and craving something only not knowing what that something is," Isabella shot back, but she didn't really look annoyed. In fact, she looked hungry, and she was already eyeing up the bags she, Ava, and Teresa were carrying, which he had to assume contained the snacks.

Clearing his throat, he took a step back. "Come on in," he invited.

"Wow, this is stunning," Ava gushed as everyone walked inside the apartment.

"So glad I got a greeting before the view stole your attention," Chelsea teased from the couch, and Ava shot her friend a guilty smile.

"Sorry." Ava dumped her armload of bags on the coffee table and moved to the couch to give her friend a very gentle-looking hug. "How are you feeling?"

"Like a bullet tried to hit my heart and got stopped by Kevlar," Chelsea replied, making Josiah feel like all the blood had drained from his face.

"I think you should stop explaining it like that, Chelsea," Teresa said with a laugh. "Josiah is going to stroke out otherwise."

"Oops, sorry." Chelsea shot him an apologetic smile, and he forced one of his own as he shoved away the thoughts of what could have happened to her if he hadn't taken off his vest and given it to her. She wouldn't be sitting here making jokes, that was for sure.

Once he'd closed and locked the door, he moved straight to the couch to join Chelsea. If he was going to survive this, he needed her close. The fact that she carefully leaned into him the moment he was at her side helped soothe away the roughest edges of his anxiety, and for the next couple of minutes, while everyone got themselves settled, and helped themselves to slices of pizza, he was able to relax a little more.

Small talk mostly consisted of the girls asking one another how they were doing. It wasn't so long ago that Ava had been abducted, had her kidney stolen. Isabella was still recovering from her seven-month-long ordeal at the hands of the organ trafficking ring, and she had the surprise pregnancy to deal with on top of it. And it had only been a matter of weeks since Teresa was abducted and some of her liver taken.

When Ava cleared her throat and reached for Nathaniel's hand, Josiah felt Chelsea stiffen beside him. This was what he knew she'd been afraid of, an announcement that her two best friends were going to leave for the other side of the country, which he was sure to Chels felt like the other side of the world.

Romantic that she was, he knew she saw the beauty in Ava and Nathaniel, and Teresa and Micah's stories, but she was also scared of losing her two best friends at a time when she really needed the support.

"So, Nathaniel and I have news. Teresa and Micah, too," Ava announced, glancing over at Teresa, who had also straightened in her chair.

"You guys are moving?" Chelsea asked, and Josiah was so proud of his girl for not letting any of the pain he knew she was feeling seep into her words.

"Actually," Ava said slowly, a grin spreading across her face. "No."

"No?" Chelsea repeated.

"Well, we talked about it, of course, with Nathaniel's job and all. But in the end, after everything we've all been through these last few months, I can't leave. I don't want to."

"Can't break up the team," Teresa added.

"Not when we're already so awesome," Tobias added

with a smile, a soft look in his dark eyes as he glanced at Isabella, his gaze then dropping to her still flat stomach where their baby was growing.

"You're really staying? All of you?" Chelsea asked hopefully.

"It's only a few more years until Micah and I are out," Nathaniel said.

"And we're away a lot anyway," Micah added. "So even if Teresa and Ava moved, we still wouldn't be with them all the time. So flying out here whenever we can is easy enough."

"Ava and I can support each other while the guys are away," Teresa said.

"We'll *all* support you with that," Chelsea said quickly, and Tobias and Isabella immediately nodded their agreement.

"We all know this is going to be rough," Ava said, "but we also know we can do it. And like Nathaniel said, it's only for a few years, then the guys are going to maybe look into getting jobs with Prey."

"So we're not breaking up the team?" Chelsea asked, her grip on his hand tightening, and he absently began to draw small circles on the back of her hand with his thumb.

"No way we can break up this team," Teresa assured her.

"Not after such an amazing win, taking down one of the biggest organ trafficking rings in the world," Ava added.

"We're a family," Tobias said, reaching for Isabella and tugging her into his lap.

"A family," Chelsea echoed, grinning at everyone, then leaning up to kiss his jaw.

"A family," he agreed, capturing her chin and tilting her face so he could kiss her properly. For six years, he'd shoved his own family away and refused to allow himself to build a new one. Now it was time to embrace the life he'd been spared and start living again.

**Having a savior complex makes working undercover to bring down a sex trafficking ring difficult for Nathan Solace in the first book in the action packed and emotionally charged Prey Security: Undercover Team series!**

Defending Nathan (Prey Security: Undercover Team #1)

*Also by Jane Blythe*

**Prey Security: Cyber Team**
RESCUING NATHANIEL
RESCUING TOBIAS
RESCUING MICAH
RESCUING JOSIAH

**Prey Security: Athena Team Series**
FIGHTING FOR SCARLETT
FIGHTING FOR LUCY
FIGHTING FOR CASSIDY
FIGHTING FOR ELLA

*Prey Security Series: Artemis Team*
IVORY'S FIGHT
PEARL'S FIGHT
LACEY'S FIGHT
OPAL'S FIGHT

*Prey Security Series*
PROTECTING EAGLE
PROTECTING RAVEN
PROTECTING FALCON
PROTECTING SPARROW
PROTECTING HAWK

SAVING OWEN

SAVING LOGAN

SAVING GRAYSON

SAVING CHARLIE

*Candella Sisters' Heroes Series*

LITTLE DOLLS

LITTLE HEARTS

LITTLE BALLERINA

**Broken Gems Series**

CRACKED SAPPHIRE

CRUSHED RUBY

FRACTURED DIAMOND

SHATTERED AMETHYST

SPLINTERED EMERALD

SALVAGING MARIGOLD

**River's End Rescues Series**

COCKY SAVIOR

SOME REGRETS ARE FOREVER

PROTECT

SOME LIES WILL HAUNT YOU

SOME QUESTIONS HAVE NO ANSWERS

SOME TRUTH CAN BE DISTORTED

SOME TRUST CAN BE REBUILT

SOME MISTAKES ARE UNFORGIVABLE

**Detective Parker Bell Series**

A SECRET TO THE GRAVE

WINTER WONDERLAND

DEAD OR ALIVE

LITTLE GIRL LOST

FORGOTTEN

**Count to Ten Series**

ONE

TWO

THREE

FOUR

FIVE

SIX

BURNING SECRETS

SEVEN

EIGHT

NINE

TEN

*Storybook Murders Series*

NURSERY RHYME KILLER

FAIRYTALE KILLER

FABLE KILLER

**Christmas Romantic Suspense Series**

CHRISTMAS HOSTAGE

CHRISTMAS CAPTIVE

CHRISTMAS VICTIM

YULETIDE PROTECTOR

YULETIDE GUARD

YULETIDE HERO

HOLIDAY GRIEF

HOLIDAY LOSS - 12/2024

**Conquering Fear Series**

(Co-written with Amanda Siegrist)

DROWNING IN YOU

OUT OF THE DARKNESS

CLOSING IN

# About the Author

USA Today bestselling author Jane Blythe writes action-packed romantic suspense and military romance featuring protective heroes and heroines who are survivors. One of Jane's most popular series includes Prey Security, part of Susan Stoker's OPERATION ALPHA world! Writing in that world alongside authors such as Janie Crouch and Riley Edwards has been a blast, and she looks forward to bringing more books to this genre, both within and outside of Stoker's world. When Jane isn't binge-reading she's counting down to Christmas and adding to her 200+ teddy bear collection!

To connect and keep up to date please visit any of the following

*There are many more books in this fan fiction world than listed here, for an up-to-date list go to www.AcesPress.com*

*You can also visit our Amazon page at:*
*http://www.amazon.com/author/operationalpha*

### ***Special Forces: Operation Alpha World***
Christie Adams: Charity's Heart
Elizabella Baker: Challenging Luke
Linzi Baxter: Dangerous Rescue
Misha Blake: Flash
Anna Blakely: Rescuing Gracelynn
Julia Bright: Saving Lorelei
Cara Carnes: Protecting Mari
Kendra Mei Chailyn: Beast
Melissa Kay Clarke: Rescuing Annabeth
Gia Cobie: Saved from Revenge
Samantha Cole: Handling Haven
Cassie Colton: Rescuing Ryder
Jordan Dane: Redemption for Avery
D.M. Earl: Claire's Guardian
Riley Edwards: Protecting Olivia
Dorothy Ewels: Knight's Queen
Lila Ferrari: Protecting Joy
Nicole Flockton: Protecting Maria
Lea Griffith: Finding Ava
Desiree Holt: Protecting Maddie
Bree Hera: Trusting the Team
Rayne Lewis: Justice for Mary
JM Madden: Rescuing Olivia
A.M. Mahler: Griffin
Ellie Masters: Sybil's Protector

Trish McCallan: Hero Under Fire
Naomi McKay: Twist
KD Michaels: Saving Laura
Olivia Michaels: Protecting Harper
Annie Miller: Securing Willow
MJ Nightingale: Protecting Beauty
C.K. O'Connor: Delaney's Bodyguard
Danielle Pays: Defending Sarina
Lainey Reese: Protecting New York
Angela Rush: Charlotte
E.M. Shue: Discovering Tyler
Heather Slade: Code Name: Admiral
Dee Stewart: Fighting for Brielle
Lynne St. James: SEAL's Spitfire
Bella Stone: Rexar
Jen Talty: Shielding Jolene
Reina Torres, Rescuing Hi'ilani
LJ Vickery: Circus Comes to Town
R. C. Wynne: Shadows Renewed
Amanda Zook: Freeing Camila

### Delta Team Three Series
Lori Ryan: Nori's Delta
Becca Jameson: Destiny's Delta
Lynne St James, Gwen's Delta
Elle James: Ivy's Delta
Riley Edwards: Hope's Delta

### Police and Fire: Operation Alpha World
Freya Barker: Burning for Autumn
Jane Blythe: Salvaging Marigold
Julia Bright: Justice for Amber
Gia Cobie: Saved from Revenge

Leyna Cohan: Embracing Juliette
Nicole Craig: Justice for Francesca
Danielle M. Haas: Crossroads of Betrayal
Deanndra Hall: Shelter for Sharla
Reina Torres: Justice for Sloane

*As you know, this book included at least one character from Susan Stoker's books. To check out more, see below.*

## SEAL of Protection: Alliance Series
*Protecting Remi*
*Protecting Wren*
*Protecting Josie*
*Protecting Maggie*
*Protecting Addison*
*Protecting Kelli*
*Protecting Bree (Jan 6, 2026)*

## Rescue Angels Series
*Keeping Laryn*
*Keeping Amanda*
*Keeping Zita (Feb 10, 2026)*
*Keeping Penny (May 5, 2026)*
*Keeping Kara (July 7, 2026)*
*Keeping Jennifer (TBA)*

## The Refuge Series
*Deserving Alaska*
*Deserving Henley*
*Deserving Reese*
*Deserving Cora*
*Deserving Lara*
*Deserving Maisy*
*Deserving Ryleigh*

## SEAL Team Hawaii Series
*Finding Elodie*

*Finding Lexie*
*Finding Kenna*
*Finding Monica*
*Finding Carly*
*Finding Ashlyn*
*Finding Jodelle*

## Eagle Point Search & Rescue
*Searching for Lilly*
*Searching for Elsie*
*Searching for Bristol*
*Searching for Caryn*
*Searching for Finley*
*Searching for Heather*
*Searching for Khloe*

## Delta Team Two Series
*Shielding Gillian*
*Shielding Kinley*
*Shielding Aspen*
*Shielding Jayme (novella)*
*Shielding Riley*
*Shielding Devyn*
*Shielding Ember*
*Shielding Sierra*

## SEAL of Protection: Legacy Series
*Securing Caite (FREE!)*
*Securing Brenae (novella)*
*Securing Sidney*
*Securing Piper*
*Securing Zoey*
*Securing Avery*

*Securing Kalee*
*Securing Jane*

## Delta Force Heroes Series
*Rescuing Rayne*
*Rescuing Aimee (novella)*
*Rescuing Emily*
*Rescuing Harley*
*Marrying Emily (novella)*
*Rescuing Kassie*
*Rescuing Bryn*
*Rescuing Casey*
*Rescuing Sadie (novella)*
*Rescuing Wendy*
*Rescuing Mary*
*Rescuing Macie (novella)*
*Rescuing Annie*

## Badge of Honor: Texas Heroes Series
*Justice for Mackenzie (FREE!)*
*Justice for Mickie*
*Justice for Corrie*
*Justice for Laine (novella)*
*Shelter for Elizabeth*
*Justice for Boone*
*Shelter for Adeline*
*Shelter for Sophie*
*Justice for Erin*
*Justice for Milena*
*Shelter for Blythe*
*Justice for Hope*
*Shelter for Quinn*
*Shelter for Koren*

*Shelter for Penelope*

## SEAL of Protection Series
*Protecting Caroline (FREE!)*
*Protecting Alabama*
*Protecting Fiona*
*Marrying Caroline (novella)*
*Protecting Summer*
*Protecting Cheyenne*
*Protecting Jessyka*
*Protecting Julie (novella)*
*Protecting Melody*
*Protecting the Future*
*Protecting Kiera (novella)*
*Protecting Alabama's Kids (novella)*
*Protecting Dakota*
*Protecting Tex*

*New York Times*, *USA Today* and *Wall Street Journal* Bestselling Author Susan Stoker has a heart as big as the state of Tennessee where she lives, but this all American girl has also spent the last fourteen years living in Missouri, California, Colorado, Indiana, and Texas. She's married to a retired Army man who now gets to follow *her* around the country.

www.stokeraces.com
www.AcesPress.com
susan@stokeraces.com

Made in United States
Cleveland, OH
11 November 2025

25802242R00174